HOW TO KEEP A BOY AS A PET

HOW TO KEEP A BOY AS A PET

DIANE MESSIDORO

How to Keep a Boy as a Pet
First published in Great Britain 2012
by Electric Monkey, an imprint of Egmont UK Limited
The Yellow Building, 1 Nicholas Road, London W11 4AN

ISBN 978 1 4052 5816 6

3 5 7 9 10 8 6 4 2

www.electricmonkeybooks.co.uk

A CIP catalogue record for this title is available from the British Library

Typeset by Avon DataSet Ltd, Bidford on Avon, Warwickshire
Printed and bound in Great Britain by CPI Group

48736/3

EGMONT

Our story began over a century ago, when seventeen-year-old
Egmont Harald Petersen found a coin in the street. He was on
his way to buy a flyswatter, a small hand-operated printing
machine that he then set up in his tiny apartment.

The coin brought him such good luck that today Egmont has
offices in over 30 countries around the world. And that lucky
coin is still kept at the company's head offices in Denmark.

For two extraordinary pet men

Didier Messidoro, my rock

Graham Cox, my star

And, always, for my mum, Christine Cox

and for her rock, Derek Banks

Totally *not* weeping under a willow

Posted Thursday 22nd July, 16:25

I'm smiling. Honestly.

Okay, if you stared really hard at me, you'd probably notice my teeth are showing slightly too much. If you were being extra picky, you might even say I'm doing a good impression of our neighbour's Shetland pony when she fancies a human hand-burger.

So, no, my smile is not the most woo hoo, let's party, relaxed kind of smile. But, still, I *am* smiling.

I'm smiling because my oldest best friend, Ben, is walking off down the lane with his arm around my newest best friend, Tash, and I do not mind at all.

I am beyond not bothered.

In fact, I'm blissfully happy for them.

Totally.

It's true that only last week Tash vowed to spend the summer with me, hunting down hot new boyfriend prospects. But I have now wiped her promise from my entire memory.

If she happened to glance back, she would be reassured by my 'Hey, go ahead, have fun' grin. Only she wouldn't be able to see it. Or me.

I'm at the top of the tangled garden that slopes up behind our patio, sitting under a weeping willow tree. It's like a giant grass skirt, so I'm completely invisible. But it's the perfect lookout, as with some cunning leaf plucking, I can survey my whole domain i.e. the lane, Sharon the Shetland's field and The Nook (the smallest cottage in the world, where I live with my mum).

All right, I can guess what you're thinking. If I'm so ecstatic about my friends getting together, why am I hunched under a tree gnashing my teeth like a psycho-pony? Good question. For which I have no less than four extremely logical answers:

1. As my plans to become an irresistible boy magnet are shredded into bitter pieces and lying around me in tragic ruins, I've decided to become a fabulously sophisticated journalist instead. So I've started this blog to practise reporting on totally hot topics and typing really fast.
2. According to *Teen Vogue*, the garden is *the* place to have an office. Ideally, you find an abandoned gypsy caravan then add the antique desk and funky leather chair you happen to have spare. I've got my lap and a wobbly deckchair at the moment, but plan to upgrade.
3. I'm being fabulously sophisticated.
4. I'm hiding.

I know, I know, hiding doesn't sound fabulously sophisticated at all. But it is, I promise. If I'd given in to my more basic teenage human instincts I would now be hanging out in the park with Tash and Ben, pretending to have a laugh when we all know they just want to get meaningful behind a bush. Instead, I sneaked past them at the school gates (not hard, they were snogging, of course, along with practically everyone else). Then I forced my thumbs to ignore Tash's text ... .

> Missed U at gate???
> B at yours in 5.
> Fancy park?
> PS Ben's with me.

Then, because I really didn't trust myself to ignore the actual Tash, I grabbed my laptopasaurus (prehistoric, weighs tons, roars menacingly every few minutes) and headed up here to my office.

I did the right thing anyway, because when she knocked, I had to grip the deckchair arms to stop myself charging straight back down to the cottage and throwing the front door open. And I felt odd, a bit hollow, and hungry, even though I'd just eaten a giant sticky bun. That's when I forced myself to smile. Mum says you feel happier automatically when you smile. And it's true, sort of.

I think I'll stop smiling now, my cheeks are aching.

Sigh. What is it with the newly smitten? Tash and Ben left ten minutes ago, but they're still only about twenty metres away. They're walking sooo slooowly. Not even walking really. Ben is kicking at the ground as he inches forward, Tash is taking teeny dainty steps in her baseball boots, making her hips about a thousand times swingier than usual.

'Ah, so sorry I can't catch up with you right now but I'm, like, totally busy.'

I just said that out loud. Risky, I know, Tash and Ben might only have eyes for each other, but I'm not sure what their ears are up to. Come to think of it, love is meant to be blind, isn't it? Does that mean your hearing works better, like a real blind person's hearing?

Luckily, the garden's quite noisy, so I should get away with it. The wind's making the willow whoosh. And all the birds are going bonkers because Johnny Depp's hissing at Daniel Craig and Jude Law (our cat and two guinea pigs – how sad is my mother?).

Wait. Ben's stopped. He's peering back towards the cottage. Now Tash is scanning the lane. She looks a bit flustered . . . Perhaps I've got it all wrong? I only introduced them last weekend. Maybe they don't feel that comfortable on their own? Maybe they're thinking about trying the door again, or even letting themselves into the garden through the side gate, Tash does that sometimes, but . . . Oh. My. God. What if the breeze is blowing *their way*? What if they're coming back because they *did* hear *every word I said*?

 4

Quick. An excuse . . . That's it, I'm writing a play. Tash knows I want to be a journalist, playwriting's connected, ish, it involves words anyway. So, I'm writing a play about . . . a busy working mother – like mine, in fact, only much sneerier. And I was acting it out under the willow because . . . it's set in a cave. And I was so lost in my dramatic performance I didn't hear Tash hammering on the door, or calling through the letterbox, 'Cir-ceee?' (that's my name, I know, weird, more later).

Perfect, right, I'll sign off now then, put the laptopasaurus on stand-by so it doesn't roar itself into a flaming ball of fire . . .

Oh. Hold on . . . No – they're not coming back here.

They've just stopped for a snog.

Me. Blog. Thursday. Upstairs. Mum's pointlessly flirting downstairs.

Posted Thursday 22nd July, 21:07

Who? What? When? Where? Why? The five questions vital to professional journalists according to the booklet the school careers officer, Mr Dire, gave me today. He was full of encouragement.

'Oh dear oh dear oh dear . . . so you want to become a journalist, er, Kirsty?'

'Circe.'

 5

'Oh dear oh dear oh dear, Kirsty, you'll need to brush up that grammar and be rather more civil to stand any kind of chance in an interview. Never start with, "Sir, see . . ." Open politely, replying directly to my question, "Yes, sir, I do."'

'No, sir, I mea–'

'Oh, you don't want to be a journalist, but my notes clearly state–'

Where do they get these people? It took at least five minutes to politely and grammatically correctly explain that my name's not Kirsty, and that I do want to become a journalist. It then took him four minutes to find the appropriate booklet in his filing cabinet, leaving just one minute of our *Vital Year 10 Consultation Upon Which Your Entire Future Depends* to plan my career. First, he smoothed down the bristles of his eyebrows (which took at least another twenty seconds) so he could actually see to read the booklet. Then he peered back at me.

'Well, young lady, you are fully aware, no doubt, that since joining us last September you have been, ahem, academically *unremarkable*. Journalism is a notoriously competitive field you know, especially for girls. Frankly, I think you'd be wise to sign up for a secretarial course.'

Gasp. Isn't there a law against that? Tash is going to check, she wants to be a human rights barrister (like a lawyer, but with a wig on top). I had to clamp my hand over my mouth to stop a major illegal swear word falling out.

I bet he didn't say that to any of the boys, not a single one of them. Okay, he might have suggested that Tim Lough consider a career as a builder rather than an astrophysicist, as he failed all his mocks, even pottery. But at least if you're a builder you can be your own boss. If you're a secretary you just book appointments for other people to do exciting things. Like, whoopdidoo.

I felt like slapping his beige cheeks with his beige tie. I didn't, of course, I'm far too sophisticated. I just stood to leave in a dignified way, raised both eyebrows archly (having tried, and failed, to raise one) and said, 'No, sir, even though I'm obviously *a mere female* I won't be training as a secretary. If journalism turns out to be too hard for me, I have a foolproof back-up plan to marry a footballer and become internationally famous for having extremely shiny hair and lots of different handbags.'

I bit my lip then, waiting for the inevitable, 'Detention!' This is a regular date for my diary since I started at Hell House, thanks to my 'impertinence' (asking questions) and 'bad manners' (pretty much anything that involves moving or speaking).

But it didn't come. Instead, Mr Dire did an excellent impression of a shocked cod, then spluttered, 'Ridic–wait–Kirst–paffaffaff . . .' Which was a relief, but I think you'll agree, was also both impolite and grammatically incorrect.

So, he was hopeless. But the booklet's great. It's called

Focus for Success: Journalism and if Mr Dire had bothered to read it he would have been shocked to find it packed with advice from a *woman* – Jess Bradley. Do you know her? She's an über-cool professional journalist from New York who never, *ever*, lets anyone get away with putting her down. Actually, she's so fabulously sophisticated I bet no one dares even *think* about dissing her, which is precisely the level I'm aiming for.

Jess wears eccentric vintage clothes that should look rubbish together but don't, usually with a big floppy flower pinned on somewhere you wouldn't expect one. And she always has vampy scarlet lips, even in the rain. She's got a magazine column called *Hot Topicals* where she writes about serious women's issues, but in a way that makes you laugh and think properly about things, instead of huffing and getting bored. And she's on lots of arty TV shows, usually making men look a bit worried but sort of madly in love at the same time.

She says, *Your reader always needs to know the key facts.* So I'm always going to try to give you those, reader, if you're out there, which you're probably not because the chance of someone finding this blog among the gazillion on the web must be, well, one in a gazillion.

The facts now are that I'm stuck up here in my room alone unless I count you, or the snoring black rug otherwise known as Johnny Depp on the floor, or the 'larger than afterlife-size' Robert Pattinson poster on the ceiling. My mum's downstairs, giggling at the news with one of her 'just friends' men, Ralph.

Wait – the giggling just transferred to the front garden. Ralph must be leaving. Excellent. I can now go down and watch TV without being suffocated into an early teenage grave by *Smarmy Beast Pour Homme* aftershave fumes.

Night-night imaginary reader.

To swoon or not to swoon
Posted Friday 23rd July, 06:19

Good morning imaginary reader.

I know, up at dawn when I don't need to be. Welcome to the countryside – it's meant to be sleepy, but somehow it keeps everyone awake. It's the same every morning. First, thousands of birds start nattering at the tops of their tweets, then Clarence the alarm cock goes off, doodle-dooing as if he's personally responsible for waking up every hen in the entire world.

This morning, Johnny Depp joined in too, mewing proudly as he dropped a snail on my pillow, interrupting a delicious dream involving R-Patz and long grass. Then my mobile started beeping when Tash texted. She lives on a farm half a mile away (Clarence is her dad's fault) and has eggs to collect and sheep to comb, so early rising is essential.

Her message said:

> OMG U R BFF Ben = swoon! XOX
> PS Called 4 U where were U?
> PPS Ooh did Jake phone re HW?

It was strange. The text made me feel happy and sad and guilty and innocent and just a tiny bit angry all at the same time. Maybe it was because Tash mentioned Jake, my latest Official Crush (who for about a split second really seemed to want to be my Official Boyfriend). I know she's only trying to make me feel better, as if I still stand a chance with him. But it's two weeks, three days, sixteen hours and . . . thirty-eight minutes since Jake winked at me after English Lit., then whispered (really close to my ear and holding my elbow), 'Hey, what you said in class about Shakespeare's ego was well smart. Want to hook up over the homework one night? Suss out all the rhyme and rhythm?'

Those were his *exact* words, I wrote them in the back of my exercise book for accurate daydreaming purposes. And the homework he was talking about wasn't just some boring essay, it involved analysing a deeply meaningful love poem (including a line about pale breasts).

As he purred the word 'rhythm', my ear started fizzing, which made my throat close up, so I couldn't really speak. I did manage a nod and an 'Mmm' though and quite a friendly smile, I think. And Jake smiled too.

But since then he's been out with Joanna Hawtree and Mita Vinod (both in Year 11 and gorgeous) snogged Charlotte Floyd (admittedly, everyone has snogged her) and done something very unmentionable with the hippy girl from the chemist's who scares the vicar because she has a tattoo on her shoulder of a Greek God with a huge spanner.

It's fair to say then that Jake hasn't exactly been sitting indoors pining for me. And now, in a twist straight out of the most tragic kind of soap opera, he's dating my form captain, the Oh So Lovely And Charming Portia Thornington. And if she *even suspected* I liked him she'd laugh her pretty head off for the rest of her entire life. At least.

So I am now Officially Getting Over Jake, which involves accidentally being in the same places as him in order to identify serious defects. I've started a list:

Jake's Most Major Faults (Visible)
* *Hair not dark enough and a bit too wavy at the back.*
* *Eyes the wrong sort of blue.*
* *Shoulders far too broad compared to his hips.*
* *Rubbish at rounders, especially bowling (maybe his arms are too long?).*
* *Doesn't play guitar.*
* *Rides his bike with no hands, which is a bit naff (though it might, I suppose, have something to do with his too long arms).*

As you can see, Jake is actually deeply unattractive. All I need to do now is stop my heart blocking my throat every time I see him and I'll be back to my usual perky self.

Sorry, I've wandered right off the subject. What was the subject? Tash's text. Yes. So, I read it, felt like all my emotions were crashing into each other inside my head, then squeezed my eyes shut to try to get back into my dream. But R-Patz kept morphing into Jake, so I gave up and started wondering in an intelligent journalistic way about vampire lips and whether they're cold etcetera. That got me thinking about Ben and Tash's non-stop snogging, and how weird it is when the two people you feel closest to in the world start to get closer to each other than you'll ever get to them.

I've only known Tash since my second week at Hell House, but it feels like forever. We're in different forms, but we bonded when I crashed into her in hockey, scored an own goal and collapsed in hysterics.

I actually have known Ben forever, though, since I was five and he was seven. His family lived in the flat above ours in London and our parents babysat for each other when we were small.

It's dead easy being with Ben as he knows the basics about me, like the kind of spooky rock I'm into and how sherbet makes me sneeze. We used to see each other all the time, to listen to music or bike to the park or just knock about somewhere. And even if Ben was busy being sporty or dating or something, we'd still bump into each other in the front garden or at the corner shop up the road.

Anyway, I've missed him like mad since we left. So I was ecstatic when he called to say he was moving to the nearest so-called town, Dullford, because his parents had come over all organic and needed a garden big enough to keep hens and carrots.

In case you're wondering, I really did want Tash and Ben to get on, so we could hang out together sometimes. But I never dreamt they'd fancy each other, as Ben always goes for fair floaty girls and Tash likes dark tragic boys. And, okay, I admit it, I never would have introduced them before the holidays if I'd known they'd fall head over trainers in split seconds.

I also admit that it was my idea to spend the summer urgently hunting down hot new boyfriend prospects because – well, let's just say it's been a quiet year, romantically. Again. But Tash was totally into it too, as there's a limited supply of dark tragic boys in our area. She finished with her last one, lean Lee, at Easter because he kept nagging her to do something far too meaningful involving black ribbon on a gravestone behind the scout hut.

Anyway, whatever. The important thing now is to think up a topic hot enough to keep me busy for five weeks. I've decided to channel Jess Bradley to inspire me, so I'm flicking through my journalism booklet . . . Ah, this could be good. I've found a picture of Jess staring out of the window of her loft apartment in Soho, biting on a leopard-print fountain pen. The caption under it says, *Jess always likes to be able to see the sky when she writes*.

Excellent. I'm going to climb back on to my bed and type while I look up through the skylight.

So whas a totttaly h ot top igg tha woujld be intrrestng?

Oushc mebbe if I squin t ?

Norr, this snit goong ta worm, the sun's shininbg on thersc reeen,, cand"t seee it priply give ma a secc;

Jess Bradley come in please . . .

Posted Friday 23rd July, 06:24

Okay, better, I'm now jammed into the tiny ledge of the tiny curved window at the end of my tiny room.

My bum's a bit folded up, which doesn't feel that classy and, unfortunately, I haven't got a floppy flower to pin somewhere unexpected. But my hair is long and curly like Jess Bradley's (though it's a huge uncontrollable frizz in a glamorous shade of mud pie). And I've put on my *Forbidden Scarlet* lipstick, which Mum has actually forbidden (and confiscated) but which I just liberated from where she hides it in her own make-up bag. I'm also biting my biro in a quite fabulous and sophisticated way for a beginner (I practised in the mirror first).

So, any second now, I will channel Jess and think of a

totally hot topic. Or at least something so wise and insightful it will make girls laugh and cry and be able to fulfil their wildest romantic dreams and most stratospherical career ambitions all at the same time.

Um

Posted Friday 23rd July, 06:29

Hmm

Posted Friday 23rd July, 06:42

Sigh

Posted Friday 23rd July, 06:57

I can't think of anything. I can't even think of a totally rubbish topic, unless you count, *How does Jess keep her lipstick on her lips when mine ends up all over my pen, T-shirt, laptop, curtains and cat?*

I think I'll take the pen out now, my cheeks are aching again.

Perhaps it's my room? Perhaps I'll only ever have tiny ideas in this tiny space? You probably think I'm exaggerating the size of The Nook. I wish. It's like some kind of sixteenth-century practical joke. I virtually have to tuck my nose

 15

between my knees to get in the front door, even though I'm only five foot three. There's one living room on the ground floor with a kitchen in the corner. Mum's room takes up the whole first floor (she has to flatten against the wall to get round her bed). And up here, in the attic, the same space is divided in two. The front half's my room with a high bunk and just enough space underneath for a chest of drawers and clothes rail. The back's our excuse for a bathroom, with a miniature hip bath, which Mum insists is the 'in thing' but means one end of your body's always cold. If you slide down to soak your shoulders your legs stick out, and if you keep your legs underwater your top sticks out. That's also a problem because with the garden sloping up into the woods behind the cottage and the window in the roof sloping down, you can find yourself being ogled by rabbits/ramblers/Mum and her animal rescue friends (who are liable to wave).

The Nook is even more ridiculous because, apart from the row of tiny cottages on the high street that have been turned into Ye Olde Curiosity Shoppes, every other house in the area looks like it's fallen out of *Pride & Prejudice*. Think towering gates and crunchy drives leading to grand mansions with columns and turrets and tennis courts and swimming pools. Though I guess they didn't have pools in Jane Austen's time. Can you imagine? *Heavens, Mr Darcy, I couldn't possibly flutter my fan in your direction, but could you do my back with factor fifteen?*

The cottage comes free with Mum's job, working for a

horse trainer, the Right Honourable Henry, and we moved here a year ago. 'Here' is The Middle Of Absolute Nowhere, deep in a home county, which means it's close enough to London to commute to work if you fly a helicopter or want to spend nearly your entire life on a train. But it's not close enough to commute to my old school or hang out with my old friends. And it feels like it's on a different planet, all trees and hills and nothing to do.

Mum's a vet, and when she's not rescuing random animals, she looks after horses. So we lived in a smart area in London, beside a huge park surrounded by stables, but as we were in a flat, we didn't stick out so much.

Anyway, I'm wandering off the subject again, which I don't think is a particularly good journalistic speciality. Also, Friday is the only school day Mum doesn't start work at six, so I have to go down to breakfast early as she insists on a 'proper catch-up'. Back in five.

Neigh

Posted Friday 23rd July, 07:35

Mum's catch-ups feel more like consultations, as if I am an actual horse or something. This morning, she ran her hand over my head like she was checking for tics, peered into my eyes, then rattled off, 'How are *you*? How is *school*? Any *prob*lems? Anything you need to *talk* about?'

And, between mouthfuls of porridge, I answered, as usual, 'Fine. Fine. No. No.' To be honest, I doubt she'd even notice if I said, 'Terrible. Dreadful. Millions. I got rampantly meaningful on a trampoline with my PE teacher yesterday.' (Who Tash and I have decided is quite cute if you squint to blur his very close together eyes.)

Right. Must phone Tash now and kill the Jake idea so she doesn't blurt out something lethal at school. Tash doesn't know quite how poisonous Portia can be. Nobody does.

Not being totally honest without lying is a bit tricky and tiring

Posted Friday 23rd July, 08:12

I was so fixated on the Jake crisis, I completely forgot about the hiding under a tree situation.

'So – where were you then – didn't you get my message?'

'Oh, um sorry Tash . . . yes I – I popped out – left my phone at home.'

This was true. I deliberately left it in my room so it wouldn't reveal my secret location if she called.

'But didn't my text show up when you got in?'

'Um . . .' I had no choice but to play dirty, 'How's Ben?'

'Ooh . . .'

Result.

'And how was your evening together – *all alone*?'

'. . . ooh, swoon, it was totally dreamy . . .'

So much for the super-sharp legal brain.

'. . . aah . . . more than dreamy . . . ooh . . . he's so fit . . . aah . . . his arms are so strong . . . ooh . . . his shoulders are so broad . . . aah . . . his stomach's so hard . . . ooh . . .'

I felt slightly suicidally bored out of my mind after ten minutes of Tash's non-stop drooling. But at least it got me out of confessing I'd deliberately avoided her.

Not being totally honest without lying is also dangerous

Posted Friday 23rd July, 18:44

Thanks to the hiding under the tree situation, I completely forgot about the Jake crisis, right up until our last lesson. Drama. How appropriate.

We were all cross-legged on the floor of the acting studio, watching Portia perform the vile school anthem. Our teacher, Mrs Stave, was crashing away on the piano and everyone (except me) was swaying as Portia warbled through vomit-inducing lyrics like, 'Hail to Hell, the beauteous illumination shines from every hallow-ed window,' while shaking her boobs as much as possible.

Tash was taking the opportunity of sitting in the shadows, behind the spotlight shining a halo on Portia's swinging blonde hair, to whisper to me about Ben.

19

'He's a spectacularly good kisser, Circe – even with tongues!'

As I can remember Ben sticking his tongue out at girls, this was a bit weird to hear, but I had to admit it was rare.

'God, Tash, that's dead lucky, so many boys kiss like puppies or hoovers.'

'Ooh – how many boys have you snogged?'

'Um, quite a few.' This was true. I'd also practised extensively on my own hand and several ice creams.

'Wow. Ben said he never met any of your boyfriends in London – I suppose you kept them apart, in case they got jealous of him, he's so fit.'

I just shrugged, hoping Tash would interpret my silence as homesickness for London – and all the adoring boys I'd left behind. Big mistake.

Tash linked her arm through mine. 'Ah, Circe, don't be sad – Portia gets bored so easily, I'm sure you'll be with Jake soon.'

I flinched and remembered I needed to tell her my Official Crush was Officially Over.

'Ugh! I wouldn't snog him if he was the last boy in The Middle Of Absolute Nowhere.'

Tash frowned. 'Really? But when we voted last week you said he had the second most kissable lips in the world, after R-Patz . . .'

I flinched again, this time because Portia was trilling out an ear-piercing, 'Hall-ellullah aaaaaah-men!'

'I've changed my mind – I just hadn't looked at him properly.' I was hissing urgently now, determined to get Tash to believe me, but she just widened her eyes and squeezed my arm so hard it hurt. 'Ouch. Honestly, I have now worked out that Jake is deeply unattract–'

It was then I realised the music had stopped – and everyone was gaping at me. Except Mrs Stave, who was glaring. Oh, and Portia. Portia was smiling sweetly at me – and clenching her hands into tight white-knuckled fists . . .

Totaliuss ridiculousicus schoolium
Posted Friday 23rd July, 18:56

Oops, forgot to mention a key fact – I got detention, hurrah, for bad manners (specifically, Disrespecting The School Anthem). So I enjoyed yet another delightful hour in the 'Dungeon of Doom', a creepy classroom under the assembly hall which smells of cobwebs, and me, probably, as it's practically my second home.

Oh, if you think I've also skipped a key fact from drama, sorry, but it's really not worth wasting any typing energy on Portia, she's so pathetic. Basically, she hissed some of her usual rubbish at me as soon as Tash was out of earshot. But I just ignored her and huffed off to detention. Then, as I copied out a passage on obedience from the Hell House Handbook (in Latin – how pointless is that?) I

 21

decided to wipe the whole unimportant catastrophe from my memory.

Mr Dire was on Dungeon duty and drummed his beige fingers on his beige tie for sixty exact minutes, which made me grin as it reminded me of my one and only detention at my old school (after a bunch of us pretended to fall asleep in RE). Our teacher got bored after about three seconds and let us out, which made us feel a bit wildly untamed. So we all bundled into the Fancy Dress Emporium on the High Street and bought cheapie fangs and glitter wigs, then hit the Rockarolla Diner and bopped round the jukebox vamping in smouldering undead ways at the cute Italian waiter.

Good job Mr Dire didn't let me out early, if I came over wildly untamed here I'd have to sit and watch a blade of grass grow until it wore off.

Is *The War Against Extreme Frizz* a totally hot topic?

Posted Sunday 25th July, 11:35

Tash thinks it is. I'm not so sure.

Ben managed to detach his lips from Tash's for long enough to play tennis at his new club yesterday, so we had a lovely girlie afternoon. Her mum made us a picnic and we bought pink sparkly elderflower at Ye Olde Minimarkete.

 22

Then we climbed the hill behind the church and lay in the grass, chatting like mad, barely even taking breaths between different subjects.

Tash told me about some new clenching exercises she's trying to reshape her bum, which she thinks looks oblong (it doesn't). Then she asked me about Ben's girlfriends in London and I said none of them were as gorgeous as her, which is true (she's all glossy black hair and dusky skin). Then she talked about Ben's muscles for a while, of course. Then she said, 'Circe, you know, this doesn't change anything. I mean, we're still BFFs and Ben's still your BBFF even though he's now my BF and really I think it's just a total plus that you're also my BFBGFF as well as my BFF – and we both *sooo* want you to hang out with us in the holidays. Really.'

I got a bit confused, but Tash looked so worried that I bit my lip to stop saying what I wanted to say, which was, 'So, BFF you're still up for hunting down new BFs with me, are you?' and instead said, 'Ah, thanks Tash, but I really *do* want to get ahead on the journalism thing this summer. I've started a blog to practise, so I'm going to be pretty busy a lot of the time.'

And she didn't say, 'But what about our vow to spend the holidays together hunting down new BFs?' which proved Ben had snogged it from her memory. She just said, 'Ooh, your own blog – can I read it?'

Yikes. I hadn't thought of that. 'God no. You'd be bored

out of your mind.' I yawned loudly to emphasise my point. 'There's nothing much on it yet and when there is it will be very journalistically technical – it's just for me to learn from really.'

'Oh, okay – what's it about?'

'That's the problem. I don't know yet – I need a juicy subject, something I can get my teeth into . . .'

'What about something useful, like . . . *How to Save the Planet*?'

Tash is quite ambitious, can you tell?

'Um, that might be a bit too much for a first assignment – maybe next term.'

Tash stood up, paced twice around a tree, sat down again, frowned at the sky and crunched through an entire apple before she replied . . .

'Hair.'

My mouth actually dropped all the way open. This is the girl who hopes to get into Oxford, study law then do 'one of the most important jobs in the world' saving humans from death and fates worse than death, whatever they are. If Mr Dire heard her he'd insist she switch to flower arranging.

'Hair?'

'Yes, hair. Think about it, you need a subject you're passionate about, that you understand, that you can learn from, that will inspire others . . .'

'Oh. And you think I'm passionate about hair?'

'Yes! But not just any hair – specialist hair, *your* type

of hair. You've tried tons of different taming methods, haven't you?'

'So?'

'Well, write up the results. Do more research. Expose the lotions and potions that fib about miracles. Interview hairdressers, other victims . . .'

Victims? I think Tash may have confused bad hair with actual torture. Okay, it is on rainy days when I bump into Jake in a corridor and he can barely squeeze by because my hair has doubled in size. But, most of the time, it's just annoying.

I was thinking all this when Ben turned up, looking very London with his irritatingly manageable sandy hair spiked up into a mohawk.

'Hey, Tash . . . Witchy.'

Ben's called me 'Witchy' since I was six and my so-called dad explained my name to him. I guess it might irritate some girls, but I don't mind it. It reminds me of being young and not caring about anything but who could run faster or climb higher. Or it did remind me of that, now it makes my heart clench a bit, because of the twisted ideas Portia's tried to plant in my head. But I've sworn I'm not going to let her get to me, so I managed to grin at Ben, as usual, and he fake-punched my shoulder.

And, yay, we really did all have a laugh together, about Mr Dire's ambitious plans for me and about Ben's über-competitive Canadian tennis partner, Chuck (really), who shouts 'Yesss-sirrr' every time he serves. And when he told Tash he'd won his match, she whooped and kissed him, but not a proper snog, so I didn't have to pretend I was suddenly fascinated by my feet and/or entirely invisible.

A jolly good fun abuse of our teenage human rights
Posted Monday 26th July, 20:22

The Hell House Head, Professor Potts, interrupted registration this morning (or rather his belly interrupted and the rest of him turned up a few minutes later). He announced that as Year 11 is going to be 'tough' and 'a shock', we have to do 'jolly good fun tests' all day on Friday to prepare for it. We've got to revise practically the whole of Year 10 again and learn some totally new stuff about jolly subjects like banking and war. Oh, and anyone who fails will get a jolly good fun detention – *on the last day of term*. How warped is that?

Comment
Posted Wednesday 28th July, 15.55, by your Studybuddy!

Hey *Circe!*

Cramming for end of year tests at *Hell House*?

Rather be having a blast with your mates or out on dates?

Don't get stressed, get a **studybuddy**!

Studybuddy.com helps you revise every subject from Archaeology to Zoology. All for the special introductory offer price of only $3.99 a month!!!

So for the easy way to get straight 'A's <u>click here now</u>>>>

Dear Studybuddy

Posted Wednesday 28th July, 16.52

If you were any kind of decent friend you would know I have nothing better to do than study. My mates spend their entire lives snogging each other and I don't have any dates. Unless you teach Boyfriendology, please do not darken my blog doorway again.

Deep sigh

Posted Wednesday 28th July, 16.55

I am the epitome of frankly disappointed. When I saw 'New Comment' pop up, I thought my imaginary reader had actually turned into a real one. I've switched on all my anti-spam security blocks now as it's quite spooky when you realise an internet robot has read your blog and thinks it knows personal things about you.

 27

Most hideously appalled over 14

Posted Thursday 29th July, 20:22

As if it wasn't enough that Hell House has teachers who look like they live in dusty cupboards and holidays so short they almost don't exist, we had to sit through an awards ceremony today – for *three hours*. Best Mathematician Under 14/Best Mathematician Over 14/Best Biologist Under 14/Best Biologist Over 14 and on, and on, and on . . . I was so bored I got pins and needles in my brain.

Every student with a parent on the Board of Governors received at least one award. Portia got two. Oh, and she's been promoted to Head Girl next term. And guess who's Head Boy? Yes, Jake. They may as well be married already.

How not to get teenage kicks

Posted Friday 30th July, 20:35

So, the last day of Year 10. How can I sum it up?

Snogging hell.

I'd prefer to leave it there, I've no desire to relive the whole excruciating experience. But I suppose if I want to practise accurate reporting I have to explain the key facts.

It started okay. Tash and I met at the spooky bus stop between our houses (it looks like a gravestone and I've never seen a bus, but sometimes I've seen a really old person waiting and the next time I've looked they've disappeared). It was already hot and sunshine splashed us through the trees as we walked along the lanes, firing revision questions at each other for the 'jolly good fun' test.

Tash knew everything. I knew almost nothing. I've a theory that some sorts of people are born to collect answers and some are born to collect questions. I'm definitely the second sort. The more I try and cram facts into my brain, the more it fills up with 'But who?'s and 'So why?'s. I wonder if it's in my blood? Or maybe it's because when I used to ask Mum about my so-called dad she'd just stare right through me? Maybe that's made me more curious than a normal person? Maybe that's why I want to be a journalist? God. See what I mean?

Anyway, after I answered 'Who founded the Stock Exchange?' with 'Why do we need to know?' Tash gave up. 'Stop! Okay, a question for you – are you going to Venetia Hitch-Scott's pool party after school?'

I frowned. I'd brought my swimming stuff, in case, but I wasn't sure Venetia had invited me. She's sweet, but so posh I can barely understand a word she says. Mum's other 'just friends' man, AJ, who talks a bit like her, explained she speaks extreme RP (Received Pronunciation, or Radical Plum as Ben calls it), which is an accent teachers in historical times invented to help rich people feel more important than poor people. Hurrah. Excellent idea, historical teachers.

'Um . . .' I stalled, 'maybe, detention permitting.'

'Oh please come, Circe. It was great last year. We played croquet and water polo and Venetia's dad set up karaoke and Portia sung right through the top twenty.'

I bared my Sharon the Shetland smile. It was becoming useful.

In fact, I kept it on pretty much all day, which dragged like a week. At my old school, the last day of term was like a party with desks. At Hell House every teacher set a section of the jolly test, then barked out a pre-holiday 'don't do this/ don't do that/definitely don't do the other' lecture, which made me want to do it all, even if I hadn't wanted to do it before.

When the bell finally went, I headed to the school gates (which were draped in writhing snoggers as usual, yawn) and found a couple-free spot to wait for Tash. But as soon as I dropped my bag on the ground, Portia smirked up with Jake in tow, wrapped all her arms and legs around him and started devouring his face. Less than a split-centimetre away from me. Scream.

My heart did its annoying throat-blocking thing, but I was determined not to let Portia see I was even a bit bothered. So I clenched my entire body and gazed at my blank mobile screen like it was the most interesting thing on the planet. When Venetia tapped my shoulder a few minutes later I nearly fainted with relief, and when she said, 'Airhairlair, Sarcy, see you back at my gaff?' I chirped, 'Yes! Fantastic!'

It took Tash and I thirty minutes to walk over to

Venetia's 'gaff', which turned out to be a humble little castle with a lake full of swans in the front garden. A stiff butler buzzed us in through the security gate and pointed us round the side of the west wing in the direction of blaring hip-hop.

The pool actually made me gasp. It was stunning, an olympic-size glittering blue oblong with a marble bar at one end and a hill dotted with thoroughbred horses at the other.

Most of the cream leather sunbeds around the pool were already occupied by loved-up couples, making the most of the last hours together before their parents jetted them off to separate exotic locations. Even Tim Lough was there, looking a bit blank as always, but otherwise happily clinging on to Mita Vinod.

Portia was already installed centre stage, thanks to her family's chauffeur. She was just about wearing a teeny scarlet designer bikini and arching her back to push her boobs out as far as possible. Jake was lying next to her, his tanned skin gleaming with oil, but I quickly made myself notice that his stomach looked too flat, almost concave, which wouldn't be very cuddly. They both glanced up as Tash and I walked in. Jake lifted his shades and winked, Portia grinned like the cat that got the cream with a side order of freshly slaughtered mouse.

I plastered my best psycho-pony smile back on and led the way to a pair of spare beds on the other side of the pool. As I lay back, my bargain basement bikini crackling with static, Tash dragged another bed up.

'Venetia told me to invite Ben too, she's so lovely, isn't she?'

I managed to 'Mmm' through gritted teeth.

Tash looked stricken. 'Oh Circe, that's okay isn't it? I assumed tha– you know, because you're best friends – I thought you'd be pleased.'

I felt childish then, and horrid, as if I was being deliberately mean to her and disloyal to Ben at the same time, even though all I'd said was 'Mmm'. So I nodded like mad and said of course I was pleased.

And I was, at first. When Ben arrived it was great, Venetia came over to be introduced properly and we all sat chatting and laughing.

But then Portia started to butt in to our conversation from the other side of the pool, giggling and squealing louder and louder, no doubt livid we were daring to have fun without her being in the middle of it. When Ben didn't even glance up as she wailed melodramatically at something Jake said, it was obviously too much to bear. She leapt to her feet, strutted along the diving board and pirouetted at the end as if she was on a catwalk. Then she clapped to make absolutely sure she had everyone's undivided attention and announced, 'Now, you must all swear not to look if my silly top comes off like it did last time!'

Predictably, the boys were all glued as Portia bounced (a lot) on the board, then launched into an Olympic standard dive. Her top didn't come off, although I'd swear she did a little shrug halfway through to try and shift it. But still, she got what she wanted, as usual. The party was all about her again. Venetia trotted off to fix her a drink, Jake wrapped her in his towel (clearly demonstrating his far too long arms) and Mita obeyed her order to 'Put on some raunchier sounds babe'.

As the air filled with a heavy bass beat, the temperature seemed to soar to 100 degrees. A few couples started to slow dance. Jake rolled on to Portia's sunbed. Ben took Tash's hand and asked if she wanted to go for a walk 'to meet the horses'.

He invited me too, but didn't, if you know what I mean, so I said I'd already met enough horses to last a lifetime. Then I hugged my knees and counted the windows on the back of the house (nineteen) before it occurred to me I could avoid all the snogging now going on by actually swimming. I quickly wove my hair into a thick plait, so it wouldn't block out the sun when it dried, then slipped into the pool.

I'm a rubbish diver (I blame heavy hair) but I'm a decent swimmer, so I did a few lengths of crawl, keeping my face in the water as much as possible. Then I noticed that Venetia and Milly Fung, unattached to boys, amazingly, had materialised on the semi-circle of marble steps in the shallow end. I swum over and sat beside them.

'Hey you two. God, gorgeous place Venetia – has your family lived here long?'

'Quite, yah, since 1642. Bit shabby now. We're opening

for teas next year, so we can restore the east wing. We'd do it this year but Pa's shooting all summer.'

I tried not to wrinkle my nose in disgust, but obviously failed.

Venetia snorted. 'Not animals silly – an epic jungle adventure. Pa and Ma are film-makers.'

'Wow, how cool is that – and they're shooting it here?'

'No, we're all going out to New York tomorrow, then on to LA, then overland to Costa Rica. What are you up to in the hols?'

'Oh, you know, the usual jet-setting. I'm going out to my back garden tomorrow, then on to the village, then maybe overland to Dullford.'

She whooped, 'Oh Sarcy, you're such a scream!' Then she dropped her voice. 'You know, this place's empty all summer, if you fancy a dip, just buzz our chap Chivvers on the gate, I'll tip him awff.'

Then, as I opened my mouth to check I'd understood, and she'd offered what I thought she'd offered, she curled her arm round Milly and they started snogging.

I clamped my mouth shut and slid down until the cool water closed over my head. Pushing off the steps towards the deep end, I was happy to spot Ben's stripy trunks in the swirling murk and swam faster, planning to creep up and ping his waistband. But as I got nearer, his body shifted and I saw that Tash was with him. And they were snogging. Underwater. Is that even humanly possible?

I somersaulted and kicked for the surface, so they wouldn't think I was some kind of perve. But then I felt someone grab my ank– ouch, my stomach feels like it's shrinking . . .

Okay, deep breaths . . . smile . . .

Right. Sorted.

So, I'd just pushed off the bottom of the pool when I felt someone grab my ankle. I kicked back, hard, guessing Tim Lough or one of his equally brainy mates was having 'a right laugh'. But the hand didn't let go, it gripped tighter, and tighter, holding me down, so I started thrashing and twis– oh, woh . . .

Hold on a minute.

Sorry

Posted Friday 30th July, 21:09

I know I'm being very journalistically unprofessional, but that horrid hollow feeling I get sometimes just came back quite badly then, and smiling didn't help at all, so I had to walk about and sing a bit to distract myself. Anyway, I think it's best if I skip to the next part . . . .

Okay, so I burst out of the water, spluttering and gasping, with my eyes stinging with chlorine and my lungs on fire . . . well, blah blah blah, whatever, you know. I was spitting mad, spinning, scanning the chopping waves, still expecting to find Tim or someone. But the face that suddenly rose up next to me wasn't grinning gormlessly. It was smirking and winking like everything was just so hilarious and then it giggled and my foggy eyes realised it was Portia and I opened my mouth to swear illegally but nothing came out because I had no air and then she said, 'Hey, babe, I've got some really juicy gossip! Have you heard about the creepy saddo in our year who's never *ever* got off with a boy at the school gates but still leeches around so she can get off on watching *everyone else* snogg–'

Argh! I'm going hollow again . . .

Enough. You know, what's the point? Maybe it's best to forget what happened next. Telling you about it isn't going to make it any better. Besides, leaving out the most horrible key facts is quite normal, I think. Newspapers do it all the time when they're writing about their favourite politicians. Let's just say things got nasty, or rather – *Portia* got nasty. Nasty-er.

But it's fine really.

She's pathetic.

And I am not the least bit bothered about her.

Besides, woo hoo, she's going to be away for the entire summer, poncing about on her darling daddy's yacht on the Costa del Swank. And, thanks to Jess Bradley, even if I don't get a boyfriend, I will be so fabulously sophisticated by the time she gets back that she won't dare try anything like that again.

So, it's all cool.

Totally.

Race against time: will girl be forced to stare into space for 31 days?

Posted Sunday 1st August, 20:27

I've been flicking through the Sunday papers, so I thought I'd try out a tabloidy headline. I also thought I'd check how I look in journalistic mode (i.e. thinking at the same time as typing) so I took a photo of myself on my mobile. It's impressive. I'm wearing a bright blue cagoule with the hood up because my deckchair's damp, my front teeth are glamorously smeared with *Forbidden Scarlet* and I'm trying to raise one eyebrow, which has made my eyes cross. I look about as intelligent as a bun.

Anyway, I've some good news and some bad news.

The good news . . . I think the weekends might be okay. It turns out Ben's planning to play tennis every Saturday afternoon, so Tash and I can hang out on our own then, at least. And Mum's around on Sundays, with either Ralph or AJ (who are *never* around at the same time even though they're 'just friends' men).

Ralph (pronounced Rafe) came over this morning with the *Mail on Sunday*, which (in case you are an international imaginary reader who has never seen it) is mainly about pot plants and facelifts.

Ralph's good point is his shiny open-topped sports car (which comes free with his shiny job in advertising) so we whizzed to The Soggy Duck for a roast. Mum and Ralph giggled about politics all the way home, but I managed to ignore them by fantasising that R-Patz was sitting next to me, and practising throwing my hair back suggestively and sideways smiling.

AJ strolled in ten minutes after Ralph roared off. He brought the *Observer*, which is mainly about foreign films and famous dead people.

AJ (no one knows his full name) is a penniless poet, all scruffy waistcoats and trailing sleeves. He looks quite groovy, I guess, for an older man. He has a sweet short-sighted collie called Meg who has an Official Crush on Johnny Depp (very unreciprocated). And he always has a totally obscure book in his back pocket, this afternoon it was *Nobody Is Here And Nobody Knows It And Why: Reflections & Essays Part II*. I asked him who wrote the book if nobody was here but he just said, enigmatically, 'Ah, you'll understand when you're older . . .' which I think is grown-up code for 'No figging idea.' Mum used to say it when I asked about my so-called dad after he left and it obviously meant nothing because now I am over three entire years older, but I still don't understand.

AJ's the least annoying 'just friends' man right now as he gave me the laptopasaurus, which has not only boosted my journalistic career but also saved me from having to beg to use Mum's fancy Macbook, which belongs officially to her boss and is 'expensive clinical equipment darling'. AJ said he was going back to 'good old pen and ink' as the computer was 'murdering his metaphors'. This is fine by me, as I wouldn't know a metaphor if one marched up and poked me in the eye.

So. The bad news . . . I still haven't found an even half-decent hot topic. I hoped the papers might inspire me, but the stories were all too gloomy. The supplements were better, until I found a totally depressing article about the actress Layla Grey. It had a column of photos headed *Layla's Love List* with these captions underneath:

Layla and childhood sweetheart: antiques heir Jordan Soames.
Partying in Dublin with Irish musician Paul Malone.
Dining out with DJ Harry Parker-Fipps during their six-month liaison.
At the BAFTAs with hot new director Leon Sykes.
In Malibu with Hollywood heart throb Chuck Hernandez.
With F1 racing driver Sergio Mazerala in Monaco.
On set with new love co-star Davy Goldstein.

Layla's only two-and-a-bit years older than me. Very deep sigh.

If I had pictures, my *Love List* would look like this:

Kissing 'Joseph' backstage at the Year Five Nativity as a swap for a Mars Bar.
Pecking a terrified Clyde Ombango on the cheek at the Year Nine disco.
Snogging Tim Hurd in a papier mâché cauldron at the Scouts Halloween party.
Snogging Tim's twin Tom at the same party because he said he was Tim.
Snogging Harif Ali at the same party because I was angry with Tim and Tom.
Holding hands with Drew Johnston during a not-quite-three-day liaison.
Nearly being asked out by Hell House gigolo Jake Weatherall.

Okay. Confession time. Nobody knows this, not even Tash, I've always been really vague and mysterious about my 'romantic' past in London.

Are you ready? Are you sure?

Right. Drum roll please . . .

I have never had a proper boyfriend.

Not even one I didn't like.

I just can't seem to get the hang of boys. It's cool if they're just mates, like Ben. But as soon as I fancy someone it all goes wrong somehow, just as it did with Jake. One minute he was very suggestively holding my elbow, the next he was suckered on to every girl in the area who wasn't me.

I really thought things might be different here. That starting over in a new place would change me somehow.

When Mum broke the news that 'financial circumstances' meant we had to sell our flat and move out to The Middle Of Absolute Nowhere I went ballistic. I had to run round and round the park to stop myself shouting at her. It seemed so unfair – stupid too. But I needed to keep myself pulled together, so I clung on to the only hope I could think of – that moving might transform my non-existent love life. But, if anything, it's got even worse.

Hold on . . . that could be useful, could it be my totally hot topic?

Why I have never had a boyfriend?

God. No. How sad and weird is that? If I was wearing a Jess Bradley-style floppy flower, it would shrivel up and die of shame.

Circe Shaw's Scintillatingly Exciting Summer Holiday Adventures: Day One

Posted Monday 2nd August, 19:08

Nothing happened.

I mean Absolutely Nothing At All.

 41

If I was writing an old-fashioned type of diary it would say:

Dear Diary, Woke up. Breathed. Went to bed.

What are the key facts right now? Well, Mum's sitting on the patio, on the phone to the animal rescue people about fostering some ratlets rejected by their mother. Johnny Depp's hissing at his own shadow. Ralph's due round any minute, woo hoo.

I'm half-typing, half-watching TV. I put the news on so I could study the reporters' techniques. But they're just wittering on about what colour shoes the women MPs are wearing, like it makes a difference to their actual brains or something, so I've turned the sound down. Maybe I should write about what colour socks the men MPs are wearing? Or pants?

Big Ben says it's seven. I wonder if small Ben's still with Tash? They were rowing down Dullford River today, all the way from the 'inspiring' village of Upper Boring to the 'stunning' hamlet of Lower Snoring. Tash did invite me but I said, 'Six hours in a boat trying not to watch you two trying not to grope each other would be just peachy, but I've decided to pull all my eyelashes out instead.'

Actually, I didn't, I just said, 'Ah, be great, but I've lots of stuff I need to do, you know, for my journalism.'

I wonder if she'll call tonight? I doubt anyone else will. Ben doesn't really do phoning. And literally everyone even half-nice at school has jetted off to their second homes in Provence/Tuscany/The Caribbean. Yawn. How dull.

Seven. God. I can stay up till eleven. Four whole hours more. I'd walk over to the paddock and give Sharon a carrot but I need all my fingers for typing. Ha. I know, I'll paint my nails in a new professionally journalistic style.

Black, white, (a teeny bit green) and bored all over

Posted Monday 2nd August, 19:47

Nails now alternate *Noir Nuit* and *Chalky Chick (Frosted Punk Princess Edition)* with *Luminous Liminous* stripes down the middle. Cool. Showed Ralph, he looked scared. Flumped on my bed now, waving them up at R-Patz. He looks unimpressed.

Circe Shaw's Triumphant First Day Back At School (in her dreams)

Posted Monday 2nd August, 20:26

Ahhh, feeling swoony. I just let my brain get lost in its favourite fantasy . . .

It's 3.45-ish on Wednesday, 1st September – that's the first day of next term.

Portia has been trying to get up to her usual charming tricks all day, but has been astonished and appalled by my new fabulous sophistication. So I'm walking out of the school gates feeling good and looking my best only better (with a smaller bump in my nose, or no bump at all, and really smooth hair and perfectly applied *Forbidden Scarlet*) when I notice R-Patz pacing around broodingly. I assume he's meeting one of the 'It' girls in my year. But he ignores them as they giggle by and stares right at me, licking his lips like I am exactly his idea of the ideal snack.

I'm so entranced I don't even notice Mr Dire's Vespa suddenly swerving out of control and buzzing lethally towards me. Just as I'm about to be gorily moped-ed to death, R-Patz whisks me out of danger, then holds Mr Dire up by his tie and snarls, 'You will bitterly regret your foolish secretarial advice, sir! Circe will be the most fabulously sophisticated journalist this school has ever produced.'

And Portia sees all this and starts salivating enviously and prowling round R-Patz, prodding at him with her boobs. He looks right through her in a disgusted manner though, because he can tell she's thinking bitchy thoughts about me. So she collapses in floods of tears and begs for forgiveness. But we both just throw back our heads and laugh charismatic vampirical laughs.

Then we snog. For a long time.

Juicy, isn't it? It made me grin. But then I remembered I'd be lucky to get even the biggest muppet in the village to be my boyfriend* and meet me at the school gates and show Portia just how excrutiatingly wrong she is about me.

So then I thought I'd better get on with my fabulously sophisticated transformation urgently instead and read some more of my journalism booklet. It says reporters starting out sometimes ride motorbikes to follow the police and be first on the scene of an emergency incident and 'scoop' the story. I'd definitely try it to get a good hot topic, but I'm not sure my old Chopper would keep up. Sharon might, I suppose, if she was in a particularly bad mood.

Oh, hold on, is that my phone? No. It's Mum's *again*. I think she's doing it deliberately.

Never mind, only 2,678,400 seconds to fill before the real first day of term.

2,678,399 . . .

2,678,398 . . .

* There are at least four major muppets in our village but not even one has ever noticed I exist.

I doubt I'll ever be able to sleep again
Posted Tuesday 3rd August, 02:37

I'm in bed with neckache, ruined nails and a brain full of angry thoughts that keep swelling up and exploding into loads of new even angrier thoughts.

It turned out Mum's last phone call was a new client in an emergency situation.

'I might be out for a few hours, darling – you'll be okay, won't you?'

I'm used to Mum's job, and being on my own, but I'm still not quite used to how pitch black it gets here without any street lights. I nodded like mad though and exuded masses of sensible maturity, so she didn't get Ralph to stay, or worse, call in our nearest neighbour, Sharon's owner Geraldine (who says she sees angels and is even more scary than her pony).

Then it hit me that this could be an excellent journalistic opportunity and I wouldn't even need a motorbike. So I quickly transformed myself into the epitome of a helpful offspring. 'Um, there's nothing on TV tonight and I don't have to get up early – can I come along, you know, in case you need back-up?'

Mum looked a bit surprised as I haven't volunteered to go on a call with her for years, but she nodded towards her Mini. 'Okay, hop in then.'

Unfortunately, Mum hasn't got a siren or even a flashing light on her car. But she slapped a 'VET ON EMERGENCY' sign on the windscreen and we hurtled along the lanes so fast they blurred into green tunnels.

After about ten minutes, we pulled up at a pair of spiked gates that moaned open like something out of a cheesy horror film. Inside, a rough twisting track led up to a properly gothic house with arched windows and gargoyles snarling out from the corners.

While Mum went to check she'd got the right place, I sat in the car enjoying feeling a bit spooked in the dark and imagining my favourite vampire swooping down and tucking into my virginal neck. I was just picturing him battling through my hair to actually find my neck when there was a tap on the window. I looked up, hopefully, and pouting a bit, only to see an old man in a tweed cap. He was pale, but I didn't spot any fangs when he smiled, so I opened the door.

He bowed. 'Enchanted. I'm Lucien, do come along and I'll rustle you up an ott chockay what. Your ma's gone straight round to young wuffess and flaying flinn.'

As no one's invented a Radical Plum–English/English–Radical Plum dictionary, I smiled and followed him, hoping for the best.

Ott chockay turned out to be a huge steaming mug of creamy cocoa. Young wuffess turned out to be Rufus, a stocky dark groom in muddy jeans and a scruffy black T-shirt. Flaying flinn turned out to be Flying Flint, a 17.2 hands high (huge) dapple grey gelding with colic (major tummy ache). An injection normally sorts colic out pretty quickly, but Mum said this case was more complicated and the horse needed to be walked round until the pain went away, because if he stopped and lay down he might twist his insides and die.

Rufus was coaxing Flint across the cobbled yard, tapping him on the rump with the end of his blue lead rope whenever he paused. The horse's head was drooping so much his soft white nose was inches from the ground and he was letting out wheezy grunts of pain.

Wincing at the sound, I nipped across to a straw bale tucked into a corner and sat down, well out of the way as Mum taught me when I was little, but within helping distance if she did need me. I then started being observant.

I suppose journalists follow the police to report on serious murders and things and nothing like that had happened. But I still hoped being in a real-life dramatic situation might help me find an idea like one of Jess Bradley's *Hot Topicals*. She uses her own daily real-life dramas to report on things like how crazy it is that girls in some countries aren't allowed to learn to read, or why pretend boobs are silly and not very convenient on buses.

It was really dark in my corner, but I thought coping in extreme conditions would be good training, so I dug my professional equipment (pen and spiral-bound reporter's notebook) out of my jeans and started making notes. Like this . . .

Who? Mum (vet), Lucien (boss), Rufus (groom),
Flying Flint (horse), Circe (me)
What? Emergency vet call-out
When? Monday 2nd August, 11.25 p.m.
Where? Stableyard (quite shabby, but nice) behind house (gothy)

Why? Flying Flint (horse) with colic (complicated case)

Then I added . . .

Other/miscellaneous/useful Atmosphere edgy. Also dark – only light from olde-worlde lamps. Mum flicking thermometer, talking (very quietly, intensely) to Lucien (nodding, frowning) who is stroking lurcher (dog) dozing on rug (tartan). Mum now shaking head and tucking hair (straight tawny bob) behind ears.

Yes, I know, my mum's hair is seriously annoying. I have my so-called dad's daft hair. Her hair used to be amazing, almost to her waist, but it's got shorter and shorter over the last few years, maybe because she's had problems with older men not taking her seriously. When I observed that, I wondered if it could be a hot topic, say, *Do bobs get more respect?* It did feel meatier than Tash's hair idea, but it didn't make my heart fizz, like things do when you know they're right.

So I carried on with my journalistic observations by studying Rufus and noticed that his thick black hair was matted and spiked with straw and his face looked a bit like a bruise, with greenish stubble on his jaw and blue shadows under his pale eyes. He looked like he hadn't slept in days. As he led Flint towards me, I smiled sympathetically and his strange, light gaze met mine for a second, then seemed to intensify, like it was boring straight through me and out the other side.

I had to stop my observations then as the horrid, hungry feeling started hollowing me out again. I tried another smile but it got worse. So I squeezed my eyes shut and shook my head furiously to try and shift it when . . .

CLACKCLACKCLACK clackackackackackackackack

. . . a deafening clattering echoed round the yard – it sounded like a whole herd of horses had galloped in. I stopped shaking my head, snapped my eyes open and gasped. It was Flint. He was shying, skittering sideways just a few feet away. His eyes rolled as he staggered and slid, his metal shoes firing sparks across the cobbles.

Rufus was fighting to hang on to him and I leapt to my feet to help. But then, incredibly, Flint found his hooves at last and stayed upright, snorting hot blasts of air out of his flared nostrils, the whites of his eyes still showing.

Knowing any movement could spook him again, I froze, watching as Rufus ran his hand down the horse's arched neck under his silvery mane and murmured, 'Whoa, steady boy,' over and over.

After a few minutes, Flint's sides stopped heaving as his breathing finally calmed down. Rufus turned to me and I smiled, feeling light-headed with relief, and thinking he'd smile too.

'You stupid little cow!'

His insult hit me like a slap. I stepped back, my cheeks burning.

He narrowed his eyes and hissed, 'What the hell did you think you were doing hiding there?'

Hiding? How dare he? If I'd wanted to hide I would have made a better job of it. I'm an expert. My shock flipped instantly to outrage. I hissed back, 'I wasn't hiding, I was right in front of you – I smiled at you.'

Rufus did smile at that, only it wasn't a smile really, his lips curled up at one side and his eyes clouded, then went sort of dead. If a snake could smile it would smile exactly like that. When he opened his mouth I half expected a forked tongue to dart out. Though maybe what actually came out was worse.

'Ooh, sorreee.' He paused, clicked his tongue to encourage Flint forward again, then put on a high, mocking sing-song voice as he passed me. 'Did I miss you flashing your pretty smile and flicking your pretty hair?'

'Wha– bu– I was just being friendly.' My voice squeaked out defensively, then I remembered I was telling the truth. 'You look wrecked – I felt sorry for you!'

Rufus spun round and opened his mouth, but I didn't fancy another tongue-lashing, so I rushed on, 'And it's not my fault you're blinder than a bat – and you should have had him on a shorter lead rope!'

I knew that last part wasn't strictly fair, but there was no going back.

He turned Flint and started towards me again. 'Oh, *really*?'

As he said, or rather, snarled that, he raised an eyebrow. Yes, just *one*! Despite everything, I had to bite my lip to stop myself asking how he did it.

'So you think you'd do better, do you? Here – he's all yours!' And with that he threw the rope at me, stomped over to where Lucien and Mum were sitting on a mounting block talking and spat, 'Your little girl's taking over!'

My fury shot straight up the rope and Flint tossed his head and backed away. The rough hemp whipped through my hands, burning my palms. I nearly lost it but jumped up and snatched the end, adding insult to injury by chipping the tips off my new manicure.

On the other side of the yard, Mum mouthed, 'Okay?' and raised both eyebrows (perhaps it's genetic?) and I forced a huge smile to show Rufus I was in fact very mature, and totally not bothered about him. I then started marching Flint round the yard, terrified every time he faltered that he'd sink to his knees, but whispering encouragement and radiating extreme calm (horses must never know you're scared, it scares them too).

After what seemed like years, Mum came over and took Flint's temperature. 'Excellent. All done.' To my disgust, she then held the back of her hand to my forehead (though I suppose I have to be grateful she didn't pop her thermometer up my bum). 'Darling, are you all right?'

I shrank away and snapped, 'Fine!' on autopilot, although by then my right arm felt twice as long as my left and my neck was so stiff I thought my head might snap off if I nodded. Worse, inside my head, my brain had been concentrating so hard on Flint, it had forgotten all about hot topics. Then I spotted Rufus, still scowling across at me, chewing hay, obviously willing me to collapse, so I laughed loudly in a very nonchalant way and added, 'Great!' though it did come out a bit growly.

On the way to the car, Lucien thanked us about a hundred times and gave Mum a massive bear hug. Rufus grunted 'Cheers' to Mum but totally ignored me, which was fine because I totally ignored him too. I only wondered why a lovely man like Lucien would hire such a nasty boy. I also noticed he smelt a bit, not exactly of BO, but not very charming either, sort of leathery and manurey and a bit salty. Gross.

As we bumped back down the pot-holed track, Mum tutted and said, almost to herself, 'What a mess. But Lucien's such a gent . . . oh and I do hope poor Rufus gets some sleep now, he looked so exhausted.'

I just shrugged and huffed a bit. I hoped Rufus would lie awake for the rest of his life feeling guilty about being such a stonking muppet. But as he is definitely The Rudest Stupidest Most Despicable Boy I've Ever Met he'll probably just laugh himself to sleep instead.

Then I remembered his vile, snaky smile and mocking

voice and that reminded me of another mocking voice and my body did that thing where it shudders all over just once, like a jolt, or the feeling you get when you accidentally touch a bug when you're little. And Mum flinched and tilted her head as if she wanted to say something important. But she didn't, of course, she just sighed and leaned forward and flicked the radio on. And I'd gone rigid inside, so I hugged myself really hard and closed my eyessssssssssssssssssssssssssssssssssssssssssssssss

Johnny Depp saved my life

Posted Tuesday 3rd August, 10:49

I was nearly killed in the night. Totally. I know I'm a teenager, but I promise this is NOT AN EXAGGERATION!

I fell asleep blogging with my laptopasaurus open on my stomach. If it had stayed like that it would have roared itself into a ball of flames, ignited the thatched roof just inches above my bed and burnt The Nook down in split seconds. Mum would have murdered me, if I hadn't already been dead, though I guess she'd have been dead too.

Instead, I woke up this morning with the laptop closed beside me and Johnny Depp snoring on top of it, with a huge snail under one paw. I guess he'd come to bring me the snail present, was attracted by the heat, climbed on and automatically shut it down as the lid closed.

Thank you Johnny Depp, almost domestic pet, fire safety expert, hero. I will never again complain when you bring me a snail, though I would still prefer flowers.

The fluffiest film stars in the village
Posted Tuesday 3rd August, 17:35

Mum just whizzed into the garden between coming in from work and going out with AJ and forced a highly unwelcome spontaneous consultation on me. When she said, 'Anything you want to *talk* about?' as usual, I said, 'No' as usual. But then she said it again, slower, as if I'd been struck down with advanced learning difficulties or something. I started crossing my eyes sarcastically when it suddenly occurred to me she might think I'd gone with her last night because I'm lonely at home on my own, so I straightened them and snapped, '*No!*' so she wouldn't draft in Geraldine. Then I had a quick intelligent brainwave and added chirpily, 'It was useful watching you work last night – observing people is part of my Special Holiday Homework Project,' (excellent new code for my blog). Her forehead did wrinkle, but she said, 'Okay then, darling, good.' Then she went back to humming about in her bedroom.

Tash and Ben are out tonight too, they've gone to see a documentary on torture at The Arthouse cinema, so no doubt they've been snogging non-stop for the past two hours. If I was feeling wicked I'd ask them over tomorrow and test them on the key facts. But thanks to my petrifyingly close shave with Death, I'm feeling very generous and grateful to be alive, even without a totally hot topic or any hope of getting a proper boyfriend.

I decided to reward Johnny Depp for his heroism with his favourite beetroot and avocado salad (he was living rough behind an M&S when Mum rescued him) and a good brushing. He's posing on the front gatepost now, looking extra fluffy and pleased with himself, a bit like the real Johnny Depp, only with a slightly purple chin.

Jude Law enjoyed his brushing too and is looking about as dashing as a guinea pig can look. Daniel Craig didn't much like his and is now hiding under a lettuce leaf, which I've told him is not very James Bond.

Comment

Posted Wednesday 4th August, 01:29, by Savvy Rose

Hey, Circe (cool name by the way), I'm your imaginary reader – only I exist! I'm live and kicking in Manhattan and, oh my gosh, I am *so* loving your blog.

I was googling for 'totally hot pics of Jude Law' (want to mail one to my best girlfriend on her birthday, she is *so* into him) when *Jude Law dashing guinea pig* flashed up. How freaking random is that? Just had to check it out, then couldn't stop reading, took me back to my crazy High School days – hilarious.

Can't help with your hot topic, sorry. But I sure can help with the boy thing. I'm a tailor on Madison, so I've totally sussed how guys operate. And I *so* know you can figure them out too, you sound awesome and you have masses of useful experience – you just don't know it. Take it from me, honey, if you want to hook a boy, just treat him like a big pet.

Good luck!

Oh. My. God.
Posted Wednesday 4th August, 10:17

I've got an actual, living, breathing, totally non-imaginary reader! In New York!

Hi Savvy Rose, amazing to virtually meet you. Welcome to Totally Hot Topics (apologies for the lack of totally hot topics).

Suspect you don't know what my name really means, but thanks anyway.

Wow! Working on Madison Avenue must be amazing. Do you make suits? Are American guys as square-jawed in real life as they are on TV? Do they smell nice? Some of the boys over here smell rubbish.

Thanks for the tip about boys being like pets, but I've

 57

decided boys are just too inconvenient and complicated. They seem to either not actually notice I even exist as a proper girlfriend opportunity. Or as soon as they do notice me they act like total plonking muppets. They will also definitely distract me from my career as a fabulously sophisticated journalist. So I'm now Officially Giving Up All Boys. Until I'm ancient. Or 30. Or 18. Minimum.

Desperately seeking Savvy . . .

Posted Friday 6th August, 09:43

Hi Savvy Rose – if you're still out there – HELP!

You're probably madly glamorously busy sewing all day, dancing all night, and going up and down skyscrapers in between, but I'm now the epitome of properly desperate.

The pet boy thing is driving me bonkers – what do you actually *mean*?

I know, I was going to totally give up boys. I did try, really hard, honestly. I even took my beautiful R-Patz poster down, but that left a gaping void in my heart. And when I switched on the TV, Orlando Bloom was being interviewed and I concentrated on not fancying him, but it was a physical human impossibility.

So, I resigned myself to being a hopeless case and started thinking about your advice. That got me thinking about all my nearly boyfriends, and Jake, of course (not in a daydreamy way, but in a cold calculating research way). But I just can't see how treating them like pets would do any good. And I'm sure you don't mean feeding them a healthy balance of meat and biscuits and stopping them leaving hair all over the sofa, but that's really the only experience I've got.

I went for a milkshake with Ben yesterday, so I could watch him. But I didn't spot any pet sort of behaviour, unless you count scratching quite a lot, but I think that was because he'd put too much mega-gunk on his mohawk. So that was no help either.

I also tried complex psychology, studying our cat and the guinea pigs and AJ's dog and even Sharon the Shetland from a distance, though only an officially bonkers person like Geraldine would ever call her a pet. I thought if I could identify any boy sort of behaviour in animals it might help me work things out. But apart from Daniel Craig being a bit pongy, and Sharon always being up for a fight like Tim Lough, I'm still clueless.

I told Tash what you said and she thinks it might have something to do with showing the boy you're boss. Is it? If I ignore the fact that Johnny Depp is in charge of me and Mum, that sounds like it might be a half-decent theory.

Or is it something to do with good grooming?

Or lots of the right kind of cuddling?

Or keeping them indoors at night?

Please write again soon or I think my brain might actually totally explode.

Bang

Posted Friday 6th August, 23:47

Special live dispatch from deepest Dullford

Posted Saturday 7th August, 15:52

Deepest Dullford was plunged into a state of shock today by an astonishing event. A gang of local boys, driven to total bored insanity by the lack of anything at all to do, dared to try a bit of breakdancing in the town square.

Less than split seconds later, a van-load of police stormed in to force the youths to stop and return to a state of yawning gloominess as they were in danger of causing unheard-of surprise and excitement. But the boys ignored the officers, even when they started waving their truncheons threateningly.

Then, just as it looked like things were going to get nasty, an unknown girl, thought to live nearby in The Middle Of Absolute Nowhere, strolled over and said quietly and with astonishing dignity, 'Okay boys, leave it.'

The unruly mob immediately stopped spinning on their hoodie hoods and returned to obedient upright positions. They then gazed at the girl in a besotted way, obviously waiting for her next command. But she just raised one eyebrow modestly, patted each boy affectionately on the head, tossed the cutest one a chocolate biscuit, then went on her way.

An amazed eyewitness described the stranger as being in stunningly magnificent control of the boys and added that she was fabulously sophisticated despite having huge hair.

Okay, okay, I might have made that up

Posted Saturday 7th August, 16.22

Although this is a real live dispatch. I'm sitting in Dullford town square outside Bev's Baps. It's not exactly funky Frith Froth in Soho where Jess Bradley hangs out. But to get a Wi-Fi connection, it was either here or in the chippy squished between the fruit machine and a tiny old man who'd fallen asleep halfway through his haddock.

I'm doing an exercise from my booklet while I wait for Tash and Ben to come back from the tennis club. I was at the club too until twenty minutes ago. I know, rubbish isn't it? So much for girlie Saturday afternoons.

Very reluctantly, I let Tash drag me along to watch Ben play an 'important' match today. I only agreed because I thought Ben's opponent, Canadian Chuck, might be cute in a checked shirt lumberjacky way. But he turned out to be the kind of sporty boy who's extra long, which isn't my type at all.

Even worse, Sally, Chuck's extra-long Canadian girl-friend was watching too. And Tash insisted I sit between them. And every time Chuck played a good shot, Sally whooped. And every time Ben played a good shot, Tash 'ooh'ed. And every time Ben hit the ball he grunted. And every time Chuck served he said 'Yesss-sirrr'. So the match sounded like this . . .

'Urgh'

'Oooh'

'Urgh'

'Aaah'

'Whoooo'

'Urgh'

'Yesss-sirrr!'

And it all started to sound a bit rampantly meaningful if you know what I mean. So I whispered urgently to Tash, 'Swap places – I know you don't want me to feel left out, but I'm far too joined in.'

But she just gasped back, 'Oooooh!' because Ben scored a point.

Then Chuck served an ace with a particularly throaty, 'Yesss-sirrr!'

And Sally squealed, 'Yeė haa – go baby go!'

And my bottled-up laughter sort of exploded out of me. And the umpire glared down from his perch and snapped, 'Be quiet young lady!' So I forced myself to think of Portia to make me feel angry instead of hysterical, but that gave me quite loud hiccups, so he asked me to leave.

This means I've officially been thrown out of a tennis club, which is definitely not fabulously sophisticated. But it could be described as quite rebelliously sassy I think, so is not all bad.

Anyway, in my exercise I'm meant to *'Write exactly what you see in approximately 150 words'*. Apparently there are *'Stories everywhere, in everything'*, and newspaper editors often need last-minute short reports to fill space if an advertiser decides not to sell things after all, or if an accident doesn't actually happen, or turns out to be totally uninteresting.

My report was based on the true facts. I mean I did scan the area for story possibilities and did see something happening. But when I typed it up it was so tedious I thought I might actually faint.

This afternoon, three local boys stopped on the edge of the town square. One boy shuffled from foot to foot, while his mates leaned against a parking meter, yawning. After a few minutes a traffic warden marched up, told them off for obstructing council property and waved his ticket pad. The boys all went pink and said sorry.

See what I mean? I understand now why some journalists work for the kind of newspapers where they can spend all day thinking up fibs.

What to remember never to say to Tash in front of Ben and to Ben in front of Tash and to any boys ever in front of anyone at all or even alone

Posted Saturday 7th August, 19:35

When Ben turned up after his match he was puffed up with sporty boy pride because he won, and huffed at me for hiccupping.

Naturally, I started to defend myself, explaining why I'd been giggling, but then realised that it might sound like I was teasing Tash in a bad way. So I swerved off and started jabbering about internet communications because Ben's really into that as he's starting a digital design course at college in September. And I ended up telling him about Savvy Rose and the blog (though not the name or web address, of course, can you imagine?).

He was dead impressed that I'd had a visitor without doing any publicity, like linking up with other bloggers or getting listed on search engines. He reckons I'll have to do all those things if I want other readers to know my blog exists as there are, in fact, even more than a gazillion blogs on the web. But I'm not going to yet, especially as I still don't have a totally hot topic, which makes my blog name worse than an embarrassing farce.

I'm in my office under the willow now, which means that I'm not literally staying in on a Saturday night, as I am in fact, out, even if it's only just a bit out.

Mum and Ralph are at Le Gingham Bistro, an 'authentic eaterie' in the next village where everything is covered in, ahem, gingham. I'm not just talking tablecloths and napkins here: the chairs, lampshades, curtains, carpets, cutlery – even the cups and saucers are gingham. It's like some kind of check hell.

I didn't reply fast enough when Mum invited me last time, and before I knew it she'd thrown a coat over me and practically kidnapped me into the back of Ralph's car. And when the waitress put the teapot on the table I wasn't looking, so I couldn't find it for a few seconds, but I pretended I couldn't find it at all, which Tash and Ben would have found hilarious. But Mum just rolled her eyes and Ralph looked like he wanted to say, 'Stop it silly teenager,' but couldn't because I'm not *his* silly teenager and he knows there is a Line he cannot cross.

This time, when Mum asked, I immediately said, 'Hmm . . .' (as if I was really thinking about it) 'sorry, can't really. I must do some of my Special Holiday Homework Project if I'm going to finish it all by September.'

And Mum said, 'Ah . . . that's a shame,' like she was really sorry (as if).

And Ralph just grinned.

Anyway, it's fine by me. I've tons of important thinking to do to try and solve the pet boy mystery, which I'm determined to unravel even if it takes the rest of my entire life.

I didn't tell Ben about Savvy Rose's theory by the way. I tried to, but I only got as far as, 'Um, Ben, do you think you're anything like a do–' when Tash butted in with, 'NO! I told you Cir-*cee* . . .' she made her eyes go glarey at that bit, 'Ben is *so* not like *Do*minic!' We don't know a Dominic, so I made my eyes go glarey back at her. Then she turned to Ben and said, 'Heisanewboyinyearelevenwithamoh awkthesameasyoursbutyouarenothinglikehim!' It all came out in one go, honestly, without even a comma, so I had no chance of squeezing in even a teeny 'but'.

It was more than totally frustrating, and dragging your best friend all the way to Dullford then not allowing her to speak is not my idea of polite. So I complained when we were on our own on the bus later.

'Why did you stop me telling Ben about the pet thing?

'Ultimate durr, Circe – it's obvious isn't it?'

'Um . . . no.'

Tash did look a bit shamefaced then. 'Oh. I thought it was, sorry. Some things are best kept between girls, that's all.'

Which made me realise it's going to be quite tricky being a BFF and a BGFF and a BFBGFF all at the same time.

'Besides, if you learn anything, I might be able to use it too.'

'What? But you so don–'

I was about to argue that she didn't need any tricks as she's a natural boy magnet, whereas I've never had a proper boyfriend. But then I remembered she didn't know that, so I turned my sentence into a fake cough, which then turned into a real cough and then I couldn't say anything at all to anyone at all for ages.

God, life is beyond complicated sometimes.

Please don't worry, I will never turn up on your doorstep or in your skyscraper lift or anywhere unexpected[*]

Posted Sunday 8th August, 09:09

In case that's why you haven't written back, Savvy Rose. I'm not even expecting to be cyber mates or anything, I promise. But if you could write just one more time, just one line to explain what you meant about the pet boy thing then I might be able to stop obsessing and get back to concentrating on finding a totally hot topic so I won't be classified as an Official Teenage Laughing Stock if anyone does read my blog.

---

[*] Proven psychological fact: I scored nine red triangles (equalled *No Way*) and only one black heart (*Way*) in the *Would you stalk him?* quiz in *Cosmo* last month.

Screech to a halt with a dramatic sound effect like a DJ scratching a record

Posted Sunday 8th August, 09:22

OMG. I am deeply ashamed of how devastatingly dense I've been. If I met me in the street I would definitely cross over to avoid myself.

My totally hot topic . . . it could be the pet boy thing! Couldn't it?

What did Tash say? Hang on a second, I need to check the blog archive . . .

Okay. Am I passionate about it? Yes.

Do I understand it? No! But I want to *so* much, which means I could definitely learn from it.

And if I could learn from it, I guess it could help and inspire others. Though I doubt there's any other fifteen-something girl on the entire planet who hasn't had a proper boyfriend, unless it's because she fancies girls instead of boys or lives in a place where there just are no boys, if there are places like that. There are places where there are almost no girls, China's one of them. Jess Bradley wrote about it, she said there are almost more pandas than girls in some parts of China. Maybe I should go and live there? But can you imagine the humiliation if I still didn't get a boyfriend? All the Chinese people pointing and gasping, 'Holy crispy noodles, she's the only girl for thousands of miles around but still no one fancies her!'

I would have to hide in the jungle and live wild among the pandas.

Basic Obedience Training For Beginners
Male Human Pet Control: Experiment 1

Posted Sunday 8th August, 23:06

Or maybe that should be p(o)et control? AJ came over for supper tonight and when Mum was in the garden picking herbs, I started my official totally hot topic research.

AJ was fiddling with the cuffs of his wafty Victorian shirt and frowning out of the window in Mum's direction. I was sitting on the sofa on the other side of the room (about three feet away) pretending to read a magazine but secretly watching for any pet-like behaviour through my hair. Then the idea struck me. Without giving my brain any time to think about why I shouldn't say it, I said . . .

'AJ.'

'Yes Circe?'

'Sit!'

I said it quite loud, in my bossiest, no-nonsense tone of voice, the kind I use in emergencies, like the time Johnny Depp tried to eat a bee.

As soon as the command was out, I went a bit rigid, thinking AJ might whip round stricken-browed and aghast like a real Victorian and spit, 'How dare you address me so, you impudent little whippersnapper, get thy filthy soul to the workhouse forthwith!'

But he didn't. He turned away from the window, walked over to the sofa and sat. Just like that.

Ta da! Result. If it was proper research I suppose I'd have to try to make him do it over and over again to come up with a scientifically statistical percentage. But I think he'd get suspicious, and I'd definitely get bored.

I was tempted to try it just one more time while he was pacing from wall to wall while Mum was fixing coffee. But he was rattling on about the tragic hidden meaning in a doorknob or something and if I'd got him to sit next to me my ears would have had no choice but to listen.

Ralph's coming round tomorrow night though, so I'm going to try and see if I can get him to fetch something.

Comment

Posted Monday 9th August, 05:45, by Savvy Rose

Hey, Circe, I'm back on the block. And, oh my gosh – I am *so* sorry, I didn't mean to take off and cause major teenage freak-out. The city got super steamy last week so I headed out to The Hamptons with the girls to cool off and ended up partying on the beach for 48 hours straight. Such a drag! I only got back to my apartment an hour ago (it's twenty after eleven, Sunday night, here).

Geez, what can I tell you? I guess I'm so used to the concept of guys as pets I kinda figured you'd get it straight off. It's all about Attitude, with a freaking giant 'A'. It's not really about showing boys you're the boss (though that sure can be useful sometimes). Honey, it's a breeze: it's about showing them that you're confident – that you know you are totally where-it's-at!

That test you did on your mom's buddy, AJ, made me die by the way. So cute. The feisty tone of your voice probably did make him obey, I figure, on reflex. But if I were you I wouldn't bother experimenting on him or that Ralph dude, they're way too old – it seems kinda like wasted energy.

Where what's at and is 'it' that 'it'?

Posted Monday 9th August, 08:45

Thanks so much, Savvy Rose. Your advice seems very knowing and wise and if you were writing to any other girl I'm sure she'd skip straight off into the horizon and catch herself a proper boyfriend in split seconds. But, unfortunately for you, this is me, and my seriously annoying brain has a question.

Where what's at?

As in, what is the 'it' in where-'it's'-at? I don't think I am 'where-it's-at' but I can't know for sure until I know what 'it' is exactly.

Portia definitely thinks she's 'it'. Maybe that's the same 'it'? She does always have a boyfriend, even if she is now stuck with one who is deeply unattractive. But if her 'it' is that 'it', I'm not sure I want it really.

Where are they at?

Posted Monday 9th August, 09:20

Desperate to talk to Tash about the 'it' question but her mobile's going straight to voicemail, so I just texted.

> SIS.
> Where-it's-at.
> What's 'it'? X

We both know that an SIS (Serious Internal Screaming) text is meant to be answered instantly or sooner, but I sent that over 20 minutes ago and I'm still waiting.

Drumming fingers

Posted Monday 9th August, 09:57

Still waiting.

Peeling polish off nails

Posted Monday 9th August, 10:32

Sigh. Might need to hire a new BFF.

Climbing the walls

Posted Monday 9th August, 18:20

Tash didn't call back for over five hours.

She was climbing an indoor mountain at Plastic Peaks in Dullford with Ben, which is about the only thing worth doing in The Middle Of Absolute Nowhere, so I actually wouldn't have minded going.

I don't blame them for not telling me, I've said no to pretty much everything in the past week to convince them I'm extremely busy with important journalistic business. Still, my heart did clench a bit when I realised they hadn't even tried to invite me. But I did my smiling thing and even managed to laugh as I realised indoor plastic mountain climbing must be the only activity in the entire world where it really is impossible to snog.

Anyway, Tash hadn't understood my urgent 'it' text, so I read out what Savvy Rose had said.

'But that's easy – "it" is *the* place to be – like a party.'

'Oh. Are you sure?'

'Definite.'

'So to control a pet boy I have to act like a party?'

'Yes. Ooh, Circe, you should have seen Ben's biceps today, he's so strong, he's got a proper six-pack too, you know just like you see on posters but never in real life and when he flexes his –'

'Tash!' I butted in. 'Do you think Ben's totally where-it's-at?'

'Oh. My. God. Yes!'

So that proved the point, I guess. And the more I think about it, the more it makes sense. If a boy thinks you're so confident that being with you is like being at a party, maybe he will want you to be his girlfriend – to have fun all the time. Though some boys don't seem to have any fun at parties but just slouch against walls trying to smoulder intensely.

But then Tash isn't like a party really, and boys are totally into her. I mean she is pretty confident (apart from the oblong bum thing) but she's not a loud, dancey type of girl. Though I guess you do get quieter intelligent sorts of parties too, or parties where it's fun but not in a lairy OTT way.

Maybe that's the secret? Maybe you just have to find out what kind of party you are, then sort of exude that at a boy? Tash would be a garden party with chill-out music and fairy lights. Portia would be a dance in hot pants on a podium type of party (but she'd be the only one allowed to dance on a podium). What would I be? A barbecue? No, too meaty and sizzly. A dinner party? Yawn. Hope not. A disco? Closer but maybe a bit too noisy. God I've got no idea.

Why is that? You know, why is it that even if you don't know someone else *that* well, you can still work things out about them from a distance. Whereas you live inside your own skin non-stop from the moment you're born, but sometimes it's really hard to work out anything about yourself. Even what kind of party you are.

This isn't another question for you, Savvy Rose, if you are still out there and haven't given up on me as a hopeless case destined to never get 'it' and/or a proper boyfriend. It's just me and my brain trying to sort things out while I'm waiting for Ralph to turn up. He'll be here before Mum gets home because she's running late thanks to a hamster emergency in Dullford. So I'm going to nip down and try to act confident and like I'm a party as soon as I've worked out what kind, then see if it makes Ralph* obedient too.

* I get what you mean about older guys but my male human practice pet supplies are limited.

Being In Command By Being 'Where-It's-At'
Male Human Pet Control: Experiment 2

Posted Monday 9th August, 22:43

I'm definitely not a disco.

I convinced myself I might be. I do love dancing in flashing lights and not having to worry if anyone's looking at you because your body's smudgy from moving around quite fast. I also love that it doesn't matter if you say too stupid things or too intelligent things to boys, because the music's too loud to hear anything you're saying anyway.

I stayed in my room to get into my new disco persona properly. I thought about changing into a dancey outfit, but decided to keep on my denim shorts and white vest in the end. Mum might not notice much, but even she'd be suspicious if she found me watching TV in silver spandex leggings and my sequinned boob tube. But I did change my stud earrings for the diamanté hoops Tash bought me last Christmas and I painted my nails with gold glitter, which is quite normal.

Then I sat cross-legged in front of my mirror, closed my eyes and imagined I was in the middle of a disco. The last actual disco I went to was in aid of the Upper Boring Bat Protection Society (which Tash and I hoped might attract gothy boys, but where no one was under 50 and the same Michael Jackson album was played over and over again until everyone moonwalked themselves into a coma). So I memory upgraded to a fantasy disco where all the boys looked like R-Patz and they were all doing that intense black-eyed thing that showed they totally wanted to spend eternity climbing trees with me on their back, but would restrain themselves from whisking me off until the end of

'Dancing Queen'. And I pictured shimmying among them in the dark sparkliness until certain bits of my body went quite excitingly fizzy. Then I opened my eyes and stared hard at my reflection while exuding a groovy disco vibe. And I looked a bit boggle-eyed, but quite friendly. Then there was a knock on the front door, so I gave my hair a bit of a groovy shake and went downstairs.

Now, I knew controlling Ralph might be tricky as he is a bit stiff. Literally. His clothes are so ironed I bet they'd stand up without him in them. But I'd prepared properly. I'd put my book on the coffee table opposite the sofa (only a few paces away, so not too demanding, but still an effort). I'd hidden the TV remote, so he couldn't ignore me too easily. I'd even put a bowl of his favourite roasted peanuts on the arm of the sofa to get him to sit in the correct position.

All went well at first. Ralph smiled, I smiled, exuding a bit of disco but not too much. I handed him a glass of Coke and he sat down on the sofa, in exactly the right place. Then I sat next to him, because I needed to be exactly the same distance from the table so there wouldn't be any confusion about him helping me just because I was further away, rather than actually obeying me.

Then I took a deep breath, batted my eyelashes funkily and exuded total disco party confidence straight at him at the same time as saying, in my best no-nonsense voice, 'Ralph, I left my book over there – please could you *fetch* it?'

And the table was right in the middle of the room, and

the book was right in the middle of the table and was obviously my book as it had a picture of a teenage girl on the cover and was also the only book.

Ralph looked at the book, then back at me, then at the book again, then into his Coke, but didn't move.

I thought then that my disco exudations might be a bit too subtle, so I widened my eyes to add a bit of a mirror-ball type glint and commanded, 'My book Ralph, on the table – could you *fetch it*? *Now!*'

This time, Ralph looked at the book, then into his Coke, then at the front door, but he didn't look at me at all and he still didn't move. So I waited, really madly comprehensively exuding disco from every pore and all my hair and both eyes.

Then his lips went thin and he said, 'Look, Circe . . .'

And I got the feeling he was struggling with the rules of The Line, so I stopped flicking my hair about.

'. . . this isn't easy . . .'

I stopped making my eyes flash. My experiment had obviously failed. Far worse, Ralph seemed to be trying to say something important, which must be hard for an ad-man with a brain full of slogans like, *Do you getti enougha spaghetti?*

'Um . . . do you need some dry white wine or a snufty of gin or something?'

Ralph jumped up so fast it was as if the sofa had ejected him. For a moment I thought he was going to fetch my book after all. But he didn't, instead he squeezed himself on to the window ledge as far away from me as possible and said . . .

'Look, Circe, I saw all the facts and figures last month when our demographical data analysts presented their research for our anti-teenage pregnancy campaign on behalf of a well-known brand of chocolate . . .'

He paused then and stared forcefully past me and into the kitchen as if there was a captivated cheering audience there and he was the prime minister talking about world death or something. I tried to look interested but all I could think was, if you were a party you'd be dinner for one in a dark room.

'Circe, you're fifteen, your, ahem, *hormones* will be raging at the moment and sometimes they'll get the better of you and this kind of thing will happen. But, trust me, it *will* pass, I promise.'

I was actually interested then. 'Um, what will, Ralph?'

'This, er . . . this *crush*, Circe.'

And I thought how in raving doughnuts does he know about Jake? And I was about to say, don't worry, it *has* passed, when he muttered, more to himself really, so I nearly didn't hear it . . .

'It's only to be expected, considering your circumstances – your father not being around . . .'

I nearly fell off the sofa then because not one single so-called grown-up has dared to say the 'F' word in front of me for about forever. And the last person on the entire planet who should is definitely Ralph who obviously knows precisely less than zero about me, or he would know I am totally not the kind of person to whinge on or slash my wrists or even bother to think about my so-called dad. And even if I was that kind of person, what would it have to do with me fancying Jake anyway? Not that I fancy him any more, of course.

And then the truth hit me and my whole body felt like it had been plunged into a bath full of the crawliest kind of spiders.

Ralph thought I had a crush on . . . aaaargh it's making the spider thing happen all over again . . . Okay, relax . . . breathe in, breathe out . . .

Are you ready for this? All right, brace yourself.

Ralph thought I had a crush on . . .

Him.

Oh. My. Every illegal swear word in the dictionary. God.

What is it with older men? Don't they ever look in the mirror?

I mean, I'm not saying I'm about to be scouted for cover girl stardom or anything but I'm not *totally desperate*. Actually I suppose I am. But, even so . . .

Anyway, while I was busy feeling covered in spiders and wondering whether to pretend I didn't realise what he meant or to yell something fabulously sophisticated like, 'Desist vain nutter,' Ralph strolled over to the kitchen like he hadn't just dropped a major bombshell and started foraging for sandwich ingredients. He carried on talking the whole time . . .

'It's a very common phenomena blah blah blah a significant problem for teachers blah blah sure you'll meet someone more suitable soon blah blah . . .'

God. What does Mum see in him? Honestly. If Ralph was a pet he would be something particularly clueless, like the ram she had to stitch up last month because he'd sat down on a goose. Or a newt.

By this time, as you can imagine, I was not feeling that comfortable and there was obviously no point trying to get Ralph to fetch my book as he'd only be doing it out of pity. And, weirdly, the more Ralph spoke, the more he kind of puffed up, like he was advertising the sensitive wonderfulness of himself to himself and he believed himself totally. He was dropping the F word like mad too.

'Blah blah your father should be here to guide you blah blah a report revealed around 40 per cent of fathers lose contact with their children blah blah absent fathers responsible for urban youth crime blah blah blah . . .'

And my brain started to get overcrowded with all the useless information he was trying to cram into it. And 'Dancing Queen' was still playing in the back of it, so I tried to turn that up to drown him out, but he was too booming. And my heart wanted to run out of the room screaming but my legs were too wobbly, so my body started sort of shrinking in as if it was trying to tuck itself down the back of the sofa.

Ralph didn't notice any of this, of course, he just droned

on and on and on as he finished making his sandwich. I thought at least he'd shut up while he ate it, so I could get one measly word in. But then he swaggered over and put a cheese doorstep on the sofa arm next to me.

'There you go, Cheeky, friends eh? It'll work out all right.'

Cheeky? *Cheeky?* Had he ever actually met me?

Ralph then treated me to an intense look that was probably meant to say, *I am very fond of you in a strictly paternal way*, but which came across more as, *I don't blame you, I am obviously an irresistible older sex symbol.*

'You might not appreciate it now,' he started ranting again, 'but your fath–'

My mouth had had enough, it spat out the first thing it knew would shut him up. 'Ralph, I have *never* had a crush on an *old man*. But if I did decide to go a bit pervy and try it I would definitely choose AJ. *He* is attractive and *he* is clever and *he* is not a puffed-up spag-bol seller but a properly tormented artist.'

When I got to 'clever' Ralph's mouth dropped open and said, 'Grnnk'.

I had obviously totally crossed The Line as far as he was concerned. But he'd crossed it first and not only crossed it but trampled on it. And he'd made my so-called dad's big grin flash in my brain like some kind of advert for missing so-called relatives, so he deserved everything he got.

I probably would have said a lot more if my legs hadn't taken over at that exact point, hurtling me through the back door. As I flew out I heard Mum's key in the front door, so I froze the other side, so she wouldn't see me pass the window.

'Hello Ralph darling, oh good, you fixed yourself a snack. I thought I'd be stuck all night, what a mess, the poor hamster needed stitches and I simply didn't trust the owner to keep the baby rats away from him, so I brought them home . . . Ralph? Gosh, you look a bit white. Sorry I'm so bloody late.'

And Ralph sort of sighed and said, 'Me too, Mags, me too.'

I knew then he'd tell Mum what happened, only it would sound like something completely different in which he is Good and I am Mad. And I had a whole hour before Tash was due to come over (Ben was at his new karate class) so I ran down the garden, shot across the lane and vaulted the gate . . . straight into Sharon the Shetland's paddock. Yes, I know – but that's how desperate I was.

And people move to the countryside because they think it's safer

Posted Monday 9th August, 23:35

Sorry about that, I had to pretend to be asleep, Mum was creaking on the spot outside my room and fake throat clearing as if she wanted to ask to come in. But I'm just not up for a consultation right now.

 83

It would be a total waste of time anyway. She'd probably check for inappropriate teenage hormonal rush in my eyes or wherever it is that hormones rush to. Then she'd give me some random 'wise' advice, but without actually saying anything about what happened with Ralph, which you might think would be better than being told off, but isn't, because if you're not told off you never get a chance to say 'But it wasn't like that' etcetera. So the fact that it must be 'all your fault' just hangs in the air like a bad smell.

Anyway, where was I? Ah yes, desperate.

I planned to sprint through Sharon's field and out the other side into Bluebell Wood, where there's an old tyre roped to an oak tree, perfect for swinging and raging. And I thought I was safe enough, because I could see Sharon munching on her hay net in her shelter on the other side of the field.

So I leapt the gate and hurtled across. And it felt wild and free with the wind roaring in my ears drowning out Ralph's plonking nonsense and my feet going faster and faster until I got that giddy almost flying feeling that kicks in when you're not sure if you'll be able to stop your legs even though they're your own legs attached to you so you should be in charge but you might just have to run on and on and on forever.

I was still about fifty metres from the stile that leads

into the wood when I heard hooves pounding across the ground behind me. I didn't look back because I knew exactly what I'd see and it wouldn't be charming. I just ran on, even faster, faster than I've ever run before. But the hooves got louder and louder and mixed with my breath gasping out of my lungs and my blood thumping in my ears.

As the stile got closer, I realised that if I paused for even a split second to climb over I'd end up with a psycho-pony clamped to a buttock. So I veered sideways and dived head first straight between the slats of the fence beside it, crash landing the other side and rolling straight into a ditch full of nettles. My hands started prickling straight away, so I jumped to my feet, blowing on them, and glared back at the fence, expecting to see Sharon baring her teeth and stamping in frustration.

But Sharon wasn't by the fence. She wasn't anywhere near it. She was where she must have been all along, still tearing at her hay on the far side of the paddock.

Instead, now bolting off into the distance, silvery mane and tail flying, was a huge dapple grey horse – Flying Flint. And crouching low over Flint's neck, obviously enjoying the gallop of his life and not giving any kind of stuff that he'd nearly killed a fellow human being, was a scruffy dark figure.

The Rudest Stupidest Most Despicable Boy I've Ever Met.

The cases against Ralph and Rufus

Posted Tuesday 10th August, 00:12

God. Why can't life be better spaced out? First there is Absolutely Nothing Going On For Practically Ever, then loads of things all barge in at the same time.

I intercepted Tash outside The Nook and panted, 'Ralph thinks I fancy him, Rufus tried to kill me and we've adopted hamstericidal ratlets – wait for me here,' then I waved my dock-leaf wrapped hands, 'I need to sellotape these on.'

Tash just gaped.

Luckily Mum and Ralph were in the garden settling in the ratlets, so I quickly taped the dock leaves round my prickling hands, then shot straight back out.

Tash wanted to know everything instantly but I was too emotionally puffed out, so we bought crisps and fizzies in Ye Olde Offy Licencee. Then we sat down at a table on the pavement outside Gina's Olde Cafeteria & Pizzeria which felt quite chic, even though it was closed and I had leaves instead of hands.

I filled Tash in on the evening's drama, then added, as a joke really, because she was looking so worried, 'God, what a mess, good job this isn't one of your legal cases, you'd never unravel it all.'

'Oh yes I would!' Tash sat up straight and put on her most intelligent expression. 'It's all dead straightforward. I'll prove it, it'll be good practice for me – like your blog.' And then she 'umm'ed and 'err'ed a bit and wrote it all down in my notepad . . .

1. Ralph is definitely guilty of being delusional.
The evidence: Circe has never done anything to make
Ralph think she had a crush (the disco exudations
didn't involve flirting, just sparkling commands).

I admitted I once practised sideways smiles at an imaginary vampire in the back of his car, which he might have seen in his rear-view mirror and misinterpreted. But Tash drew a diagram which proved the angle would have been all wrong. He was also driving, so she said he wouldn't have had enough spare brain to notice, because the male brain can only do one thing at a time properly. I felt a bit strangled then because I remembered Mum saying exactly the same thing to my so-called dad at a gallery when he was explaining one of his paintings at the same time as eating olives and he stuck one behind his ear on its little stick.

2. Ralph is also probably having some kind of major
spanner crisis.
The evidence: he is only a 'just friends' man, but he
definitely fancies Mum.
3. Rufus is mentally mad, or actually blind.
The evidence: no remorse if he saw me – or he didn't
see me.

So that was all great, but it still left me totally confused about 'it' and pet boy control and what to do about Ralph. So then Tash wrote out a plan of action.

a) Pity Ralph.

This idea is excellent as it gives me a definite way to behave when I next see him, rather than just screaming. Tash says it will also give me back my 'power', whatever that means.

b) Forget about trying to work out 'where-it's-at' until Savvy Rose replies because it could mean something totally different in New York.
c) As we both know roughly what confidence is, think about that instead and how it might make a boy act like a pet.

Then we opened our crisps and crunched through them without speaking because too much had definitely happened too quickly. And when Tash started talking again and it was about the general tastiness of Ben I was relieved. And I asked lots of interested questions about their date at Plastic Peaks, and I didn't even mind that all the answers involved describing his muscles.

Oh, and, yes, they *did* snog. Sigh.

Back at square one, or even a bit before that

Posted Tuesday 10th August, 18.36

Mum asked me to stick around at home to keep an eye on the hamstericidal ratlets as it's their first day here. So in between feeding them, I've been thinking on my own all day and I've filled half my notebook with ideas and even some properly worked-out graphs with my nearly-boyfriends on the vertical axis and things I'd said to them on the horizontal and none of it really made much sense. But then scraps of memories started flying about in my head, like this:

Clyde fancies Jane . . . you're just not his type . . . straighten your hair for Drew, he'll like that more . . . forget it, Sanjit's far too hot for you . . . no point calling Dan, he was only joking . . . Jake winked at Joanna, not you, laugh ha ha ha, ignore him . . .

And in between all the scraps a nagging voice started up saying something over and over again and it made my nose wrinkle. But it is true, and useful, I think, and might be why the disco experiment went so wrong.

Basically, Savvy Rose, I haven't actually got any confidence to show boys.

Is there something else I can show them instead?

Not anything physically personal, obviously. Charlotte Floyd shows things like that all the time, but her boyfriends never last more than a week, and they're not very good quality in the first place.*

* This is not bitchy, it is factual, Charlotte's last boyfriend got caught stealing two seedy saddo films and three bags of pickled onion Monster Munch from the corner shop in Lower Boring.

Comment

Posted Wednesday 11th August, 17:40, by Savvy Rose

Hey, Circe, okay, I have a break because a client's late for an appointment, but I've gotta be quick.

1) The 'it' is kind of your life force, honey. Energy. Pizzazz. Chutzpah. Your party idea isn't so far off, but it's way overcomplicated. You have great spirit, Circe, I can tell that just from the way you write – relax, believe in it.
2) Nope. Portia's 'it' sounds like a whole different 'it'. Portia seems pretty damn sure she's better than everyone else (which, of course, makes her the complete freaking opposite).
3) Uh uh. Sorry, there is NO alternative to confidence. But if you haven't got it right now it's no big deal – just fake it! I know you can. Remember that horse you looked after – if you'd let him see you were jumpy, he would have gotten jumpy too, wouldn't he? It's exactly like that.

Hope that's covered all your questions.

And, oh my gosh, that Ralph dude was way out of line, but older guys get confused real easy, Circe. And it's not about getting guys to fetch things or roll over – though it sure feels fabulous when they do! It's more about remembering they're pretty darned straightforward. If I were you, I'd quit the experiments – or go practise on a boy your own age.

Quickly too because Mum just called me

Posted Wednesday 11th August, 18:20

Hi Savvy Rose. Thanks so much. Re. point one. It's sweet of you to say that about great spirit, but if you saw me right now you might take it back as my cheapo gothy burgundy mascara has run badly and is making me look like a zombie, only more miserable. Point number two is excellent news, that's a relief. Point three I need to think about. It sounds easy, but there's something itchy about the horse theory, I just can't quite work out what.

And about experimenting on boys my own age, I get what you mean, but what can I do? My only proper boyfriend prospect has been proven to be very physically unfanciable after all. He is also extremely busy on the Costa del Swank making sure a certain charming person is nicely covered in sun cream.

Apart from him, every other boy with even the teeniest bit of cute potential in the whole of The Middle Of Absolute Nowhere is on holiday thousands of miles away (except Jonah Frazer who is in a teepee on a lentil retreat in Cardiff because his parents are vegans).

Comment
Posted Thursday 12th August, 07:17, by Savvy Rose

Hey, Circe. One last thought before I crawl into the sack. What about practising on that moody guy, Rufus? He sounds kinda cute. Night-night.

Something to do with the time difference
Posted Thursday 12th August, 08:01

Or maybe it's the language barrier, or both, and you must be tired after a whole day measuring arms and legs and things and that can make lines blur and words read differently and everything.

Please don't feel bad. Exactly the same thing happened to me after my so-called dad went out for The Longest Walk Around The Block In History and Mum was having her 'tired time'. I wasn't sleeping much, and when I had an English comprehension test I read every single word of the story really carefully. But all I could remember at the end was that the hero was a Prince, but not who he loved or why she went bonkers or who he killed or who killed him or why there was a ghost.

So, really, don't worry that you missed a few crucial facts. Here they are again:

1) Rufus is The Rudest Stupidest Most Despicable Boy I Have Ever Met.
2) He could have killed me and didn't even bother to check he hadn't.
3) He smells.

All this, of course, makes him totally unsuitable as a pet boy, even a practice one.

Besides I did an experiment on A Boy Of My Own Age last night

Posted Thursday 12th August, 08:04

Just need to feed everything i.e. myself, cat, guinea pigs* and hamstericidal ratlets, then I'll type up my official journalistic report.

* Actual, not male human.

Are First Impressions Important Or A Total Waste Of Time?

Male Human Pet Control: Experiment 3

Posted Thursday 12th August, 10:55

Mum was calling me last night because Ben had turned up. I was in the garden but she thought I was up in my room with headphones on, which just goes to show how much some mothers don't notice about their daughters.

It was weird to see Ben without Tash joined on to him somewhere and my first thought was, *Oh My God, she's dumped him*, which came with a little 'hooray' that I didn't consciously think but happened spontaneously and felt awful, like a kind of mean sneeze. So I switched to feeling sorry for him, even though he looked happy* chatting to Mum while she made tea. Then I thought, *Argh, he's dumped Tash*, which didn't come with a 'hooray' because she so doesn't deserve to be hurt. Also, she is now so smitten by his muscles I'm not sure she'll ever get over them, even if she ended up dating Matt Dudley who has pumped so much iron he's made his head shrink.

But then he said, 'Hey Witchy, Tash sends a big kiss.' And it turns out she's vegging in front of the TV after a long day helping to get her dad's rare sheep ready for The Middle Of Absolute Nowhere Summer Show on Saturday. So Ben thought maybe I'd be up for doing something with him.

This, of course, got me totally confused. The cleverish

side of my brain was huffing, *No, tell him where to stick his something, you are his second choice and any port in a storm* (which is a metaphor, I think). But the soppy side was just dancing about and cheering. And that argument could have dragged on for hours, but then the fabulously sophisticated journalist side kicked in with, *Wise up! This is an excellent hot topic opportunity, he is A Boy Of Your Own Age.* So I said, 'Ben, it's great you're here, you can help me with my Special Holiday Homework Project.'

He frowned and popped a tennis ball out of his jeans pocket (he always has some kind of ball on him, it's a sporty boy thing) and tossed it from hand to hand a bit wistfully. So I added, 'And we can go over to Bluebell Wood to do it and I bet a bun you can't throw that all the way across Sharon's paddock.' And he perked up straight away and said, 'Kiss your bun goodbye, Circe Shaw.'

Ben threw the ball so hard it cleared the stile and we could stroll after it as Sharon was out doing her job. She has to pull a little cart around all the local villages so Geraldine can sell her homemade cakes (which are very good) and homemade meditation CDs (which are very bad, unless you're the type of person who likes to listen to grown women pretending to be whales).

We walked through the wood and up the hill to a fallen oak trunk to watch the sunset. Now most of the time I don't even notice that Ben's seventeen, not seven.

But it really showed then because he didn't do a Tarzan impression on the swing or climb a tree, even when I said, 'Right, I want to practise conducting a journalistic interview on you.'

Instead he shrugged. 'Okay, let's do book-ends.'

So we sat back to back and it felt great leaning against his shoulders, not in a romantic way, of course, but in a chair-like, spine support way. And I thought, if Ralph's got any kind of point about absent so-called fathers it must be connected to missing that bigness to lean on.

I recorded the interview on my phone. I would upload it as an audio file but I'd need to edit out too much because there was lots of umming and some really loud blackbirds so it's quicker to write:

Me: This is Circe Shaw interviewing Ben Vincent at 20:37 on Wednesday 11th August.

Ben: Oh, what, you're recording this, Witchy? You didn't say that before.

Me: Of course, I am a professional, almost. Don't worry, it is extremely confidential and I won't reveal my sources, even if I am badly tortured.

Ben: Will it be on your blog?

Me: No! Well, um, yes, but only excerpts and nothing of a sensitive or private nature and I never reveal where we live and I've changed everyone's surnames and the school name, so it's over 100% anonymous and private. Besides, no one reads my blog except Savvy Rose and I'm not sure even she does any more.

Ben: (tossing his ball from hand to hand) Er, okay, what do you want to ask me – nothing about Tash?

Me: (going red because I had wanted to ask him about Tash) NO! How dare you! Do you think I'm some kind of paparazzi slimemonger? I want you to talk about . . . um . . . an ex-girlfriend – who can have a secret alias.

Ben: Er, okay . . . who?

Me: A proper girlfriend, one you were really into – how about Stac– Shelly.

Ben: You mean Stac–

Me: (raising eyebrows) We're calling her *Shelly*.

Ben: Ah, right.

Me: So, this is an interview for a totally hot topic I'm researching called . . . (long pause because I had the pet boy thing in my head but remembered Tash didn't want me to tell Ben about that, so had to come up with something new) . . . *First Impressions: Important Or A Total Waste Of Time?* What first attracted you to Shelly?

Ben: Who?

Me: (tutting) Shell-eee.

Ben: (silent)

Me: (hissing) *Stacey*.

Ben: Um. Don't know. She was just great, wasn't she?

Me: (because I thought she was a bit too deliberately floaty myself) Hmm. Okay. But can you be more specific about the *first thing.* Was it her floaty hair, or her floaty clothes, or maybe the fact that she seemed like she was sort of 'where-it's-at' in a floaty way?

Ben: Where what's at?

Me: 'It' you know, like pizzazz, her mojo, like, her funky spirit.

Ben: (pause while Ben chokes a bit) Her f-f-fun-*funky spirit*?

Me: Okay – how about her *floaty* spirit?

Ben: Definitely not. I'm not really into floaty girls.

Me: (pause for me to sigh very deeply because he so *is or was* before Tash) Was it something she said or did?

Ben: Er . . .

Me: Or didn't say or didn't do?

Ben: Er . . .

Me: Or her laugh, or her smile?

Ben: Er . . .

Me: Or the way she walked or danced or played netball or something?

Ben: No. I first saw her in physics, she sat down opposite me . . .

Me: And?

Ben: You know – it was her shrug. When the teacher asked her a question she just shrugged . . . that was it for me – like POW!

Sigh. The entire male human species is destined to remain an absolute mystery forever. At least.

I gave up after that. The sun was licking the sky orange and making me want to relax. So I suggested we play 'If', a kids' game we've played for years, which is still a laugh even though we're really adults now. It started with things like, 'If you were a biscuit, what biscuit would you be?' when we were small. Then we both got into music and it would be more like, 'If you were a rock god, which rock god would you be?' Now we're teenagers, we're properly intellectual, so the last time we played, Ben asked, 'If you were a type of weather, what type of weather would you be?' (I'd be a sort of whirly breeze with a bit of heat in it. Ben would be midday sunshine, of course.)

Anyway, I had a brainwave then, and asked, 'If you were a type of party, what type of party would you be? And Ben answered without even pausing, 'A victory barbie after the singles final, with massive burgers and everyone cheering because I've just won – Wimbledon!' And he grinned then just like he had won and I wished not for the first time but probably for the millionth that my brain could be more like Ben's. Then he said, 'If you were a party, what type would you be, Witchy?'

And because, as you know, I have given this very question some serious thought already yet still not worked it out, I said, 'Hmm . . . god, I've no idea.'

Which Ben found so absolutely hilarious he nearly fell off the tree trunk. When he'd finally stopped laughing, he said, 'Come on Circe, it's obvious – you're Halloweeeeen!'

* Ben and his family are specialists in Looking On The Bright Side which was useful in London as they never tried to talk about our 'situation', but just gave us practical things like pies.

Is Halloween a good thing to be?

Posted Thursday 12th August, 21:42

Or an extremely bad thing?

I know it's not really about being like a party. But it can't help, can it? I mean if I'm accidentally exuding a Halloween vibe it might be putting boys off before they've even spoken to me. I love Halloween – but it's basically about dead people isn't it? I haven't seen many real dead people, or even any, but I don't think you'd want to party with them. And you wouldn't want to be spooky every day, even lean Lee only wears his tragic eyeliner on Saturday nights.

I did try to get more out of Ben. Luckily we were still doing book-ends, so he couldn't see the importance in my eyes.

'Oh, um, so why do you think I'm like Halloween – is it my name?'

And he said, 'Yeah . . .' so I smiled, relieved.

But then he laughed, a bit nervously.

And I said, 'What? I can tell there's a "but" – what is it?'

'Er . . .'

'Do I look scary or dead or something without realising it?'

And he said, 'Er . . . no, it's not that – it's nothing.'

Which, I'm sure you'll agree, is about the most annoying thing any boy can ever say to you when you know there definitely is Something, and it's probably BIG.

So I giggled carelessly as if it didn't matter at all what he was thinking, then asked, really flippantly and laughing all the way through, 'Or I suppose ha ha I look like I might ha ha ha cast a mean spell hahahaha on a boy ha ha?'

And it actually made me feel a bit sick saying that out loud but I suppose all the laughing can't have helped either as it made me gasp for air a bit.

'Don't be a doughnut, Witchy, course not . . .'

And I had to actually sit on my hands then to stop shaking it out of him and I said, 'So WHAT IS IT?' which came out really really loud and shrill and echoed round the wood so I did sound kind of scary.

And Ben said, 'Leave it, Witchy, it's just your name, I was thinking out loud.'

'Thinking out loud about *what*?'

'Nothing, all right – do you reckon I could get up that tree by the time you counted to ten?'

'WHAT?'

And Ben laughed again and said, 'Durr – it's just your

spooky black cat!' and laughed some more like it was all a hilarious joke.

But somehow it didn't sound true, and I didn't believe him. And I still don't.

Comment

Posted Friday 13th August, 07:21, by Savvy Rose

Hey, Circe. You know, you're right, I can feel bushed after a whole day measuring arms and legs. And yes I sure do misunderstand things sometimes. But *not this time*, honey!

I got the message loud and clear that Rufus isn't exactly your idea of a dream date – but that's exactly what makes him the perfect freaking practice boy. Don't you see? If your experiments go wrong it won't matter a damn because all you'll have lost is a 'rude, stupid, despicable, possibly insane, definitely smelly' boyfriend you didn't want in the first place.

That's not entirely totally stupid

Posted Friday 13th August, 08:15

I hadn't looked at it that way at all. I need to think . . .

Major problem

Posted Friday 13th August, 08:45

Okay, so I get the idea that it won't matter really if my experiments go wrong. But what if they go right? I would get stuck with a pet Boyfriend From Hell.

It would be a bit like when Mum brought home that disturbed Staffordshire Bull Terrier, Thug, and he bit my so-called dad, then he bit Mum, then he bit me and I had to have two stitches, so Mum put a muzzle on him and took his macho parts off him. But even though he acted like he hated us, he really wanted us to love him. And he wouldn't take no for an answer about sleeping on our beds, which was a bit like trying to sleep with a live bomb snoring next to your face so we all had to lock our doors at night.

I'm glad Tash will have to spend at least seven years at judge school

Posted Friday 13th August, 19.21

She might need more.

I think she actually might be *too nice*. Not in an eyes-extra-wide-when-smiling (at your boobs) kind of way like the vicar, but in an expecting-everyone-else-to-be-nice-because-she-is way.

I just got back from Tash's farm and shot straight up to my office to avoid witnessing a horrific scene in the cottage. Ralph is taking Mum to his advertising agency's summer ball, so he's turned up in a white suit and flowery bow tie which is making me wince even from a distance. Mum's wafting about in a halter-neck dress. Tash would probably say they look 'dreamy'. Vomit.

She texted me at exactly the same time as Clarence the alarm cock went off this morning:

> No Ben 2day!
> Fancy coming over
> for goss and sheep
> grooming?!? X

And, like last night, lots of thoughts all rushed into my head at once and had a big argument . . . *Don't go – she wouldn't ask if Ben was around. Go – she only doesn't ask because you always say no. Don't go – she'll want to know if Ben said anything about her and you'll end up torn like a rag doll between lovers. Go – no you won't, he didn't say anything.*

Honestly, it is beyond tiring being me sometimes. Anyway, finally (thank you Jess Bradley) the fabulously sophisticated bit of my brain kicked in and yelled, *Get up, get dressed and go now! You have two vital questions to research.*

a) Am I a Halloween party?

 104

b) Is it a totally suicidal idea to try to make Rufus my practice pet boy?

So I went.

As soon as I walked up the drive, I was glad my fabulous sophistication won the argument. It's pretty much impossible not to feel happy at Honeyhill Farm. The buildings are made of stone the exact colour of honeycomb and nestle in meadows sprinkled with wild flowers and sheep.

Tash's mum and dad used to be in a folk band which made me a bit worried about tambourines at first. But it's all right, her dad does pick up a ukelele sometimes, but usually everyone groans so he laughs and puts it down again. Her mum hums a lot in a soft, lilting accent as she's originally from Sri Lanka. Her older brother, Sid, plays drums, but I've never met him as he's been away on his gap year since we moved here.

It turned out all the sheep grooming had actually been finished, apart from hoof shining and fleece fluffing up which can't be done until tomorrow. So we were roped in to help with the food stall, which involved ladling pickles and jams and honey from huge jars into small ones, then sticking on the labels Tash's mum was writing.

I know, I know, it sounds deeply boring doesn't it? But it was fun. Really. And for hours and hours we didn't talk about Ben or Rufus or pet boys or mad older men or anything even slightly worrying. We just laughed at how sticky we were getting. And Tash's dad told us funny stories about how the sheep deliberately behaved badly at the show last year. And when I finished jarring-up all Tash's mum's onion marmalade she clapped, then sneaked up behind me and gave me a hug, which made me feel a bit quiet for a while.

Anyway, we didn't finish until about five. And although it had been nice forgetting everything, my vital questions hadn't gone away. So as soon as we collapsed on our backs in a heap of hay in a barn, I took a huge deep breath and asked, 'Tash, do you think I'm like a Halloween party?'

'What? No way, Circe – you're far too bouncy and funny.'

And I didn't particularly like that description of my budding fabulous sophistication, but was so glad that she hadn't said 'yes' that I smiled anyway. Then I took an even deeper breath and said, 'Savvy Rose thinks I should try to practise the pet boy thing on the despicable Rufus.' And my nose wrinkled up as I spoke because I thought Tash would laugh it off as ridiculous.

Tash popped up like toast out of the hay beside me. 'That's brilliant!' She sprung to her feet and started pacing so fast it made me dizzy watching.

'It is? Why?'

'Because he obviously really doesn't like you – he might even hate you!'

'Thanks. And that is excellent because?'

'God – loads of reasons . . . because it'll be such a huge challenge, so much more satisfying – like training a vicious

Rottweiller instead of a piddling poodle! Imagine, if you can get Rufus to be your pet, the boy world will be your total oyster!'

'But isn't that a bit, like, *advanced*?'

'What do you mean?'

'You know, um . . . like a *total beginner* driver taking their first lesson in a Ferrari with no brakes or something?'

'But you're not a total beginner, are you.'

'Of course I a—'

I literally said that. I was a mere 'm' away from revealing my utter cluelessness. It felt like I was teetering on the edge of a cliff and for a split second I was tempted to jump, to bare my shame and confess that I'd never had a proper boyfriend.

But then, with my mouth still wide open on the 'a', an image of a certain totally insignificant but extremely irritating person's vicious smirk flashed up in my mind. I clamped my mouth shut, then snapped out a lightning fast 'I am *not*!'

But Tash was frowning and her mouth was forming another question. I rushed on, my brain snatching at the first thing it found in my head, 'Of course *I am not* exactly Portia though, am I?'

Tash stopped pacing and planted her hands on her hips. 'Portia? What's she got to do with anything?'

Heat prickled across my chest. I rolled quickly on to my stomach before it reached my cheeks and mumbled, 'Oh, you know . . .'

'No, I don't – what?'

And I closed my eyes tight and inhaled the sweet, dusty smell of the hay and desperately searched around in my head for something sensible to say, but it was full of Portia's pathetic whispers so all I managed was, 'Hmmph.'

Saying anything else would have involved too much revealing of too many annoying incidents. And if I said them out loud it could somehow make them seem important, which they're totally *not*. Even worse, if Tash didn't believe me, I wasn't entirely sure I could still be her friend, which would not only be horrible but also complicated because of Ben. And as I was thinking all this, Tash was obviously doing some thinking too.

'Oh. My. God. Circe, I'm such a rubbish friend . . .'

And my heart skipped a beat and I thought she'd been remembering the past year at school and putting things together and working it all out and now she'd believe me for sure and be on my side and then I might not even have to worry about becoming totally fabulously sophisticated in less than four weeks or transforming my so-called love life enough to get a boy to meet me at the school gates as soon as humanly possible next term.

'I'm so sorry, what with Ben and the holidays and your pet boy stuff, I'd forgotten all about it . . .'

I held my breath.

'You're still not over Jake, are you?'

Deepest kind of sigh.

I know I can't expect you to understand why that question pinned me flat on my face for the next few minutes, because I haven't explained properly what Portia gets up to at school and/or the pool 'incident'. But it did. I couldn't speak at first, which Tash took to mean that I was still totally into Jake. And she sat down beside me and squeezed my arm and stroked my hair I think, though it's hard to know for sure as my hair's so big it's not always possible to tell when someone's touching it.

Anyway, it felt nice that she cared, and going along with the Jake story was much easier than telling the truth about Portia, or confessing that I'm a total beginner when it comes to boyfriends. And, if I'm honest, I guess I do still think Jake is fanciable, even with his too long arms. So, eventually I rolled over and said, a bit sulkily, for extra effect, 'No, s'pose not.'

'Oh Circe, you poor thing – don't worry. Portia's just a bit, you know . . . deeply insecure . . . I'm sure she only went for Jake because it was obvious he was interested in you, I bet it'll all be over by half-term.'

I was so stunned by the deeply insecure idea my mouth dropped wide open and couldn't say anything.

'And, by the time it's over, you'll be ready to step in with your new pet boy powers.' Tash was up and pacing again, almost talking to herself. 'And Rufus, well, he's probably not actually nasty at all, just really shy.'

She suddenly dropped to her knees in front of me and

stared hard into my eyes. 'Circe, you know what this means, don't you?'

'Um . . . no.'

'Savvy Rose is right! Rufus really is the perfect practice pet boy. Not just because he doesn't like you – but because you're into someone else . . .'

'Oh.' Tash's excitement wasn't infectious.

'. . . no one can get hurt or annoyed. It'll be like pure science – there will be absolutely no emotions involved at all!'

And that did actually make me feel a bit excited, because science and journalism are definitely linked. In her column last week, Jess Bradley reported on a clinical lab test that proves putting 'gravity defying' cream on your face doesn't actually make your face get higher, it just makes your brain a bit more worried.

I enjoyed a quick daydream involving being presented with a major journalistic award for scientifically proving that boys are exactly the same as pets. Tash's excited clap jolted me off stage.

'Ooh, and Rufus doesn't go to Hell House, does he? He works for that Lucien guy. So whatever happens or doesn't happen won't matter at all. No one at school will ever know – *Jake* will never know. How cool is that?'

I had to admit, that was cool, not because of Jake, because of Portia.

Tash stuck out her hand to pull me up, then shook it. 'So, settled, you'll try a pet boy experiment on Rufus.'

I nodded, my mind already busy planning some in-depth Rufus research and preparation. It would take at least a week, maybe two.

'Excellent,' she said. 'And as he's horsey, he's bound to be at the show, everyone horsey goes. You can do it there – tomorrow.'

Tomorrow might be about five years too soon

Posted Friday 13th August, 19:26

Do it there. At the show.

Tomorrow.

Do *what*? Exactly?

Okay. I am absolutely not panicking. I probably *do* know what to do, I just have to read back through Savvy Rose's messages again.

SIS! URGENT TRANSATLANTIC MESSAGE TO SAVVY ROSE

Posted Friday 13th August, 21:04

OH. MY. GOD. WHAT DO I *DO*?

In the last two hours all I've been doing is lots of realising. Probably more realising than I've ever done before.

First, I've just been over all your advice again and

realised I haven't a clue about what I actually have to *do* to get myself a pet boy.

Okay. I know it's about being where-it's-at and having a pizzazzy type of spirit. Puzzling over that got me thinking how it was so much fun at Honeyhill today that I didn't look at my watch at all. And I realised that Tash's family are naturally where-it's-at. So maybe it's genetically born-in and Tash has it and I never will, because when I'm with Mum and Ralph, or even Mum and AJ sometimes, I just want to be where they're not.

Then I forced myself to think back to the way it was with my so-called dad and remembered I didn't look at my watch when I was with him. But I think he did look at his watch, which means he wanted to be where I was not, which wasn't a good thought. Although it wasn't a realisation, because you'd have to be a pretty stupid type of abandoned daughter not to see that was totally obvious.

After that I realised that not being where-it's-at is a bit like not having long legs: if you haven't got them there's no point worrying about not having them.

So I decided to concentrate on faking some confidence, like I did with Flying Flint. But then I remembered that idea felt itchy, like something wasn't quite right, and I realised (see what I mean?) that it's because horses – and all other pets – don't speak. Ever.

This is a crucial point, you've got to admit. It was easy to get Flint to believe I was confident. He didn't expect me to have an intelligent conversation about things we had in common, or football. You can talk nonsense to animals most of the time, or use the words everyone uses like 'whoa' or 'steady'. As long as your tone of voice is right they're okay.

Which means I have another urgent question to go with WHAT DO I *DO*?

WHAT DO I *SAY*?

An instantly understandable reply sent before eight a.m. British time (about three a.m. New York time, I think) tomorrow morning will make me definitely the epitome of the most relieved teenager on the entire planet.

I'd probably be a rubbish vampire bride

Posted Friday 13th August, 22:17

I've had to leave my office and come indoors because it's pitch black outside and there are actual bats flapping round the moon. And although I know they have special on-board equipment that stops them bumping into humans, I can't help thinking that if one did accidentally get into my hair it might never find its way out again.

My laptopasaurus is also almost too hot to touch because I've been on it all evening. So I'm going to turn it off now and prepare myself in every other way I can apart from knowing what to actually do tomorrow.

I'm going to work out what to wear. Then I'm going to

 113

dress up in it and film myself on my phone practising exuding natural confidence at the same time as saying something intelligent about a subject I have in common with Rufus. It will have to be horses, I suppose, although his hair is messy like mine, but saying something about that might be too physical so early on in our relationship, or even before it.

Dressing a bit like a horse might help, I think

Posted Friday 13th August, 23:21

Right. I'm ready, in theory. I have my outfit sorted out at least. Skinny grey jeans. Black ankle boots. Silvery top with a scoopy neck and glitter buttons down the back and one long sleeve and one short sleeve which will appeal to boys who really like looking at arms and boys who prefer arms to be mysterious, which is useful because I don't know which type Rufus is. And its silveryness (especially combined with dapply grey legs and hoof-like boots) might also remind him of Flying Flint which is probably a good thing as he definitely likes Flint even if he hates me.

I'm going to tie my hair back as he was so rude about it before, but leave a floppy bit at the front to hide behind if I need it.

And I've worked out what I want to say and how to say it after filming myself on my mobile. Are you ready? Okay, here it is . . .

'Oh,' (look of mild but quite pleased surprise), 'Hi, how's Flint?' (head tilt). I might also nod to look extra genuine. But I must not under any circumstances raise one or more eyebrows (which does unfortunately make me look a bit terrifying, however hard I try).

'Oh, hi – how's Flint?'

I just said that out loud and it sounds right, friendly but nice and short. And I've checked and it is an 'open question' which are the best kind for mingling at parties according to Jess Bradley as they stop people just saying 'Yes' or 'No' then moving away to talk to someone more interested in them.

Mum and Ralph aren't back yet, so I've the run of the cottage which is more fun than it sounds as if you try even to walk fast you bang into walls or ceilings pretty quickly. But I have found a recipe for an 'Organic Facial Revitalising Overnight Mask' in the *Daily Mail* Ralph left on the sofa and we've got similar sorts of salad ingredients in the fridge. I'm going to blend it now and go to sleep wearing it, so I wake up looking bright-cheeked, which might make up for not being where-it's-at.

And I'm not going to worry at all that Savvy Rose hasn't answered yet, because if it's my Friday night it's her Friday day and she's probably at work. And I'm going to sleep well, trusting that she'll post a comment so wise and under-standable that tomorrow will be a total breeze and Rufus will forget he's a psychopath and start eating out of my hand like the sweetest type of puppy.

I bet this never happened to Kate Moss

Posted Saturday 14th August, 01:17

Johnny Depp is sitting on my pillow licking his lips and my glamorising avocado and coleslaw mask has gone. Have to get up to wash cat spit off my face.

Properly awake and even more properly annoyed

Posted Saturday 14th August, 01:31

Heard Mum and Ralph talking in deafening stage whispers, so I slammed the bathroom door and swore really illegally in a You Have So Woken Me Up voice. I almost hoped Mum would come up and shout at me, so I would have an excellent excuse to shout back. Then I realised, as if I hadn't done enough realising already, that the one good thing about The Nook must be that it's not next door to anyone. So, however loud things got, the neighbours wouldn't complain and the police wouldn't turn up like they did once in London.

But Mum didn't come up. As if. It just all went a bit instantly silent, then I heard the front door close softly, so I crept to the window without turning the light on and saw Ralph blow her a kiss (vomit) then get in his car.

Mum had put a shawl on over her dress and she hugged it round her and started to walk up the path towards the cottage. But then she sort of jolted and spun round and marched back down it and I thought for a disgusted moment that she was going to give Ralph an actual kiss, but she didn't. She just waved him off then crossed the lane and climbed the stile into the paddock. This could look a bit suicidal, but Sharon tolerates Mum, so I'm not worried about her being bitten to death. She's probably just checking the water trough or something.

But it is weird knowing Mum's out there alone in the dark. And it's making me not sleep, which is highly inconvenient and definitely not good for the natural confidence I need to build up by tomorrow.

Where was my mum when maternal instincts were handed out?

Posted Saturday 14th August, 01:57

She just came into my room. Without knocking or anything. *What was she thinking?* Not only is that a Comprehensive Breach Of Privacy, it is also like crossing The Line, only worse because she is supposed to be my Actual Flesh And Blood so you'd think she'd know just a teeny bit about My Needs. I was still awake, but I squeezed my eyes shut and slid the laptopasaurus under my duvet to cover up its roaring. She hiccupped when she left and her breath smelt of coconuts. She may have been tipsy.

Shudder

Posted Saturday 14th August, 01:59

Or she may have been licking Ralph's slicked back hair.

Tomorrow is now officially today

Posted Saturday 14th August, 02:03

'Hello, how *is* Flying Flint?'

'Oh . . . hey there Rooffee . . . how's the big FF dude?'

'Might I bid you a smashing afternoon, Master Rufus? How fareth dear Flint?'

'Yo, what's goin' down with the Flintmeister?'

As I'm still awake I've decided to use my time intelligently, instead of counting sheep that keep turning into rabid Shetlands.

'Oh hi – how's *Flint*?'

Do you think that last line sounds better? I do. I think emphasising the 'Flint' gives it a bit of extra hidden depth. And it sounds like when Meg won't sit for AJ first time so he has to really insist. And I get the feeling that Rufus is the kind of pet boy who might be a bit disobedient like that.

Comment

Posted Saturday 14th August, 07:08, by Savvy Rose

Awesome! I'm so freaking happy you've decided to try out on Rufus – give your friend Tash a high five from me.

Okay. I'll sure try to make this instantly understandable . . .

What do you need to *do*?

First. Lighten up, honey! Don't make this into some huge deal. Remember, you don't even *like* this guy – this is just research to help build up your fabulous sophistication.

Next. Remember, if you haven't got it – fake it! Get confident. I bet you were telling yourself it was all going to be okay with that big horse you looked after; that you knew what you were doing, so he'd be fine. Just mess a little with the message! Tell yourself it's all going to be just dandy because you are unique and gorgeous and clever and funny and Rufus would be so darned lucky to win you as his girlfriend. Even if you feel like a freaking dumb-ass doing it. Even if you don't believe it (yet). Repeat it, over and over, until it gets to be like an upbeat soundtrack playing behind all your other thoughts.

And don't you dare give up on being where-it's-at! If you can't get your head round the concept, go with the party idea, I guess it's not so way off. Hey, and ignore Ben's Halloween rap, he's an old buddy so he's thinking of you in a whole different way. For what my virtual opinion's worth,

119

I think you sound cooler than a disco – more like a hip gig in the East Village. Picture a groovy underground hang-out with quirky live acts. Add that thought to the happy music in your head. Say it aloud right now, 'I am totally where-it's-at – and way cooler than a disco!'

So you get that going on in your head, then when you see Rufus, act like he's delighted to see you. If he doesn't come over to you straight off put it down to shyness and go over to him, smile at him like you mean it, right into his eyes.

Now, about what you say. Guess what? Men are so like pets it's freaking scary. If you've got that confidence down (even if it's fake) it *is* all about tone of voice at first, they really don't much mind what you say. I once got a date with a cute guy in a deli after reading him my grocery list.

But, if you feel happier being prepared, have a few ideas lined up. Sure, go ahead and ask Rufus about the horse. Even better, ask him about himself. Every guy's favorite subject is himself. Cats are perfect pet examples of this – do they care that you don't want them to curl up on your cashmere? Uh-uh. It's all 'Me Me Me'.

Now GO GIRL!

Endless (but very quick) thank you

Posted Saturday 14th August, 09:38

Phew – thanks so much, Savvy Rose. I think your advice is quite instantly understandable, but I'm going to write all the points on separate sheets of paper, spread them on the floor of my room and stare at them hard until they sink into my brain. I will then do the right thing automatically as soon as I see Rufus.

Is this the definition of self-inflicted masochism?

Posted Saturday 14th August, 11:15

Okay, so it's another sunny summer Saturday and 99.9% of my classmates will, depending on time zones etc, now either be:

a) Swanning about on swanky beaches
b) Lazing about at swanky villas
c) Dancing about in swanky clubs.

There is Jonah on his vegan retreat, of course, who is probably plaiting beansprouts. And Tash will be fluffing-up sheep. But I bet not one person is studying. They especially won't be studying how to make a boy who doesn't like you and might even hate you want to be your practice pet boyfriend even though you don't want him as any kind of boyfriend really.

Officially No Big Deal

Posted Saturday 14th August, 11:35

I really like that idea. This experiment on Rufus is not important at all. The more I think that, the happier I feel. The more I stare at all the other things written on the sheets of paper, the less I want to go to the show. But *LIGHTEN UP – DON'T MAKE IT SOME HUGE DEAL* just made me smile, a real smile, not a put-on smile, and it feels a bit like confidence. So whatever else is going on in my head, what I'm going to think most is that this is just a trivial little piece of research. And what Tash said about it being pure science fits with that too. He does not care a stuff. I do not care a stuff. No emotions will be involved at all.

Communicating In A Calm And Confident Manner
Male Human Pet Control: Experiment 4

Posted Saturday 14th August, 18:06

Arrrrrrrrrrrrrrrrrrrrrrrrrrrrrrrrrrrrrrrrrrrrrrrggggggggggggggggggggggggh!

What is it with boys?

Back at home, in my office under the willow tree. Alone.

 122

If the world repaid hard work fairly, I would now have an adoring pet boy curled up at my feet. Instead, I have a snoring pet cat curled up on a very bad poem about a jar.

This is beyond disappointing as I set out with such a straightforward plan today that it could not have gone wrong. All I had to do was meet Tash at her family's stall at lunchtime so we could spend her break hunting Rufus down. Once we found him, she would distract anyone he was with by giving them a Honeyhill Farm leaflet and/or get his attention by handing him one before melting nonchalantly into the background. I would then say my line perfectly. He would then ask me out.

Simple isn't it? Okay, I had overlooked a few key facts:

a) Mum would be at the show
b) Ralph would be at the show
c) AJ would be at the show.

I cycled to the showground. It's three miles away, which doesn't sound far, but is when you're dressed up like a glamorous sort of horse and only two of your gears work properly and all the hills go up and hardly down at all.

When I got to the top of the last hill, the view made me slam on my brakes. I'd expected a couple of tents and a coconut shy, but at least a dozen marquees bubbled across the fields like big stripy mushrooms. Squeals of laughter, tannoy announcements and even the beat of new-ish pop echoed round the valley. The countryside almost looked exciting. I crunched my Chopper into top gear and flew down the hill, feeling a bit like Boadicea going into battle.

As soon as I'd padlocked my bike to a fence I called Tash.

'Hey, I'm here.'

'Hurrah, at last. You're late. I was worried you'd changed your mind. Mum's taken the first lunch break now. Come and help me till she gets back.'

'Where are you?'

'Farmer's Market Square, it's like a little precinct made of straw, our tent's next to the *Wicked Wellies* stall, just behind the ferret hurdling.'

The show was teeming with the masses of The Middle Of Absolute Nowhere who'd been watching grass grow for weeks and were now desperately running around trying to squish a whole summer of fun into one day. Hurrying through the crowds, I kept my eyes peeled for any likely potential proper boyfriend material as I still wasn't exactly relishing the idea of approaching The Most Despicable Boy I'd Ever Met, even if it was Officially No Big Deal and strictly scientific. But the only boys I spotted were standing around enthralled by 'events' like the greenest bean competition and the hedge trimming race, which told me everything I needed to know about them quite quickly.

I found Tash serving behind a table loaded with the jars we'd prepared, smiling thinly at a trio of little old ladies clucking over chutney. 'If you really can't decide, why don't you each take a different pickle – then swap so you get to try them all?'

'Oh no, best not, maybe onion marmalade then . . .'

'But we've some already, dear, we went through all that ten minutes ago.'

I grinned over their bobbing heads. 'Ladies, you know you can "Buy 3 – save 50p" with our special lunchtime offer.' I squeezed behind the table next to Tash, then frowned at my watch. 'Oops, it's already two – sorry, you missed it!'

Tash's eyes widened, 'Er, that's not strictly tru–'

'Golly, that would have been nice . . .'

'Oh dear, we are silly, making such a fuss – could we, um . . .'

'Hmm, well . . . I'm bending the boss's rules really, but just for you.' I bagged up the jars they were now thrusting desperately at me. 'That's £5.50 . . . thanks. Enjoy!'

I blew on my fingertips as they bustled out.

Tash tutted. 'Okay – impressive, but very naughty.'

'Pah. They loved it.' I did a little dance, feeling a bit light-headed with wheeler-dealer success. 'People need to be told what to do sometimes, like pets – like boys!' I'm deeply ashamed to admit I then dissolved into hysterical giggles, which morphed into the usual uncontrollable hiccups. I blame the sleepless night and a huge pre-pet boy experiment adrenalin rush and perhaps too much sun on my face and one arm. 'Tashhh-ic . . . wat-ic – water-hic-hic . . .' I spluttered.

Tash dashed out the back to the little makeshift kitchen, leaving me bent double, gurgling and hiccing like Mr Dire's backfiring moped.

'When you're ready . . .'

I froze mid 'hic'.

Only one person I knew spoke with that hissing mocking arrogance.

The Rudest Stupidest Most Despicable Boy I've Ever Met.

All the swear words I know and lots more exploded in my head like some kind of appalled fireworks display.

'. . . if it's not too much trouble . . .'

If there was a degree in sarcasm Rufus would get Honours with an extra gold star.

It would have been logical to stand up then, smiling confidently and exuding where-it's-at-ness. But my logical brain just wasn't involved in things at that moment. My small stash of fabulous sophistication had also upped and sashayed out. So I stayed bent, feigning extreme interest in the grassy floor and desperately trying to swallow my hiccups, which turned them into sort of strangulated pig snorts, which made the sheep in the pen in the corner of the tent start bleating.

About a thousand snorts later, I heard Tash stutter, 'O-o-*oh* – sorry! M-my friend seems to be, er . . .'

A plastic cup appeared under my nose. I grabbed it and gulped, sloshing most of the water down my chin as my brain scrabbled around for pet boy information. Unfortunately, all it could find was ohmygodohmygodohmygodohmygod ohmygod . . .

Then Tash said, 'Okay, the honeycomb bar . . . that's £1.20 please.'

Rufus was obviously about to leave. More swear word fireworks went off. There was a real risk that if he disappeared into the hordes we'd never find him again. Finally the pet boy machine started to groan into life . . . ohmygod oh my gorgeousness, oh I am so unique, oh this is so no big deal blah blah blah . . .

I grabbed a huge jar from the floor as an excuse for snuffling around under the counter and pinged upright. Rufus flinched, but at least he looked at me, so I stuck to my plan, hugged my jar and smiled right into his eyes. 'Oh, hi!' (expression of mild but quite pleased surprise) 'How's *Flint*?' (head tilt, nod).

He blinked. 'What?' (expression of irritated distaste).

I'd forgotten just how weird his eyes were and really had to clench my chin to keep my friendly smile on. 'How's *Flint*?'

'Oh, right – it's *you*.' (hiss plus frown). Then he snatched the change Tash was offering, turned away, and strode out. Just like that. He didn't even bother to pretend to answer my question.

Tash's mouth fell open. 'Was that *him* – Rufus?'

I nodded, a bit dumbstruck.

Tash swore properly. This is important to mention. Tash *never* swears properly. 'He *is* awful – totally despicable. Quick, go after him!'

Now, I don't think I would have done, it's all very well building up fake confidence in private so you almost believe you have it. But it's completely different when you try to wave your confidence around a bit in public and someone practically rips it out of your hand and stamps it into the parched dry earth. So, really, all I wanted to do was fold myself up small and store myself under the chutney table until the world ended. But I couldn't imagine Jess Bradley doing that. And the hollow feeling in my stomach was starting up, which made me a bit angry and energetic. Then the last person I would have requested in my moment of need if God or Buddha or Whoever had bothered to ask swaggered in. Ralph.

Tash spotted him too and dug her elbow into my ribs. 'Look, it's poor Ralph – god, I bet his sad spanner's a bit hot in those leather trousers . . .'

'Ugh, don't even think abo–'

'Ooh, Circe – it's a sign – GO, *now*!'

Ralph was closing in, no doubt remembering some recent statistic that confirmed me as a hopeless case of teenage delinquency. I contorted my face into a withering glare of pity in case he thought I'd seen him, but shot straight past as if I hadn't, my eyes fixed on Rufus's shaggy hair winding away through the crowds.

Outside, the sun hit me, so I clamped on my cheapie seventies shades (which I love for their funkiness, but which aren't actually that see-through). Then I barged forward saying 'excuse me, sorry' etcetera, but not really thinking about what I was going to say to Rufus if I caught up with him, which was a mistake.

I did have Savvy Rose's soundtrack playing in my head though, only it went like this: *I am (illegal swear word) unique and (illegal swear word) totally (illegal swear word) where-it's-at and how (illegal swear word) dare (illegal swear word) Rufus (illegal swear word) not answer my perfectly (illegal swear word) friendly and reasonable question (three illegal swear words).*

So all that was going on in my head and my body was getting hot in my tight horse outfit as I was moving pretty fast and my eyes were really busy trying to see through my shades and hair when . . .

BOOF

. . . I hit what felt like a brick wall, only it bounced me off, which bricks probably wouldn't.

And it growled, 'Ow, what the he–' which bricks definitely wouldn't.

Rufus.

Either I'd been walking fifty times faster than I realised or he'd stopped, which my legs and eyes hadn't planned for.

I'd like to report though, that despite being the epitome of flustered, I took a deep breath and thought, *I am gorgeous and he is extremely happy to see me.* Then it dawned on my brain he may not have heard me properly at the stall, what with all the bleating, so I said again, 'Oh hi – how's *Flint*?'

And he said, 'Are you stalking me, mad girl?'

Which wasn't exactly the response I'd hoped for.

'As if! You are severely paranoid! Of course I'm not . . .' I assured him in a totally sane voice, if you think a mouse on helium sounds totally sane. Then added, 'I was, um . . . just walking behind you.'

He rolled his weird eyes and turned away.

'Wait! I have a highly logical reason . . .' I had, I'd just channelled Jess Bradley to come up with it. 'I thought you'd lead me to Flint – so I could check he's okay, you didn't answer my question, I was worried . . .'

He huffed and turned back, reluctantly. 'Your mum came to see Lucien a few days ago and looked Flint over. He's perfectly fit. Didn't she tell you?'

'No, of course she didn't – my mum doesn't talk to me, I mean of course she talks to me, but not in a normal way, you know, with details.'

It was the truth, but to my disgust my cheeks started to burn, probably because it was also possible that Mum *had* told me but I'd forgotten to bother to listen.

'Ah . . .' his lips curled and for one triumphant second I thought he was going to smile, but then he scowled instead, '. . . well, you know now.'

'Fantastic, great, I'm glad. Good.' I then noticed I was

still hugging the huge jar from Tash's stall and that it must look a bit mad, so I thrust it at him, 'Oh and you forgot this, special offer, for one day only, a free jar of honey with every bar of honeycomb!'

He took the jar in the stomach like a rugby ball, then laughed, but not in a 'lucky me' way but in a 'you are mere dirt' way and pushed it back at me.

'No thanks.'

'Don't you like honey? It's homemade, really delicious.'

'Love it.' He raised one eyebrow.

I frowned and followed his smirk down to the jar in my hands.

It was empty.

Poetic Injustice

Posted Saturday 14th August, 18:37

Sorry, I had to restart the laptopasaurus, it began to roar, maybe in sympathy at my utter humiliation, maybe because my sunburnt arm is radiating so much heat. I've now slapped thick white calamine lotion on, so it looks like I'm greased-up to swim the channel, but only with one arm.

So, there I was staring down at my empty jar, wondering if I could squeeze myself inside and roll myself quietly away never to be seen again, when I heard an 'Ahem'.

I peered up through my fringe. Rufus had turned into Ralph.

'Argh!' I greeted him on instinct, before remembering I should be feeling sorry for him and his spanner. I then accidentally pictured it sweating in his leather trousers, and although I haven't actually seen a spanner close up in real life, so it looked sort of, well, like an actual spanner, only curled up, it was still a truly gross thought. So, instead of saying 'hello' in a pitying way, I said 'Argh' again.

'Hi Cheeky – boy problems?' He squeezed a finger under the collar of his stiff pink shirt and stretched his neck like a turtle trying to escape its shell. 'Bit old for you, isn't he?'

My mouth dropped open and loads of illegal swear words would have fallen out if I wasn't struck dumb with speechlessness. What was he *thinking*? Didn't he remember that even if he was one of Mum's 'just friends' men, he was precisely Less Than Nobody to me. And what about The Line? Did he think because he'd crossed it once it didn't exist any more?

I was too furious to meet his eyes, so I stared at his hair, which was slicked to his head so neatly it looked like a plastic clip-on.

'A. My name is not "Cheeky", it is Circe. B. Not that it is any of *your* business, Ralph, but Rufus is nothing to do with me, he's a client of Mum's.'

'I know *exactly* who he is – Rufus Strakes. Your mum's been watching the jumping with him and Lucien. Listen

Circe, between you and me, he's bad news, I'd steer well clear if I were you.'

How random is that?

Actually, in The Middle Of Absolute Nowhere, it's not that random. Everyone who lives here likes to think they know everything about everyone else who lives here. And if they don't know it, they make it up.

'Circe, your mum worries about you enough already . . .'

What? Since when? Mum barely notices me. I seriously considered bopping Ralph on the head with the empty jar, but suspected it would just slide off. Instead, I glared at him pityingly and exuding raw female power. Then it hit me that he might, just might, know something about Rufus that could help with my pet boy experiment, which as you can probably tell, wasn't exactly going according to plan.

'What do you mean, bad news?'

'I can't go into it . . .' he tapped his nose, 'discretion. Let's just say he's troubled – he's *trouble. Capiche?*'

The TV commercials for Ralph's spaghetti client all involve macho mafiosi men kissing tomatoes. Sometimes it really shows.

'And two wrongs don't make a right, Circe.'

'Thanks a lot Ralph.'

He started puffing up again. 'Only last year a segmented survey of critically fractured families proved that traditional values are of tantamount importance in consumer choice. In short, Circe, what a vulnerable girl like you needs is a nice,

steady chap from a good solid family – not some angry scruff
with prob–'

Ralph droned on and on. I turned my ears off and
scanned the crowds for an escape route. There was no way
I was going over to the showjumping now, not with Mum
cosying up with Lucien and Rufus. And I didn't fancy going
back to Tash to report on my total failure.

'. . . I tell you, if I ever meet him I'll give him a piece of
my mind . . .'

Was he talking about my so-called dad again, or Rufus?
Either way, I so did not need to hear it. I had to bite my lip
to stop myself yelling, 'Shut up, sad person – you are
obviously mentally breaking down with a mid-life spanner
crisis!' as since Mum's 'tired time' there are certain things
I'm forbidden to say and I'm pretty sure that would be one
of them. Then I saw it, an escape, in the shape of a sign over
a small tent beside a saddlery stall:

Rhyme & Reason
Drop-In Workshops
with popular local poet AJ Auden-Oates

'. . . appalling behaviour, some people don't deserve to
have chil–'

'AJ!' I cut in, desperately.

'. . . over sixteen per ce-cen-tt-t.' Ralph nearly choked
on his latest statistic and whipped round.

'The poetry – I promised I'd pop in. Been delightful,
Ralph, as always. Bye.' And, I admit, I actually ran away.

Ducking into AJ's poetry tent seemed like a good idea at the time. The perfect safe haven from Ralph. A bit like hiding in a church if vampires were chasing you (and they weren't the sort of vampires you wouldn't mind catching you). I planned to slip in and out again as soon as humanly possible, unnoticed by the poetic types busy searching their tortured souls. But when I got inside I saw only one chair was occupied, by a tall lady who looked a bit like an unravelling mummy she was trailing so many mauve chiffon scarves.

AJ was pacing on a small stage at the front, looking worried. He pounced on me. 'Circe! Fantastic to see you – you're just in time for my two-thirty!'

'Oh no AJ, I just wanted to –'

'To join in! Of course. Brilliant. And you brought along an object, good, so that's your inspiration for today . . .'

I followed his intent gaze down to my jar, then glanced across at the mauve lady and saw she had a heart-shaped floral photo frame on her lap. Her eyes, framed by long fake purple lashes, were glued to AJ's face. She would have been very pretty in a china doll sort of way, but the effect was a bit destroyed by the fact that the low cut V-neck of her frilly mauve blouse revealed a patch of curly black chest hair.

'. . . intriguing, Circe, an empty vessel with an illustration of a bumble bee on the lid – naive, yet potentially organically complex . . .'

'AJ, um, sorry, really, I can't sta–'

'So are you thinking maybe a classic sonnet about nature? Or perhaps you could consider the emptiness itself, you know, the space inside, what that space really means – what it *is* . . .'

Maybe AJ was getting me back for my pet experiment, maybe he was just desperate not to be left alone with the besotted mauve 'lady'. Either way, I figured I owed him a favour, for giving me the laptopasaurus, if nothing else. So I let him push me into the nearest chair and whistle for Meg, who trotted over and sat heavily on my feet. And that was that.

Two of the longest hours of my life later, I emerged blinking and clutching probably the worst poem ever written about an empty jar. Possibly the only poem ever written about an empty jar.

The one good thing about the afternoon was that I learned a bit about metaphors, which might help with my fabulous sophistication. And that's even more important now, because with Rufus being the kind of pet boy you could spend the rest of your life chasing round a field, it's likely to be my only defence against Portia next term.

Oh . . . hold on . . . I can hear Mum's Mini coming up the lane. I hope she hasn't brought back a 'just friends' man. I've had about a thousand times more Ralph than I can take today. Actually, I've had about a hundred times more AJ too. Right, hold on, I need to pluck a few willow leaves so I can

get a better look . . . She's parking . . . the sun's reflecting off
the windscreen on the passenger side, so it's hard to see . . .
Is she, by some miracle, alone? No. Surprise surprise. Which
one is it this time? Ralph? No. Not slicked down enough. AJ
then. But his hair looks wrong . . . maybe he's got some kind
of ruffly poetic hat on . . . No. It looks like . . .

Oh.

My.

God . . .

Revenge by hamstericidal ratlet

Posted Saturday 14th August, 19:15

Okay, so if you haven't already guessed, the person who
climbed out of Mum's Mini was not a 'just friends' man, but
a potential pet boy.

Rufus looked the usual total mess, even wearing his
cream show jodhpurs and polished tan-topped riding boots.
His hair stuck up like he'd lost a fight with a bramble bush
and, though he was too far away to sniff, I was pretty certain
his faded black T-shirt would smell. Even if I did manage to
make him my pet boyfriend and keep him till the start of
term, he was the perfect male human example of not the
kind of buff boy I'd want to snog at the school gates.

He glared round with his fists clenched at his sides as
if he was looking for something he was really angry with.

My skin prickled as I wondered if I was that something. I doubted he'd hunt me down just because I'd tried to give him a free empty jar though. And while Mum wouldn't exactly win any medals for parenting, I hoped even she wouldn't have offered to drive him here just so he could attack me.

But still, my first instinct was to hide, which was a bit of a pointless instinct because I was already hiding, accidentally, under my tree. So I tuned my brain into my other instincts, to work out why he was here and what I should do next.

Rufus stamped up the path behind Mum but instead of disappearing into the cottage, they came straight through the side gate into the back garden. I gasped internally. I couldn't come out now even if I wanted to because they'd see me and my ingenious secret office would be revealed.

They were ten metres away, almost directly below me, peering down at something out of sight, I couldn't think what, then I heard Mum warn, 'Whatever you do, never let them anywhere near any other small pets . . .'

Of course, the hamstericidal ratlets!

'No worries. Apart from the horses, we've only got Digby – the lurcher.'

I leaned forward, fascinated. I'd never heard Rufus say such a long sentence. His voice was deep and drawly with the usual bit of a hiss it.

Mum handed Rufus a pipette. 'So you can give them

their milk solution with this and feed them a little apple peel. It's not too tricky, my daughter's been managing – but watch your fingers.'

Managing? Thanks Mum, for that vote of confidence. Feeding killing machines, even really small ones, is no mean feat, and I'd pulled it off without a scratch.

Rufus leaned over the cage. 'Ouch!'

I grinned, then bit my lip guiltily, then remembered no one could see me and grinned again. That would teach him for nearly murdering me and being rude. Revenge by ratlet.

'Little sods. They're quick.' Rufus stood up again. 'Do you reckon they're like this because they were abandoned?'

'Who knows? It could be mistreatment, the owner was pretty clueless.'

'And it's okay for me to take them?'

He didn't sound keen. I didn't blame him, the ratlets are basically two sets of buck teeth rolled in balls of dingy grey fur with red tails worming out at the back.

'Yes, darling. Please, it's so good of you. The animal rescue centre's rammed. And we can't keep them, they're making Jude Law and Daniel Craig very jumpy.'

'Oh, er . . .'

I grinned again, then winced realising Rufus might think I was the sad fanatic naming pets after my fantasy older men.

Mum pointed across to the other side of the patio. 'The guinea pigs!'

'Oh, right.'

I couldn't see Rufus's face, but I was pretty sure I heard him smirk. Go on, Mother, tell him the names are your idea . . .

'Ah, and here's someone who'd pop these chaps in a sandwich if he had half a chance – this is Johnny Depp.'

I was now cringing so much my neck started to ache.

'Interesting names.' Rufus bent down to stroke Johnny Depp. 'Very . . . original.'

Go on Mum – tell him *now*, tell him it's *you*, tell him what you told me the one time I dared ask. 'It's just such fun, darling, isn't it? I love watching people's faces when I say I live with my daughter and Johnny Depp!'

That was before we got Jude and Daniel. For a while we fostered a couple of lady rabbits too, David Bowie and Mick Jagger. To say Mum's got an odd sense of humour is sort of an understatement.

'Thanks darling – we rather like them.'

No *we* don't! I wanted to call Johnny a proper name – Dracula or Robert or something.

'And she's not into the rats, your daughter – she wants to just *get rid* of them?'

Rufus sneered that, like I was some kind of heartless rodentist hitwoman.

'Oh she does, yes . . .'

Thanks again Mum. For the record, I'm not really into the ratlets but I haven't said a word about actually *getting rid* of them. Typical. When I do say something Mum doesn't hear it, now it seems when I don't, she thinks she does. I am beyond misunderstood.

'. . . she'll be very glad to see them go. Besides, she's far too busy to look after them, she's got a big homework project for school, and she's hardly ever here – always dashing around having fun with her friends.'

Sigh.

'Yeah, I bumped into her at the show – or rather she bumped into me.'

Yikes. I wasn't sure I wanted to hear his description of our encounter. I tried to turn my ears off but couldn't, they were too interested.

'Really?' Mum laughed. 'I am surprised. I didn't think she was going – when I told her about it she swore it "wasn't her thing".'

I bristled, thinking she'd misheard me again. Then my mind flashed back a few weeks, to Mum pointing out the show's ad in the local paper and me huffing it off.

Rufus laughed vilely, then said, 'I can see that, she was dressed a bit er, crazily, like she was off clubbing.'

I was *not* dressed crazily – I was dressed like a horse. And for a very logical and sane reason.

Mum laughed too. 'That's Circe all right darling – bit of a rebel, rather a character.'

Argh. I am *not* a character. I am totally *normal*. Can you imagine how livid I was then? I had to hang on to a willow branch to stop myself tearing down the garden and putting everyone right on who I am and what I think and what I do and why. But I didn't want to watch my entire pet boy plan dissolve into smithereens in front of my very eyes. And I could also see it might come across as violent, rather than confident. I don't think it's very where-it's-at-ish to be spending your Saturday night alone under a tree either.

Anyway, as Rufus raised one eyebrow, I gritted my teeth expecting some cutting retort, but he just checked his watch. 'Right, I'd better get back, Lucien will be waiting, you know – saddles to polish, mucking out to do . . .'

'Gosh, busy busy busy! Well, I hope you'll be okay carrying the cage, keep the towel on top so they can't nip you through the bars. As I said, I'd happily drop them off tomorrow, but I really can't drive you back tonight, I promised to wait in for my friend Ralph.'

'It's no hassle, it's only about twenty minutes across country.'

'Quicker on Flint though, eh? I saw you bolting past the other night.'

Rufus laughed a bit flatly, but totally remorselessly, as he picked up the cage and moved to leave. 'Yeah, he's quite nippy too.' Then, as I stamped and yelled internally at him, he added something really unexpected. 'Look, if Circe *is* hacked off about this, tell her she gets visitation rights – you know, if she wants to drop by the stables to check we're not starving them.'

Oh My God. My internal yelling morphed into cheering. Rufus had just handed me the perfect excuse to try out another pet boy experiment.

Mum waved him off. 'Oh I'm sure she won't. As I said, she's really not keen.'

Sigh. Is there somewhere you can take daft mothers to get them trained to be wise ones?

Quick, someone pass me an Oscar

Posted Saturday 14th August, 19.33

I watched Rufus climb into Sharon's paddock (Sharon, very unfortunately, was still at the show). Then, as soon as he was safely out of sight, I slipped out of my office and followed Mum indoors. Conversations With My Daughter aren't exactly her strong point these days, but if I was going to take up Rufus's offer, I needed her to tell me about it. I also needed his address as I hadn't followed the route before and searching internet maps for 'stables in woods' in The Middle Of Absolute Nowhere (which probably has more stables in woods than any other place on the planet) could take the rest of my life.

Luckily, I knew exactly how to play this one.

'Mum – where are my hamstericidal ratlets?'

'Oh, hello darling. You'll be pleased to hear they're on their way to a new home.'

I gasped, '*What?* Where?'

'At Lucien's, he offered today – he's such a star.'

'Oh no! I'll *really* miss them . . .' I let my voice trail off and flumped down on to the sofa tragically.

'Sorry Circe, but I thought you didn't much like them.'

I looked hurt. 'No, I was just *worried* about them, they were so . . . vulnerable.'

'You said they were the epitome of demonic, darling.'

'Mmm, demonic in a *cuddly* way though.' I gazed wistfully towards the spot where their cage had stood. 'Now they've gone, it looks so empty . . .'

Mum started to look a bit sad too, and wary. 'Oh dear – do you want a bun?'

A bun is Mum's answer to every emotional question since her 'tired time'.

I knew I had to be careful, so I turned down my emotions, but mumbled, 'No, not hungry.' Then whispered, as if I didn't mean her to hear, 'If only I could have said goodbye . . .'

'Ah, well, that *can* be fixed, if you feel that strongly – Rufus did mention you could pop round.'

Result. I made my face look astonished. 'Oh! Did he mean it?'

'He seemed to.' Mum frowned down at the bun she'd just put on a plate. 'He is rather a moody boy though.'

I crossed my fingers behind my back. 'Is he? I don't really remember him . . .'

'Mmm. Are sure you want to bother darling? It's going to be another lovely day tomorrow, AJ and I are driving down to the coast to swim – you're very welcome to come with us.'

I would rather eat my entire beach towel, but I shook my head regretfully. 'Thanks, but I've got my big holiday homework project, remember, I don't want to be out all day.'

'Oh, yes . . . hmm, if you like I could tell AJ to come later to give you time to work in the morning.'

I heaved a sad sigh. 'No, honestly, I need to see the ratlets, it really is important to me.' That was true, anyway. 'So . . . if I could get the address?'

'Ah, right, yes, well, if you're certain . . .' she scribbled on a post-it note and stuck it to the fridge. 'There. Now are you going to come to Le Gingham Bistro with Ralph and me tonight? There's a special seven-course *Summer Show Extravaganza Menu.*'

I exited, fast, stage right.

Sliding about (and nearly drowning) in teenage confusion

Posted Saturday 14th August, 21:49

I feel a bit weird. And I smell a bit weird too. Johnny Depp just slinked into my room, took one sniff and shot out again. I might need to have another bath.

I've spent most of the evening soaking in Mum's aromatherapy oils to help me think wisely and make my skin feel confident. I mixed up ten drops each of *Relaxing Nirvana, Ecstatic Utopia, Stimulating Samsara* and *Calming Karma*. I also added a dash of *Pre-menstrual Paradise*, even though I'm not, just in case.

I couldn't think at all at first, as the bath was so slippery my bum couldn't get a grip and kept sliding away towards the taps, shooting my legs out of the water and dunking my head under. I slid backwards and forwards for about ten minutes before I had a brainwave and grabbed the rubber gloves from the tiny cupboard under the tiny sink and put them on my feet so they could grip the end of the bath. I could then lie fixed in position with my mouth and nose just above the water. It felt a bit rigid and definitely not fabulously sophisticated, but at least I could breathe enough to think.

As soon as my body got still though, my brain started sliding about wondering why Ralph warned me off Rufus. I don't trust him one bit, of course, but it's still odd. If I was a normal daughter I'd ask Mum about it, but we just 'don't go there' any more – talk about men, even of the boy type, that is. We hardly talk properly about anything any more, have you noticed?

Anyway, all the oil must have helped because I quite quickly came to the conclusion that it didn't make any difference. I already knew Rufus was the Rudest Stupidest Most Despicable Boy I'd Ever Met, Ralph probably just thought so too. If anything, that just made my experiments even more unemotional, which somehow did make me feel a bit more naturally confident.

Ouch, I just scratched my nose and the spiciness of my hand practically set my nostrils on fire. I reek. And I feel a bit dizzy too. Is it possible to overdose on aromatherapy oil? I think I'd better check the labels.

A plan, if I survive the night

Posted Saturday 14th August, 22:21

Excellent. I am an official OD case, the labels all say *This oil is highly concentrated, add a maximum of three drops to your bath*. And there's a diagram showing how it enters your bloodstream through your skin.

I worked out that I added about forty-four drops, minimum. Gulp.

As it's already pumping through my heart, it's probably too late, but I had a shower anyway because I definitely wasn't going to be able to sleep in my own smell. Then I nipped down to peel Rufus's address off the fridge, in case Ralph comes back tonight and accidentally on purpose throws it in the bin. It was stuck to an old feeding schedule Mum wrote last term when we took in three tanks of fish, a tank of terrapins and a snake rescued from a dodgy pet shop, and had to time things precisely or everyone would have eaten each other. And I remembered how it all seemed far too complicated to sort out before school, but how the schedule fixed it in my head and made it much easier. So I've worked one out for tomorrow:

10.00 Wave Mum off while exuding busy studiousness (hold calculator).

10.01 Head-to-toe body clenching to instil natural physical confidence.

10.15 Shower, wash hair.

10.30 Comb knots out of hair.

11.00 Dry hair as flat as possible while faking confidence (aloud) in mirror.

11.15 Dress like someone who really cares about hamstericidal ratlets and definitely not 'crazily' and/or as horse.

11.30 Apply subtle glitter mascara and three coats of *Forbidden Scarlet*.

11.40 Leave home, walk to Knight Ridge (where Rufus works).

12.00 Arrive, say hi, drink polite cup of hot chocolate.

12.10 Bid moving farewell to hamstericidal ratlets.

12.15 Properly treat Rufus like a pet so he asks me out on a date.

12.25 Say yes.

12.30 Say goodbye and leave (triumphant).

Comment

Posted Sunday 15th August, 09:45, by Savvy Rose

Whew. Totally bushed. Just got in from *the* wildest night Uptown, but had to hit your blog before I hit the sack as I could *not* wait to get the gossip on your experiment.

Oh my gosh. Fate threw you one hell of a curveball with Rufus turning up at Tash's store like that. But, hey, good job – I'm real proud of you. You kept working that confidence – and I have a hunch it might have worked a little magic too. Like Rufus thinks it's a cool idea to come over and pick up the killer rats, even though he knows he'll have to walk all the way home carrying them? Uh-uh, doesn't sound real logical to me. If he's so darned busy, why didn't he take up your mom's offer to drop them off? Eww, I think someone may have started a crush . . .

Good luck later – though something tells me you won't need it!

Quick question between clenches

Posted Sunday 15th August, 10:02

Wow – *really?* I mean do you really think Rufus might actually be interested? He's so naturally appalling it's impossible for me to tell. I suppose when he told Mum I could visit the ratlets he was almost nice-ish. But what if he does like me, even a tiny bit? Doesn't that change things? Shouldn't I start playing hard to get now? Maybe I shouldn't go over today at all, but wait a week or something? Savvy Rose, if you're not asleep/too tired to type – help!

Comment

Posted Sunday 15th August, 10:08, by Savvy Rose

Hey, I was just about to log off, mighty glad you caught me; now, this is *important* . . .

Do not, I repeat, do *not*, under any freaking circumstances, play hard to get! Sure, it can be useful sometimes, but *not now*, before the flirting's even gotten started. You need to hook the boy's interest real good before he'll give a damn. Start to act as if you don't like Rufus already and he might just stray off.

Listen, honey, you *are* where-it's-at. Okay? Be confident enough in that to compliment Rufus. Tell him he's brave for taking on the rats, don't be scared to make him feel real special. Think of him as a wary dog you're coaxing towards you.

Now – gitt girl! You gotta stick to that schedule!

Making A Boy Feel Special Even If He Isn't
Male Human Pet Control: Experiment 5

Posted Sunday 15th August, 14:54

Welcome to experiment five, which will be reported in a properly non-emotional scientific way to reflect my growing fabulous sophistication as a trainee professional journalist and woman of the world who has a date. Yes. You read correctly. Woo hoo. I'VE GOT A DATE!

I have taken the first step towards getting a proper boyfriend who I can adore. Or rather, I have taken the first step towards getting a practice pet boyfriend who I don't like.

I can officially report that I really don't like Rufus at all. Not even a bit. This is quite good in a way, when I realised it this morning I instantly felt less nervous about faking confidence and being where-it's-at and making him feel special all at once. Though it might be quite bad in a way too, as it could be difficult to snog him, which I might need to do as I'VE GOT A DATE!

I arrived at Knight Ridge five minutes late because I had to hold my head really still all the way to keep my hair flat. I pressed the metal buzzer at the gates and stared at the circle of perforated dots underneath, expecting a, 'Halt, who goes there?' or something. I'd already formulated two answer options, depending on how friendly the voice was, either, 'Good day, it is I, daughter of your veterinarian surgeon and former guardian of the hamstericidal ratlets, here to check on their welfare,' or 'Hi, it's Circe.' But the speaker just crackled, then the gates groaned open.

As I walked in, my brain started nagging my feet to stop and let it think for a minute, but I knew it just wanted to persuade me to get scared, so I ignored it and marched quickly up the rough drive. It wound uphill through thick woods for about five minutes so I was quite puffed out from determination by the time I rounded the last bend. But as I spotted the first snarling gargoyle on the roof of the house, I practised a confident smile up at it, preparing to greet Lucien and accept another one of his yummy hot chocolates.

'Oh. It's *you*.' A bored drawl wiped my smile off.

It was Rufus.

'No it's someone else entirely.' (Savvy Rose, I'm sure you won't approve of that reply, but honestly, he sneered '*you*' so despicably that my mouth said it on reflex, like if someone slaps you and you slap them straight back.)

'Very cute.' Rufus was sitting at the top of the steps leading up to the iron-studded front door. He squinted down at me, his weird eyes flashing in the sun, then he sort of deep sighed as if I was exactly his idea of the biggest waste of time in the world, 'I thought you were Lucien's lunch guests.'

'Sorry to disappoint you.'

He tugged a bit of straw out of the mop he passed off as hair. 'They're vile bores, Hickstead adjudicators.'

I stared at him.

'You know, *showjumping judges*. You do *live* with your mum don't you? She *is* an equine vet isn't she?'

I'd been hesitating because I was trying to work out if he'd almost given me a compliment. 'Oh, um, I *do* she *is* – I knew what you meant I was just . . .' what was I 'just'? I couldn't tell him the truth. I backtracked, 'I mean, I was just trying to remember, my mum and me, like I said, we don't talk much, properly, about horses – anything.'

'Yeah, I got that.' He raised one eyebrow. Infuriatingly. Then he looked me up and down, but not in a meaningful way like Jake used to, more as if I was a horse, which was weird because he hadn't yesterday, when I was actually dressed as one.

I transferred my weight to my toes and lifted my heels, which Tash says makes thighs look more graceful. Maybe Rufus would find my fetlock muscles so charming or my mane so shiny that I wouldn't have to bother with making him feel special, he'd just ask me out straight away. I smiled in anticipation.

'You're dressed exactly the same as me.'

'What?' I feigned extreme surprise. 'No I am not!' This, I admit, wasn't strictly true. I was wearing battered trainers, my scruffiest jeans and a faded black T-shirt. I thought he'd automatically think this was not a crazy way to dress, unless he thought he dressed crazily himself. It was meant to be a subliminal effect though, I didn't expect him to actually notice.

'Yes, you are.' He leaned back on his hands, stretched his legs out and nodded down at his body, 'Look.'

I looked, but made my eyes go blurry because it felt a bit personal and if I thought about that too much I would either do my tomato impression or start to laugh hysterically. I did notice his T-shirt logo though, a faded picture of a horseshoe with 'Prime Pony Feeds' curling round it.

'Rubbish, my T-shirt's totally different.' I grabbed its hem and pulled the logo away from my body to demonstrate. It said 'Bat Protection League Disco – fangs for your funkin' support!' which I thought would be good to get across my caring-for-small-mammals nature and add a party vibe at the same time.

Rufus just smirked despicably.

I glared at him. 'Oh, and I don't see you wearing these either.' I lifted up my hair to show off the large purple plastic hearts dangling from my earlobes.

'Very sophisticated.'

I beamed, then realised he was being sarcastic and huffed, 'Anyway, it's not exactly unusual is it, what you're wearing? I mean probably about 95% of all teenage guys in the world are dressed exactly like you. It's a total "I'm too cool to care how I look" uniform, isn't it?' I then gasped internally as I realised this probably wouldn't make Rufus feel very special and made a mental note to put that right immediately.

But then he said, 'Fair enough. What about you though,

you're a *girl* – don't you care how you look?'

'Yes, I mean no, but yes sort of, well, um, not obsessively or anything, I eat buns and things, you know . . . as long as I feel good – and clean – not smelly . . .'

I know I know, I was in a bit of a tizz then, as you can probably tell.

Rufus was smirking but his lips were twitching at the corners as if they really wanted to smile but he wouldn't let them. 'Your perfume is very . . . unusual.'

Sigh. I'd loofah-ed at least three layers of skin off in the shower, but I'd probably need an actual blood transplant to get rid of all the oily aromas completely. I wondered if I was now doomed to smell like *Nirvanan Utopian Samsaran Karmic Pre-menstrual Paradise* for the rest of my entire life.

'So?' His eyebrow was up again.

'So what?'

'Why are you here? Did you not trust me about Flint?'

'Oh. No. I mean, yes.'

'So?'

'Um . . .'

Okay. I need to point out here that my brain had sort of switched off as Rufus was doing his weird staring right through me thing. Luckily, a buzzer sounded in the hallway behind him.

His eyes rolled. 'That'll be the Hickstead lot now.'

I snapped out of my trance, realising I had only a few minutes to work my pet boy magic. I took a very deep breath, told myself this was purely scientific and no emotions were involved at all and said, 'You do look great in your clothes, Rufus, even if they are a bit samey.'

His eyebrow shot up again, but he didn't smirk, so I stood up a bit straighter and smiled an extra confident where-it's-at type of smile. 'And you're very brave!'

His eyes narrowed to slits. '*What?*'

The sneer was back. I rushed on, 'To dare to take on the pets from hell!'

He frowned, but looked slightly less evil.

'The hamstericidal ratlets!'

'Oh, yeah, right . . .'

I finally remembered why I was there. 'That's *why I'm here*, Mum gave them away without asking me . . . I didn't get to say goodbye – I'd like to see them, one last time . . .' I did the trailing off sad voice thing again.

'Ah. Oh. Your mum said you wouldn't want to . . .'

I shrugged. 'Like I said, Mum isn't exactly the world's top Circe Shaw expert.'

'Right.'

'Are they okay?'

'Course. I've set them up a decent run in my room – but . . .' we both turned at the sound of car tyres crunching up the drive, 'I've got to sit through this ruddy lunch with Lucien.'

I smiled and nodded wistfully and forced myself to look admiringly up at him as if that made him extremely special.

'I guess – if you're not too busy with your *homework* . . .'

I blushed then, not because he had sneered that, although he had, but at the thought that basically my 'homework' was him. I desperately wanted to tear my eyes away from his and stare at the ground until my cheeks stopped embarrassing me, but his eyes were sort of boring into my brain and out the other side* again so it was a physical impossibility. But I thought I may as well make the most of a cringe-making situation, so I imagined he was a big wary dog who was only growly because he needed a bit of encouragement and I said, 'When you do that with your eyes you look frighteningly intelligent.'

And he laughed, which I suppose is about the equivalent of a tail wag. So I smiled a lot more confidently than I felt. Then he said, 'Look, can you come back tomorrow?' Then he checked his watch. 'I've promised Lucien I'll help settle in a new livery pony at half-two, so . . . same time again, 12.30-ish?'

It was weird then because my mouth wanted to say, 'Hmm, maybe, if I can fit you in, I *am* pretty busy tomorrow.' But I realised the old (pre-Savvy Rose advice) Circe would have said that – and she'd got me precisely nowhere in the proper boyfriend stakes. So I swallowed hard to shut her up, grinned, and nodded.

And Rufus jumped to his feet and trotted down the steps towards me, and for an appalling moment I thought I'd encouraged him too much and he was expecting a quick snog, so I stepped back and sucked my lips in. But he totally ignored me, just strode straight past with his hand stuck out and said, 'Gents, morning, Lucien's schooling Lone Ranger, he asked me to take you straight up to the manège.' Then he disappeared around the corner of the house trailed by three tweedy men.

And not even a wave goodbye wasn't a very flirty end to my experiment, so I felt a bit flat for a minute. But I reminded myself that Rufus was a particularly difficult potential pet boy and that I didn't need to actually like him, so in fact my first experiment had been 100% successful.

I HAD A DATE!

* What Rufus does with his eyes is nothing like what R-Patz does. It's hideous, as if he knows exactly what's going on in your brain but doesn't find even one tiny thought of any interest at all.

Okay, so it might not, strictly speaking, be an actual romantic date

Posted Sunday 15th August, 15:03

But it depends how you define a date doesn't it? This is how I define one:

- It must involve a potential pet boy asking me to meet him.
- That meeting must be at an agreed time.

 158

- And at a specific place.
- No other people must be invited (although other pets, such as hamstericidal ratlet twins, can also be present).

So, I HAVE GOT A DATE! It also feels good for my natural confidence to believe I have, so I'm going to.

I do see that there weren't any sort of romantic bad intentions in Rufus's invitation. When Drew asked me out, he winked, 'Leave it to me – I'll get us *good seats*.' Which I knew didn't mean he'd get front row tickets so we could see the latest *Harry Potter* better, but back row tickets so we wouldn't see it at all. And we didn't. Instead I put up with 125-minutes of intensive suction and when we came out my lips were blue and I had a bruise on the end of my nose. So, in a way, it's a relief Rufus doesn't have any intentions, although I suppose he'll have to get some if he's going to become my practice pet boyfriend.

Anyway, I'm not going to worry about that right now, I'm going to slap on factor 50 so I don't frazzle before MY DATE and bask in the sun and my own experimental glory.

Innocent as charged

Posted Sunday 15th August, 16:27

Tash said she'd pop round later this afternoon so I was going to wait till then to spill the juicy details of my experiment. But my thumbs got too excited, so I texted her.

> Guess what . . .

And she texted straight back (even though she's meant to be out on a long sporty bike ride with Ben).

> Oooooh what?

I sat on my hands to keep her in suspense for a few seconds then shot back

> I've got a date!

And she shot back

> OMG!!!!! XOXOX
> How? When? Where?

And I shot back

> Cos I'm total
> top expert in
> Male Human Pet
> Control! 12.30 tom.
> In R's bedroom.

And she shot back

OMG SIS
Don't move.
C U in 5.

Tash arrived about two minutes later. It turned out she and Ben had sportily cycled as far as the park, then got too overcome with an urgent need to get meaningful and set up camp behind a bush all day. Her hair was full of twigs and her flowery blouse was inside out. She dumped her bike on the patio at the bottom of the garden and scrambled up the steep lawn to where I was basking at the top.

'God Circe – are you bonkers?'

I sat up. 'What?'

'Durr.' She crossed her eyes. 'A first date – in a boy's *bedroom*?'

'Calm down Tash, it's fine . . .'

'It is so *not*! He's not even a nice boy, he's a totally despicable boy, you said so yourself – millions of times.'

'Tash, really, it's the only place we can meet – there's a good reaso–'

'Oh pur-lease, give me a break.' Tash was standing below me, so her face was on the same level as mine. She wagged her finger. 'Even Charlotte Floyd wouldn't fall for that!'

'Objection! Stop pointing, I'm not some vile villain on trial at the Old Bailey!'

'Sorry, but you really shouldn't –'

'Argh! Let me speak. Rufus has a good defence. He's adopted the ratlets and he's keeping them in his room. I'm using visiting them as an excuse to try another experiment.'

'Hmm. Can't he just pop them out of the cage and take them downstairs, they'd both fit in the palm of his hand.'

'My dear learned friend Tash – you've seen their teeth!'

'Ah, good point. Still a bit odd though, isn't it?'

'No, honestly, it hadn't even occurred to me. Especially as he has no romantic bad intentions.'

'What? So, it's not actually a date then?'

'Well, it depends how you define a date – as far as I'm concerned, it is.' I reeled off my logical bullet points, but I could tell Tash wasn't really listening. She'd obviously decided that legally it wasn't a proper date so there was nothing to worry about. This was good as it shut her up and a few minutes later she babbled a bit about Ben's six-pack, then hopped on her bike and sped off. But it was bad too, as once she'd gone I just couldn't get back into triumphant basking mode. I couldn't help thinking that maybe she was right, which made me a bit confused about what stage of pet boy training I'm at. And now I'm wondering if I'll have to go through the whole Making Rufus Feel Special routine again tomorrow. Sigh.

Comment

Posted Sunday 15th August, 16:59, by Savvy Rose

Hey, Circe – you know what I think?

I think YOU HAVE A DATE!

Atta girl – you were awesome! You're right, Rufus is obviously not the most straightforward kinda guy, but you rose to that freaking challenge like the classy lady you really are! And did you notice how he responded to your compliments? That was no coincidence, they worked! Give yourself some credit, honey.

I get that no 'romantic intentions' could be a deal breaker, but I figure he *does* have them. Sure, *do* keep on making him feel special though. This pet is still a few metres off, if you want him to feel safe enough to come closer, he needs some more encouraging hints.

Remember, Circe, this isn't about false flattery. You were lucky to get away with that 'intelligent eyes' line. Watch Rufus – imagine you're watching a cat. They're such amazing creatures, you'd be thinking, 'that was a cool jump off that roof/I wish I could climb a tree like that/wow what silky fur'. Really notice what's special about Rufus – trust me, there will be something; every guy has something.

But if you really can't think of anything genuine to say, remember you don't necessarily need to say anything. You can do a heck of a job just with your physicality. Lean towards him, not away from him. Don't cross your arms defensively. Try not to make any sudden unpredictable movements that might make him back off.

And hey – as always, relax, remember it's no big deal – have a blast!

I suppose there are cats and cats
Posted Sunday 15th August, 18:47

Just followed Johnny Depp around for an hour to practise and all I thought was, get your bloodied paws off that snail/bird/guinea pig/bunny/pony you spitting maniac.

In the middle of my room buried under my entire wardrobe
Posted Sunday 15th August, 23:01

What do you wear for a date* in a boy's bedroom? I've searched online and scanned all my mags and can't find any even slightly appropriate fashion tips. I did find a fascinating old *Hot Topical* column of Jess Bradley's about not being a victim of a fashion industry in which three-foot-small men dress six-foot-tall women in cling film because they want to steal our power. But it didn't help really. I know Rufus thinks something like my horse outfit is crazy, and he wasn't too impressed by me dressing the same as him either. But that leaves me almost nowhere. Half my wardrobe is jeans and Ts, the other half is, well, pretty much glitter.

* Which also might not be a date at all but just a routine hamstericidal ratlet farewell.

Comment

Posted Monday 16th August, 04:32, by Savvy Rose

Oh my gosh, you know guys are like pets when it comes to clothes too.

You can learn a lot about a boy from his style. So it's good to figure out whether you're dealing with a slick pure breed or a shaggy mongrel. Rufus sounds to me like a scruffy type, but maybe with a touch of pedigree blood.

Mirroring a guy's style can be useful. I got totally into the fifties when I was dating a rockabilly dude. As soon as I decided I wanted out, I slipped back into my usual little black dresses and he picked up the vibe, so it was much easier to split.

So, you weren't so way off dressing the same as Rufus (though it's amazing he noticed – like he was looking real close, take that as a compliment).

Okay. What to wear? Honey, if you feel good, you'll look good too. So I would always say, dress for *you*.

If a guy's right, and worth a dime, he'll fall for what's inside you. But, if your outside is a good representation of that, it sure can help some. So if, say, you feel wild and quirky, don't make like an emo chick just because you think it will rock his world. Your quirkiness will break out sooner or later and mess with your heads. Better to keep your integrity from the get-go, then you'll both know where you are.

Hey, that's not to say you need some kind of uniform, mix things up as much as you like, moods change, seasons change – fashion's meant to be fun. Dress one day as a boho hippy, the next as a gothic vamp if the spirit moves you. As long as it feels natural and you're enjoying it, you're being true to yourself.

Hilarious – try this one at home

Posted Monday 16th August, 08:11

Lying in bed with Johnny Depp sussing out which males are what kinds of pet from their clothes. This is where I'm up to so far:

> Ralph: flashy Dobermann with a touch of fancy poodle
> AJ: dramatic, but quite complicated, wafty type of tropical fish
> Ben: sporty, friendly Border collie/Labrador cross
> Jake: very posy prancing thoroughbred dressage pony

And what about the most crucial – Rufus? Well, I thought about Savvy Rose's 'scruffy type with pedigree blood' and it didn't seem quite right. I just can't convince myself he has any type of class. So I've decided Rufus is a scruffy, possibly cunning, very hissy, moggie tomcat, liable to pounce without warning. Which, as you can imagine, isn't very reassuring for a first date in his bedroom, but which has helped me choose an outfit.

Appealing To A Boy's Natural Animalistic Style
Male Human Pet Control: Experiment 6

Posted Monday 16th August, 15:58

It's 3.15 and I've just got back from Knight Ridge. Yes, you read right – *3.15*. This means that, subtracting walking home (and dancing about a bit) time, I was with Rufus for nearly two hours. Non-stop! Totally alone, apart from ratlets. And even if it didn't start out as one, in the end it was DEFINITELY A PROPER DATE!

Okay, I still don't like him. He was still mainly despicable and smelt a bit, of manure. He also glared about six times, hissed three times, swore really illegally once (but so did I), sneered too many times to keep count and was quite stupid precisely twice. His romantic bad intentions are still a bit hidden too – but they *do* exist. I think.

I arrived at exactly 12.30-ish and walked up the drive

talking myself through all the things I've learned from Savvy Rose. I practised the new physical things too, I stopped by a particularly grumpy-looking tree, pretended it was Rufus, then leaned towards it without crossing my arms. This made me realise that my arms cross quite automatically, because I really had to pin them to my sides to stop them. So I decided to keep my hands in the pockets of my denim shorts as much as possible.

My shorts, by the way, represented agility (for Rufus's pounciness) and it was really hot too, so made temperature sense. Above them I was wearing Mum's old eighties off-the-shoulder grey and black stripy baggy lurex top which is both scruffy and a bit like a tabby moggie. I completed the ensemble with some of my own natural quirky fabulous sophistication, wearing my chunky silver and fake-emerald cocktail ring and the polka-dot pumps Mum bought me for my fifteenth. I also sneaked my so-called dad's old leather satchel out of its hiding place (Mum doesn't know I bought it back from the charity shop where she sent all his stuff). It's quite scruffy and has a strong leathery saddlery-type smell, which I thought would be nice and familiar to Rufus and would also mask any last traces of my oily OD.

By the time I reached the house I felt pretty well-prepared. I waved at the gargoyle snarling down from the roof and almost skipped round the last bend, half expecting Rufus to bound forward with a rose between his teeth. He didn't, of course. Instead I had to knock three times and wait about forever (five minutes at least) before he threw open the front door, grunted, flashed his eyes a bit, then disappeared into the murk at the back of the hallway. I followed him in, assuming that's what the grunt meant and heard him say, 'Yeah yeah yeah . . . Right . . . You know, whatever.' Then there was a loud jangling click as he hung up Lucien's olde-worlde-style phone.

It all sounded very passionate. My stomach flipped as a hideous possibility occurred to it . . .

What if Rufus had a girlfriend already?

Maybe it was someone from school who was away somewhere exotic? I could waste the next two weeks experimenting on him, only for him to fall back into her arms on the first day of term. I would not get my snog at the gates, or get Portia off my back. In fact, ultimate nightmare, if his girlfriend was in Portia's gang it could make everything worse. I had to act fast. The moment Rufus reappeared, looking as charming as usual (frowning, glaring, clenching his jaw, hands bunched in fists), I asked, nonchalantly, 'Um, sorry, I couldn't help hearing . . . I guess that was *her*?'

He glared even harder. 'What? No, no chance.'

'Oh.' That had told me less than nothing. I stared at my polka-dot toes and imagined what a professional journalistic detective like Jess Bradley would ask. 'So . . . doesn't your girlfriend ever call then?'

'My *girlfriend*?'

'Yes.'

Rather weirdly, he threw back his head then and said, 'Ha!'

I realised my arms were crossed, uncrossed them, shoved my hands in my pockets and leaned forward. 'Ha?'

'I thought Lucien had told . . . I thought you meant my so-called moth– oh, never mind . . .' He rolled his eyes. 'No. It wasn't my girlfriend!'

Growl. Sorry Savvy Rose but I decided then that your 'boys are straightforward' idea must be totally wrong. It was like he was deliberately giving me answers without any information in them. 'Oh, so your girlfriend usually calls in the evening does she?'

Rufus's mouth twitched in a despicable *I'm not going to laugh because you are just so inferior to me* way, then said, 'No. She doesn't.'

I bit my lip – that really did sound like there was a 'She' in existence, but I still needed conclusive proof. I had actually managed to notice something special about him while all this was going on, so I decided to change tack. 'Your hair's looking cool today, gelled spikier like that – does your girlfriend prefer it that way?'

He laughed then, in fact he laughed so much he had to lean his hands on his knees to stop. I laughed along with him a bit, my fingers crossed in my short pockets. Eventually, he straightened up. 'Look. I don't have a girlfriend all right, that was my da–' he paused and ran his hands over his eyes, 'it was my stepfather.'

The way he said that, 'stepfather', sort of emptily, made me feel a bit sad for him, then sad for myself, which was annoying so I pinched my thighs quite hard through my pockets so I'd think about that instead.

While I did that he laughed again but not in a happy way, which was odd, but then he did something even odder. He raised one eyebrow and stuck his right hand out towards me. I just looked at his eyebrow, then down at his hand, then back to his eyebrow. Then he nodded to the massive wooden staircase curving away from us and said, 'Come on then.' And I thought, *Oh. My. God. Tash is right, he is even more despicable than I've given him credit for.* And he raised his eyebrow even higher and said, 'Don't you want to see your ghastly rats?'

Then it was my turn to laugh, relieved, and I let my eyes look into his again and he blinked then waggled his fingers. My hand still felt reluctant to join in, but I told it not to play hard to get and tugged it out of my pocket and he grabbed it and pulled me up the stairs. This was quite nice. His hand felt firm with just the right grippiness. And, although it didn't make my entire body fizz like Jake's hand did when he held my elbow, it didn't make my skin crawl either, like when Tim Lough 'accidentally' brushed his hand across my knee in rounders.

Rufus's room turned out to be up a second curving flight of stairs, in the attic, like mine, only his was about five times bigger. It was also perfectly tidy, which was a bit shocking. All the boys' rooms I'd been in before were tips. I don't think I've ever seen the floor of Ben's room. Here the floor was clear. Ben's walls were always plastered with posters too, of cars and footie stars and floaty girls. Rufus's were bare, apart from a showjumping calendar over his bed.

I peered at it. Each day of August, until today, was crossed off and there was a thick black ring round Sunday 29th August. As I frowned at the date, wondering about it, trying to remember if Mum had mentioned another horse show, Rufus's hand squeezed mine so hard I nearly said 'Ouch'. But then he let go completely, slipping his fingers from mine and making me blush for no apparent reason. Stepping away from him to hide my face, I did some more quick journalistic observations. I noticed there were three arched windows and the one opposite the bed opened on to a little balcony with its own gargoyle, which made me 'Ooh'.

'Wow. You really do like these guys, don't you?'

I frowned, because I could only see one gargoyle, then turned to see Rufus crouching by a chicken-wire tunnel running the length of the room and realised he was talking about the hamstericidal ratlets, which I'd forgotten again.

'Ooh!' I repeated quickly, in the right direction this time, 'I do, yes.' I crouched down next to him and forced myself to look at them fondly. 'Hey, remember me, guys?'

'Oliver and Harry.'

I beamed. 'Excellent names – if they'd stayed with us

they would have ended up as Bruce Willis and Harrison Ford or something.'

'Oh yeah.' Rufus sank to the floor, crossed his legs and leaned back on the heels of his hands. I did the same, without making any sudden movements. 'Your mum's seriously into film stars, isn't she?'

'She thinks it's hilarious, it drives me a bit nuts to be honest.' I snatched my hand away from the cage as the ratlets stuck their teeth between the bars. 'Ah, little angels!'

'Here, I saved their elevenses so you could feed them.' Rufus put a pile of apple peel and two cocktail sticks in front of me. 'Your mum's cool though, you're lucky . . .'

My mouth fell open. As I was scrabbling around for something to say back, he surprised me again.

'Do you think she's lonely?'

'*Mum?* God no, she gets on well with her boss, and she's got lots of animal rescue friends – and, of course, Ralph and AJ for dinners *à deux* and things.'

'What?' Rufus snapped. 'Are you *serious*? Are you telling me your mum has *two boyfriends*?' He hissed that so nastily the ratlets started squeaking, no doubt thinking a ferocious cat had stalked into the room.

Serves me right, I suppose. After the strangely pleasant hand-holding incident I'd lulled myself into a false sense of security, believing he might not be that despicable after all. 'No! Don't be a doughnut – they are both *just friends*.'

'Yeah yeah yeah, whatever.'

I glared at Rufus, completely forgetting I was still meant to be making him feel special (sorry Savvy Rose). His bottom lip jutted out and he was rolling his eyes – again. It was getting boring.

Worse, it reminded me of, well, *me*, on the one occasion Mum bothered to explain herself, last Easter Sunday. Ralph and AJ had accidentally turned up at the same time and filled the cottage with soft centres, hard stares and a really horrible mix of aftershaves, while I was trying to watch an important lesbian snog scene on *Hollyoaks*. By the time they'd drunk about a hundred cups of tea each and stomped off in opposite directions, I was spitting mad at being subjected to the kind of complicated romantic problems I should be subjecting Mum to, but never did. I tried to shut my mouth up by stuffing it with strawberry creams, but it had finally been pushed too far and spluttered, 'So, which one are you going to choose to be your proper boyfriend then?'

As soon as I said it I felt sick and started praying in case there was anyone influential hanging about in the sky to listen. But Mum just laughed, 'Gosh, neither! I'm perfectly happy being a footloose, fancy-free singleton. AJ and Ralph are just friends – and they always will be.'

And I hid behind my hair and checked her face and she really did look quite happy as she carried on, 'Honestly, I'm finished with men, darling. Us women don't *need* them nowadays, you know, we can get along rather wonderfully without them.' But her eyes went all blurry, like they had in her 'tired time'. And then she ripped open a pack of hot-cross buns with her teeth and ate one in two seconds flat, without even stopping to toast it or put on butter and jam.

So, I could see why Rufus wasn't entirely convinced. And I remembered that he'd called his mum his 'so-called mother', so maybe he was just down on mums for some reason. A bit like me feeling anti-all-dads sometimes and finding it hard to watch when Tash's dad hugs her. I also remembered my experiment was not supposed to involve any emotions and this was all starting to feel a bit too heavy, so I changed the subject. Or tried to.

'So, where's Lucien today?'

'At an auction in Kent – is your mum still married to your dad?'

I flinched, but managed not to cross my arms, mainly because I had a cocktail stick in each hand with a ravenous ratlet attached to the end of each one. 'Oh, um, no, I mean, yes, sort of, I think, maybe . . . I don't really know.'

Rufus swore then, quite a lot. 'And they call themselves *Grown-Ups*. Where is your dad? Lucien said you'd just moved down from London – is he still up there?'

Only two other people have asked me this since we moved to The Middle Of Absolute Nowhere. Portia was the first. Tash the second. It didn't take me long to make up my mind to tell Rufus what I'd told Tash.

I dropped a ratlet (who immediately dragged the

cocktail stick off and ate it) and shoved one hand back in my pocket and crossed my fingers. 'No – he's an artist. He's stuck on a remote island working flat out pretty much stranded there's no airport and boats only dock about once a year if ever.' As I said that, I saw it, really vividly, white foam crashing over jagged rocks, my so-called dad's wide grin crinkling his eyes, his mad hair blowing all over the place in the wind as he swept brilliant blues and greens across a huge canvas propped up against a tree.

'Sounds romantic.' His sneer was back again.

My mouth fell open but nothing came out, mainly because there was still nothing in my brain but crashing waves, so I just shrugged.

He opened his mouth again, then shut it, then barked, 'Drop it!'

And as he was the one who brought up the whole boring subject of so-called parents I thought, *plonking muppet*, and glared at him again.

But then he snapped, 'Stickstickstick!' and grabbed at my hand. And I finally understood and let go of the other ratlet just as it gnawed its way to the top of the cocktail stick and sunk its razor-sharp molars into my thumb.

I shook it off and swore illegally all over the place. Rufus yanked me to my feet, marched me to the bathroom and stuck my thumb under the cold tap. The bite wasn't actually that painful, but it was bleeding quite spectacularly. While he went out to the tack room to get the first-aid kit, I watched my blood spiralling down the plughole and enjoyed a quick daydream involving R-Patz sniffing me out, popping me on his back and making off with me across the treetops. By the time Rufus came back I was feeling quite passionate, instead of wounded, and sideways smiled at him a bit seductively almost by accident, then said, 'Sorry.'

And he said, peeling a plaster and sticking it over my cut, 'For what?'

And I thought, good point, because I guessed apologising for accidentally smiling seductively because I'd been fantasising about my ideal vampire probably wasn't the best idea. So I looked into his eyes as confidently as I could and said, 'Sorry for being clingy about the rats – I can see you really care about them, I'm very happy they've got such an excellent new parent.' Which I thought was a good excuse for oversmiling, but hadn't really thought would make him feel that special. But I think it did, because he didn't let go of my hand straight away, but held it, and did the weird staring through me thing again, but it didn't feel such an insult this time, and did actually make me fizz a bit more, though I still think R-Patz probably deserves most of the credit for that.

And then he said, 'Look, there's a film on Wednesday night at The Arthouse, one of my mates helped train the horses in it. It's about Keats. You fancy coming?'

And I didn't shift from foot to foot and pretend I really wasn't bothered if I went with him or not, like I did when

Drew asked me to go to the cinema. I held Rufus's pale gaze and noticed that his pupils were really dilated and thought, *you are very lucky because I'm going to say yes*. Then I said, 'Yes.'

Rufus said, 'Right. I've got to get on, the new livery pony will be here any minute. Let's meet by the bus stop in the village, we'll need to get the 6.30.'

'Fine, okay,' I said without crossing my arms, even though his voice was a bit sneery again.

'Good, see you then, let yourself out.'

And with that he turned on his heel, stomped out of the bathroom and took the stairs about four at a time, as if he couldn't get away fast enough. This was a bit of an anticlimax I must admit. But, on the positive side, if an evening at The Arthouse (which is all plushy and extra dark) watching a film about a poet's passionate love affair isn't a proper date, I really don't know what is.

Date number two is officially BFF certified

Posted Monday 16th August, 17:23

Yay! Just told Tash everything over the phone as she's at Ben's watching him fix his bike (his biceps are 'mega' when he pumps up his tyres). Anyway, she agrees this time – I *have* got a date. Apparently she has a highly seductive secret weapon especially for romantic cinema encounters. She's going to pop over with it tomorrow morning on her way to watch Ben fix Canadian Chuck's bike.

Comment

Posted Tuesday 17th August, 01:00, by Savvy Rose

Hey well done, honey, just read *Experiment 6* and I'm so excited for you, give yourself a big fat 10 out of 10, you sure are getting the hang of this now.

There was only one thing that kinda stuck in my throat – what you said about not telling the truth about your dad. Now I have no freaking idea what he's done or where he's at (and don't sweat it, I couldn't give a damn). But one thing's for sure, lying to a guy can get complicated. I have a buddy whose pop's in the can for fraud and she's got herself into a whole lotta trouble hiding it from guys. If you get the chance, tell Rufus the truth, whatever it is. If he's a decent boy it won't make any difference to him – I'd bet my bony ass on it!

Culture shock

Posted Tuesday 17th August, 08:18

Thanks Savvy Rose, but don't worry about me, really. I've seen *Oprah* and stuff like that and I know you're all really

179

into 'fessing up and letting it all hang out over there. But over here, we find that far too gushy and keeping stuff in comes much more naturally. Anyway, it's only a white lie and it might not even be that. My so-called dad's not in prison and he did used to daydream out loud about going off to live on an island. Besides, I've found through real-life factual bad experience that it's better to tell a fib, rather than tell the totally boring truth. It's just easier that way. Also, I know Rufus put a plaster on my thumb quite caringly yesterday, but I'm still not convinced that he is a decent boy.

Presenting the Super Deluxe Charm-Enhancing Pouncelator

Posted Tuesday 17th August, 10:16

Tash has just been and gone in a cloud of musky perfume and rampant hormones. She left a vampy velvet wriststrap with a black feather dangling off it. She says I should wear it on the arm nearest Rufus and use it to make his hand tingle 'accidentally' when he dips into my popcorn. This, she insists, will give him exactly the right kind of romantic bad intentions for the cinema, if he didn't have them in the first place. I'm not so sure. In pet boy terms it might make him pounce too fast. When Johnny Depp saw it, he was so excited he fluffed up to twice his usual size.

Are there any special pet boy rules for cinemas?

Posted Tuesday 17th August, 21:22

Savvy Rose, what do you think? Should I wear the Pouncelator or not? And do I carry on making him feel special? And should I let him snog me now I know he is a bit interested? I have scientific proof of this – when he asked me to go to the cinema his pupils were totally dilated which means either:

a) The bathroom was dark.

b) He'd taken brain-mashing drugs to turn him into a starey imbecile.

c) He really is a vampire and fancied lapping up a bit of thumb blood.

d) He liked what he was seeing.

The answer is definitely d) because:

a) The bathroom was really sunny.

b) He'd been with me for over an hour and I was watching him closely as if he was a cat pretty much the entire time so if he'd popped/sniffed/injected anything I definitely would have noticed, especially as my London school trained us to spot plonking junky behaviour after a gang of glue sniffers caused a pile-up at the roller disco.

c) Okay, the stories are to die for, pardon the pun, but really have you ever met an actual vampire? And if there was one living in England do you think he'd hang about in The Middle Of Absolute Nowhere with Nothing At All To Do when he could sprint to Oxford Circus in three seconds flat?

d) All the mags agree that pupil dilation is a sign of attraction, and the pet theory also backs this up as Johnny Depp's eyes dilate so much they turn into mirrors just before he pounces on something. True, he usually wiggles his bum a lot too, and Rufus didn't do that, but still.

Comment

Posted Wednesday 18th August, 02:03, by Savvy Rose

A *Pouncelator*? Wild idea. And hey, why not? I guess it won't do any harm, honey.

I can't think of any specific rules for movie theaters, but a pet is more likely to pounce in the dark, for sure. The only rule about pouncing is that you get to call the shots – if you don't want to make out with the guy, don't. End of. Going somewhere dark, to the movies, anywhere, is *not* giving a guy permission to pounce. You do that with your body language once you're there *if*, and only *if*, you want him to.

So, see you how feel. If you decide you're not ready yet, sit up straight, pin your elbows to your sides, use your popcorn tub as a barrier between you. And don't, of course, *ever* be afraid to simply say, 'Uh-uh. No.'

But, oh my gosh, yeah! If you're into him enough, go for it, leave your arm on the rest between you (sure, Tash's bracelet sounds like it could help) and swivel your body and face a little in his direction. Even if he can't see it, he'll sense it. Like when you're in your room at night and you know your cat is in there with you, even though you can't see him.

Have a nice date!

Exuding Meaningful Body Language In Dark Situations (With Pouncelator)
Male Human Pet Control: Experiment 7

Posted Thursday 19th August, 09:54

I stared at Rufus for at least ten seconds before I recognised him last night. Not just because I had my seventies sunnies on, but because he turned up looking almost nice. His hair was tidy-ish and he was wearing clean blue jeans and a plain white shirt which made me realise his skin's quite olivey, rather than grubby.

He didn't peck me 'Hello' or anything, but did stand really close while we waited for the bus and he smelt of piney aftershave, which made exactly one butterfly flutter in my stomach. This was much easier to cope with than the millions that hatched whenever Jake used to stand close to me. I hoped it was down to my new natural confidence. Though it was probably more to do with Rufus being despicable* instead of gorgeous.

The Arthouse is on the other side of Dullford, on the outskirts of Upper Boring. The bus journey took about forty-five minutes on The Middle Of Absolute Nowhere 'Express' which creaks through the countryside at about 5 miles an hour. We sat near the back, which was empty, but the engine was really noisy, so we didn't say much, just smiled quite a bit. Rufus did point out a fallen tree-trunk he'd jumped on Flint though, and I pointed out the entrance to the Right Hon. Henry's huge stableyard (he has over fifty horses).

Rufus asked me if I rode then and I said, 'Course, Mum taught me when I was little and I used to help out at a school on Saturdays to get free lessons. But I haven't ridden for ages – since we moved. All the stables round here are private and Henry's horses are too valuable.'

Rufus frowned, then drummed his fingers on the back of the seat in front. 'Hmm . . . I can't promise anything, but Bubbles, the new cob at our place, might be good for you and she desperately needs to get fit. The owner can only ride a few times a month – I'll ask him if you can try her out if you want.'

I grinned so much my ears started to ache. 'Would you?

God, I'd love that – I'm not that good, but I really miss it.' As I spoke, a little worry climbed into my head though – that Rufus had decided he just wanted me as a friend. That's exactly what happened with one of Ben's mates, Todd Mitchell, who I fancied like mad, but who went from very suggestively flirting to only wanting to muck about and play football in less than twenty-four hours. And I just couldn't get him to be interested again once I was his goalie, even though I pinned my hair alluringly on one side and wore all my make-up at once. So I made a big decision then. While Rufus was gazing out of the window, I got the Pouncelator out of my fabulously sophisticated evening bag (made from a beret I folded in half and sewed a zip in) and slipped it on to my wrist.

When we got to the cinema and I saw Rufus had booked seats in the middle row, I was even more worried about his lack of romantic bad intentions. But when the lights went down for the adverts, I swivelled and leaned towards him and laid my wrist on the armrest between us so he really couldn't avoid the Pouncelator. And he leaned towards me too and whispered right into my ear, 'Pass the Liquorice Allsorts,' and his hot breath felt extremely meaningful. And as I handed over the pick 'n' mix bag, his fingers touched mine and it definitely seemed deliberate.

So things were already feeling exciting as the film started. And when a big piebald horse trotted across the screen after about ten minutes, Rufus leaned in again and said, 'That's the horse my mate Jim schooled.' And he was so close his lip touched my earlobe and made it fizz. And I whispered back, 'Gosh, amazing,' in a way designed to make him feel special, even though the horse had trotted in a pretty average way. And his left shoulder started to press against my right shoulder and I think everything would have gone well, if I hadn't actually watched the film.

It was so beautiful and romantic, all about twinkling stars and broken hearts and starving poets being ill. Everyone seems doomed, at least, but then, just as you start feeling a bit cheerful because it looks like things might turn out happily after all, the hero dies. Just like that. And his poor girlfriend is left tearing at her bonnet and screaming at walls because she misses him so much.

As I watched her wailing, I felt like all the Liquorice Allsorts I'd eaten had rolled into a big stripy ball and stuck in my throat and my eyes started to sting as if they wanted to cry. But I can't cry any more. I haven't cried any proper tears for nearly three years. So it just hurt and made my body go rigid, including my Pouncelator arm. And I suppose Rufus must have felt that because his body language changed from being pouncey to being, well, sort of sensible. He slid his arm around the back of my seat and stayed really still, as if he understood something about me. And although I knew he didn't, not really, it still felt nice.

On the way home on the bus he put his arm round me

again. And when he said goodbye just up the lane from The Nook, he didn't try to kiss me, even though I'd 'pulled myself together' like Mum's doctor used to tell me to do and I'd deliberately stopped by a suggestive-looking bush. He just stared through me in his weird way, then tugged me towards him and gave me a big hug, like Ben would, only without lots of backslapping. And that felt nice too, but I'm really worried that he'll only want to be friends now, even if I wear all my make-up at once.

Bubbles is my only hope. Rufus said he'll call me in the morning if her owner says it's okay for me to ride her. If he says no, I wonder if he'll call at all? Maybe he'll just use Bubbles as an excuse not to bother with me any more?

Not that I'd be fussed, of course. Mum's right. Us women *so* don't need men these days. Not even slightly. Not even for scientific journalistic purposes or for shutting up beyond poisonous bitches who blatantly lie and hiss and leak vicious poison about a person's most private life all over the place.

Right. I will now shrug unemotionally and go about my business as normal.

* Older women might find Rufus less despicable. I noticed the hippy girl smile very meaningfully at him as she was locking up the chemists.

No call from Rufus yet

Posted Thursday 19th August, 11:50

 187

Still no call from Rufus – I guess that's that then

Posted Thursday 19th August, 12:02

Although his phone might be faulty

Posted Thursday 19th August, 12:21

It did look quite old. Or maybe he lost it on the way home. He could still be on his knees scratching around in a ditch. Maybe I should go over to his place, in case? But Lucien must have our landline, for Mum, so he could use that. But he might be too embarrassed to ask for it. Although if I had to describe Rufus as a pet, 'embarrassed' would definitely not be a word I'd use.

Or my phone might be faulty

Posted Thursday 19th August, 14:46

Waved my phone around a bit then walked up a hill to max the signal. Now worried I gave Rufus the wrong number. I gave it to him by calling his phone though. Can that go wrong? Can numbers get muddled up in the air on the way?

Testing testing . . .

Posted Thursday 19th August, 15:14

Just texted Tash to call me to check my phone. She buzzed back in seconds all gaspy and giggly.

'Ooh, you're phone-testing. Is Rufus meant to call?'

'Umph.'

'Ah ha! You fancy him, don't you? You think he's hot!'

I tutted a lot. 'How dare you – I am a professional, I do *not* fancy him, he is pure science, you know that.'

'He's pretty dishy for a guinea pig though, isn't he?'

'Ugh. No, he's dead scruffy and nothingy-looking – and his eyes are weird.'

'I thought they were pretty piercingly meaningful – he's got a fit bod too. Ooh, did the Pouncelator work?'

'No,' I answered truthfully. 'I think he just wants to be my friend.'

'Oh.' Tash stopped being gaspy, 'Are you sure?'

'Practically. He said he'd call me about going riding tomorrow. If he does I'm going to wear all my make-up – to test him.'

'Really? But boys don't usuall–'

Tash hardly wears any make-up and I could tell she was about to go off on one of her judgy lectures, so I butted in, 'Sorry, got to go, while we're nattering he might be desperately trying to get through.'

'In a desperately *friendly* way?'

'Yes.' I hung up.

I thought he might have left a voicemail message

Posted Thursday 19th August, 15:16

While I was talking to Tash, but he hasn't. Sigh. Just turned my phone off and on again really quickly to boost the battery. God, it's lucky I don't care or I'd be going a bit frantic by now.

He's probably run off with the hippy from the chemist

Posted Thursday 19th August, 15:17

She's welcome to him, I was deeply bored already

Posted Thursday 19th August, 15:18

He is actually beyond boring

Posted Thursday 19th August, 15:19

And if you spent too much time with him his eyes would give you a headache

Posted Thursday 19th August, 15:20

I am only waiting for Rufus's call because of some automatic teenage hormonal response syndrome or something. I do not like Rufus at all. Not one bit. I am now going to wipe him from my entire memory. Totally.

Rufus who?

Posted Thursday 19th August, 15:21

Oh, ooooh, my phone just beeped, pleasepleasepleasepleaseplease . . .

Good news and good news and maybe bad news

Posted Thursday 19th August, 15:38

Rufus must have called the exact split second my phone was off, he left a message, woo. And, I get to ride Bubbles, hoo. But, boo, his voice sounds totally flippant and romantic-bad-intentions devoid (an excellent new word meaning 'empty of' I learned from the film last night). And the fact he didn't want me to call back tells me he is not even slightly desperate to hear the sound of my voice. I bet the poet in the film last night would have eaten his own quill for a chance to hear his girlfriend's voice on the phone, if there had been phones then.

Here's what Rufus said . . .

'*Circe, right, I just got hold of Bubbles's owner, we're on for tomorrow if you're still up for a ride – say two? If I don't hear, I'll guess that's okay. Cheers.*'

See, no suggestive 'hope you slept well' or smitten 'thanks for a wonderful hug last night'. He didn't even sound sneery. I think I prefer sneery in a way, at least it sounds like he has some kind of human feelings going on in his brain.

As seen on *How To Look Good Naked*
Posted Thursday 19th August, 19:31

Which is quite an interesting programme I think, even though I don't really understand why the presenter ever wears any clothes at all as he's meant to be the ultimate superhero of nudey confidence.

Anyway, as I haven't done this for a long time, I'm practising putting on all my make-up at once to look more womanly and less matey. I've propped my mirror in the window of my room and I'm kneeling typing with the laptopasaurus on the window ledge so I can describe what I'm doing accurately.

Hair

One streak of *Mad Mane* in *Silverstruck*. Both sides of head.

Face

Light Up Your Radiance foundation all over.

Zappit concealer on nose bump and freckles.

Shake & Shimmer dusting powder on top.

Blushbabe on cheeks. Both sides of face.

Goldbeam highlighting cream on cheekbone. Right side only.

Eyes

Wowbrows pencil, then *Glossibrow* setting gel.

Rainbow Spirit eyeshadow palette (I only used pink, green, orange, purple and a tiny bit of blue though as red and yellow are a bit OTT).

Sassy Smudge kohl in *Deadly Nightshade*.

Mega MAXXXX Pump Up Boost N Curl mascara in *Jettest Black* (3 coats).

Lush Lash gel glitter in *Purple Haze* over the top.

Lips

Forbidden Scarlet lipstick (3 coats).

Neck, collar bones, ears

Sun In The City bronzer in *Tropical*.

Oh, and I've stuck a tiny gold heart on my right cheekbone as a subliminal 'don't just be my friend' message.

The sun's not coming in through this window any more

so I'm going to lie on my bed now with my compact mirror to check the effect close up under the skylight.

My face is almost too heavy to lift

Posted Thursday 19th August, 19:41

I think my make-up looks pretty fabulously sophisticated though, in a disco way. I'm going to sashay nonchalantly through the living room now, to see if Mum and AJ notice anything alluringly womanly and far more naturally irresistible about me.

Hmm . . .

Posted Thursday 19th August, 20:00

I'm not sure how that went. They definitely noticed something different. AJ sort of squeaked when he saw me, but maybe he's just a bit wary of glamorous make-up since the mauve lady at the show. Come to think of it, wearing lots of make-up didn't make the mauve lady look particularly alluringly womanly, but maybe that was because she was a man.

Anyway, when AJ squeaked, Meg, asleep on his feet, opened one eye and growled at me (which is almost unheard of and not very flattering) and Mum looked up from the crossword, raised both eyebrows and said, 'Gosh, darling, are you going out somewhere very dark?'

That made me a bit angry because she knew I wasn't, as I'd said I was staying in. She also knew I went to the cinema with Rufus yesterday as I'd left a note on the fridge. And, even if talking is a bit of a taboo subject between us, you'd think she might have at least bothered to remember as I am her actual only daughter. I rolled my eyes. 'No. I went somewhere very dark *last night*. To The Arthouse.'

And she said, 'Ah yes . . .' and I thought for a minute she might actually ask me something about my life and/or Rufus. But she didn't, of course, she just turned to AJ. 'You saw that film about Keats, darling, didn't you – was it any good?'

And although I can understand why she asked him about it and not me, as he is an expert on poets, being one himself, it was still annoying. So I glared a bit as AJ wafted his sleeves about and said, 'Sensitively directed and as poignant as one would expect, but I was rather disappointed in the heroine, she was a tad wishy-washy.' Then he nodded at me. 'Not something anyone could accuse you of, Circe, you are what I'd call the epitome of vivid!' I wasn't sure that was a compliment, but I quite liked the sound of it, so I let myself smile at him. And he smiled back, then said, 'Pretty nifty with a metaphorical stanza too!'

I cringed all over. There was no way I wanted to get into any kind of discussion about my jar poem, even if I was the epitome of vivid. So I just laughed like he'd made the biggest poetic joke in the world and fled back upstairs.

In the middle of my room buried under my entire wardrobe again

Posted Thursday 19th August, 21:43

Okay, most of my outfit tomorrow is easy – I have to wear jods, boots and my hard hat for riding, but what about my top? Do I go practical and wear what I'd normally wear to ride – i.e. a T-shirt – and risk Rufus thinking my laid-back attire means I just want to be friends? Or do I go in a more girlfriendy-type top, my glitter vest maybe? I obviously can't wear my sequinned boob tube or I will definitely end up looking far too topless. Maybe any kind of glittery top will be a bit much in broad daylight with all my make-up on too?

Sorted

Posted Thursday 19th August, 22:15

Thanks to my iPod, which shuffled to one of my so-called dad's seventies albums. It reminded me of the racer-back vintage Led Zeppelin vest I bought at Camden market last year. And that reminded me of my black genuine faux leather gloves, which could pass as riding gloves and which make my arms look more toned somehow and also give a bit of a non-friendly meaningful edge and will look good with the Pouncelator which I still definitely need. The whole ensemble also accentuates the rock-chicky side of my personality. And as it's mainly black my make-up shows up better against it. Right, must start to take my make-up off now if I want to be in bed by midnight.

Comment

Posted Friday 20th August, 04:21, by Savvy Rose

Hey, Circe. Oh my gosh, your look sounds far out! But, you know, I'm not sure you need to be so full-on. It seems to me that Rufus does dig you, but didn't try to make out as he was sensitive enough to suss that the movie made you feel kinda freaky. My honest advice at this point would be – whoa!

I once dated a guy whose folks owned a ranch and I remember seeing a kid chasing round and round trying to catch his pony, hollering and whooping and rattling a bucket of food. But the more he did it, the further away that pony scooted. What I'm saying is – don't try too darned hard. Creating new make-up looks can be fun, and going OTT for a party once in a while's a total blast – but most guys get turned off by lots of make-up. If there's one thing a full face of powder and paint says loud and clear it is, I am so *not* confident in who I really am.

If you're still worried, go ahead and use a little extra make-up if it boosts your confidence – but to highlight, *not* cover. Remember, more than anything, to let your feelings show in your expressions and body language, make them shine from your eyes. If you want to neck with him, think about that as you look at him, look into his eyes then glance down at his lips – *show him*!

Oh, and your outfit? Won't you be kinda hot in a black tank and pvc gloves? Maybe something cute but cotton to keep cool – have you got any broderie? Pardon me if I'm way outta line here, but I so wanna see you get your pet!

It's not that I'm being rebelliously teenage or anything

Posted Friday 20th August, 09:38

But I just tried on the antique lace camisole AJ gave me for Christmas, which is the only broderie-type thing I have in my wardrobe and, well, it's pretty, but it's just not Me. And you did say I should be true to myself, so I'm sticking with Led Zep.

What you said about make-up does sort of make sense, so I might cut down a bit, although I think it's risky. I did actually try that staring at lips thing on Todd, but he just carried on pelting me with footballs. So, if Rufus stays too friendly, I reserve my teenage human right to glam up.

Exuding Meaningful Body Language In Daylight
(With Pouncelator and Make-Up)
Male Human Pet Control: Experiment 8a

Posted Friday 20th August, 18:36

Back in my office, dizzy and weak at the knees, but for all the wrong reasons.

I biked to Knight Ridge this afternoon as it's easier to cycle than walk in riding boots. It's also quicker and I was running late due to last-minute snogging practice on a tub of chunky monkey, which melted all over my pillow and into my hair.

I locked my bike inside the gates and walked up the drive because it's so steep and I wanted to arrive looking severely kissable, but thought actually physically panting might seem a bit too rampantly keen. As I turned the last corner, I made sure my eyes were radiating unfriendly 'snog me' looks and my bottom lip was pouting alluringly.

'Oh hello there young lady – golly, you look absolutely furious, what's up?'

I flinched and switched all my kissable exudations off. 'Oh, hi Lucien, um, nothing, I'm just a bit hot.'

'Right-oh, well, you've a jolly nice treat in store, Bubbles is a fine mare, good solid hack. Young Wufess is tacking her up now. Fancy a cuppa while you wait?'

'Great.' I followed Lucien through to the kitchen where he pointed me to a chair at the round table overlooking the yard, then handed me a mug of steaming tea. 'Thanks – and thanks so much for today, you know, getting me a ride.'

'Pleasure – least we could do, after what you did.'

'Oh. After I did what – help with Flint?'

'No no, giving Wuffess your chaps. He mightn't say much, but it's made a diff.'

I had no idea what Lucien meant. 'Um . . .'

'Marvellous what pets of one's own can do, isn't it?' He nodded at the lurcher snoozing in a wicker basket by the Aga cooker. 'He's always loved Digby, of course, but Oliver and Harry have perked him up no end. Perhaps he feels they're in the same boat and all that.'

I finally twigged. 'Oh, you mean giving up *the rats*. That was nothing, really, I think they're hid–' I choked to a stop, remembering I was meant to be fond of them. 'I mean, they always *hid* a lot, in their straw, so, um, I don't miss them that much.'

'Jolly decent of you anyway, I'm no blinking good at this sort of thing, I can keep his mind off it, keep him busy, but I don't for the life of me know what to say . . .' Lucien trailed off as Rufus emerged glaring from a stable and cursed up at the clock over the tack-room door. 'Ah, righty ho, I think his nibs is ready for you!'

I downed the rest of my tea and let myself out of the back door.

As soon as Rufus saw me he spat, 'You're late.'

I opened my mouth to spit something vile back, but

then he squinted at me. 'You look different . . .'

I held my breath, and exuded appropriate adjectives out of my eyes, *fabulous*, *sophisticated*, *womanly*, *alluring*, *stunning*, *kissable* . . .

'Are you ill?'

Sigh. 'No I am *not* – I am extremely well thank you.'

'Good.' He didn't look convinced. 'You'll need to be. Bubbles's owner was delighted you were up for exercising her, she's been out at grass for three months.'

'Brilliant,' I fibbed, as having my first ride in ages on a horse raring for a gallop wasn't ideal.

Rufus shot the bolt back on the nearest stable door and led out a pretty but tubby dun mare with a shiny sandy body, feathery white feet and flowing black mane and tail. I gathered up the reins, slipped my toe into the stirrup, pivotted and jumped on, half expecting her to take off as soon as my bum hit the saddle. But she didn't even lift a hoof, just turned her big face round to look curiously at me and batted her long sooty eyelashes.

As Rufus walked Flying Flint out of his loose box at the other side of the yard, I leaned down Bubbles's neck, gently tugged on her soft ears and whispered, 'Hey sweetie, be gentle with me, I'm a bit rusty.' When I straightened up again, Rufus was mounted. I'd only seen him galloping off into the distance before, and had to admit, up close, he looked good. As I watched the muscles in his thighs and forearms flex and strain to hold Flint back as he tossed his mane and skittered,

Rufus looked up and his eyes flashed and his lips curled at the same time. My cheeks burnt, but I forced myself to hold his gaze in a suggestive and unfriendly way, hoping my layers of make-up (I did wear it all in the end, as I realised glamming-up on horseback would be tricky) would hide my embarrassment at being caught ogling his arms and legs. I guess you would approve though Savvy Rose as I think it made him feel special.

He trotted over and looked down on me, as he was sitting two and a half hands (nearly a foot) higher. That did make me feel quite womanly in an old-fashioned, 'Ooh aren't you tall Mr Darcy' way. So I thought I may as well work that and tried to heave my bosom a bit, but it was a physical impossibility in my Bounce-Ban sports bra. So I tried fluttering my eyelashes, but that wasn't a big success either as four coats of mascara and the heat had made them too sticky.

Anyway, Rufus didn't seem to notice any of my feminine wiles and just barked, 'Okay, we'll try her in the enclosed manège first, then hack through the woods.' He leaned down to check the girth on his saddle and peered at me closer. 'God, aren't you hot in those gloves?'

'No, they are excellently ventilated riding gloves!' I lied, thinking of the Pouncelator feather tucked into my right cuff. I'd decided it might look a bit too keen in broad daylight, so only wanted to expose it in case of a pet boy emergency, i.e. if Rufus didn't attempt to snog me by approximately mid-afternoon.

Far from being raring to go, Bubbles was still in holiday mode, so it took over ten minutes to plod to the riding school, which was only a few hundred metres up a track through the woods behind the yard. Rufus found this absolutely hilarious and cantered backwards and forwards while Bubbles dragged her hooves and munched her way through anything edible we passed.

The school was a rectangle of dark grey sand at the top of the hill. A heat haze rippled over it, making it look more than a bit hellish and making me mumble, 'Um, it's sweltering, maybe we should give this bit a miss?'

Rufus rolled his eyes. 'Get in there, we need to put you through your paces.'

This charming exercise involved Rufus strutting around in the middle of the school sneering and shouting, 'Come on, wake up! Trot on. TROT ON!' or, 'PATH-ET-IC, you can do better than that, shoulders back, heels down, KICK KICK!' and, 'Canter CANTER NOW *NOW*!'

Every time we stopped, which was a lot as Bubbles's favourite pace was motionless, she let out a sigh that rumbled right through her body and shook me in the saddle, then looked round at me as if to say, *What is this boy on?*

After half an hour, I was aching all over, sweat was pouring down my back and I'd swallowed at least three flies. I let Bubbles grind to another halt, dropped my reins and slipped my feet out of my stirrups to stretch my legs. 'Enough!' I grumbled, 'this is agony, Rufus. Bubbles is fed up and I am gasping for water. I have never been so hot in my entire life – it's probably against the law!'

'Don't be such a wuss!' Flint reared up a bit then, but Rufus stayed perfectly balanced in the saddle as if to demonstrate his utter superiority.

He then kicked into a canter from halt, which was annoyingly impressive, and started circling round Bubbles, prodding a finger at me and drawling instructions. 'You need to get your act together . . . your hair should be tied back . . . your position is sloppy . . . your hands are too high . . .' Round and round and round he went, and on and on and on . . .

I switched my ears off and started humming 'Dancing Queen'.

'Stop singing!' he commanded, pulling Flint up in front of me, and looking me up and down despicably. 'And no wonder you're hot,' he spat. 'Take those bloody stupid rubber gloves off!'

Then he threw his head back and laughed. A lot.

Something snapped in my brain.

I admit it, Savvy Rose, I totally forgot everything you taught me about making boys feel special and using encouraging body language etcetera and I crossed my arms and yelled, 'It has nothing to do with my gloves, it is *all your fault* – you are the epitome of a psychopathic sadistic nightmare!'

Which was at least quite unfriendly.

'You're also long-hair-ist – AND MOODILY RUDE!'

I waited, scowling between Flint's ears into Rufus's pale glaring eyes, wondering if maybe, just maybe, he'd realise he'd pushed it too far and say sorry.

He didn't, of course. His lips started to curl vilely, then his shoulders started to shake, then he opened his mouth and started laughing again. And this time he laughed so hard he had to let go of his reins and clutch his stomach.

And, without even thinking, I peeled off my sopping wet gloves and I squashed them into a sweaty little ball and threw them at him, hard. And he ducked and Flint shied away, but I didn't see if they hit him because the next second Bubbles's huge bum shot up in the air and everything went dark.

**Exuding Meaningful Body Language In Daylight
(With Pouncelator, Without Make-Up)
Male Human Pet Control: Experiment 8b**

Posted Friday 20th August, 19:17

I came round face down in the dirt with a numb chest and a weight on the small of my back. I lay still, gasping for breath and trying to work out whether I'd snapped my spine or punctured my lungs or both.

'Circe?'

I could hear the voice clearly, and the bees buzzing and

birds twittering in the background, so my ears were all right, which I hoped meant I hadn't cracked my skull open. I wiggled my toes, they seemed to work. The weight on my back moved, ran up my spine between my shoulders to touch the nape of my neck, then down again. It was a hand.

I remembered Rufus, shuddered, coughed, and spat some sand.

'Hey gorgeous, welcome back. You had me worried for a minute there . . .'

Gorgeous? The hand stroked up and down again, then again. My brain decided that was nice and made my body fizz. My skin also prickled into goosebumps. This all felt rampantly meaningful and very inappropriate as I still didn't actually know that I wasn't at least a bit paralysed or even dying. But once the fizzing started, I couldn't make it stop.

'Don't try to speak yet, you went down flat, you're winded, breathe slowly . . .'

I tried, but certain private parts of my body had started sort of throbbing now and my breath was coming quite fast. I told my brain it was just post-traumatic sexy syndrome or something and nothing to do with liking the sound of Rufus's deep slow voice, or the feeling of his hand stroking my back. But my brain didn't believe me and started imagining all sorts of things involving rolling around in sand. I could have stayed like that happily for hours if Rufus hadn't said, 'Okay, if you still can't speak, I think I should call Lucien . . .'

'Grrmph-nooo!' I said.

'Ah, that's better – does anything hurt?'

'Urr-nrrr.'

'Good, can you move?'

'Mmm.' I realised I could then, but still didn't much want to.

'Right, roll over on to your side if it feels okay . . .'

His hand was still on my back, but it had stopped stroking. I rolled over, keeping my eyes closed, feeling a bit naked somehow, even though I was pretty sure I still had all my clothes on.

'Oh, wow.'

Or maybe I hadn't? I snapped my eyes open, blinking away grit. 'What?' My face felt bunged up. I gasped, 'Ooh, do you think I've broken my nose?' I'd always wanted to break it, just a bit, to get rid of the bump.

Rufus grinned. 'Hope not, it's a pretty cool nose.'

My mouth fell open. He reached forward and ran a finger over the bridge. I winced, not just because he would definitely notice the bump, if he hadn't already, but because it felt like he was rubbing sandpaper into my skin.

His face was so close to mine by now, I thought I might as well take the opportunity to do the glancing down at his lips and back to his eyes thing. So I did, two or three times. But he just grinned again, clapped the sand off his hands, sprang to his feet and said, 'Right, let's get you down to the yard and clean you up.'

Is it possible to die of total humiliation? If it is, I would have, fifteen minutes later, back in the bathroom. When I looked in the mirror I actually yelped. My face was coated in a thick layer of grey sand. I suppose my make-up had overheated, so when it hit the dirt it sort of acted like glue. Only my *Forbidden Scarlet* survived, probably because of its top quality non-stickiness. But even my lippy didn't help, I looked like a tarty coalminer. And I didn't have any supplies on me to do emergency repairs. Basically, I had no choice but to wash my face and go back downstairs, gasp, with *no make-up on at all*.

When I went down, I nearly died of humiliation again outside the kitchen. I was a few steps from the door when I overheard Rufus saying, 'Don't worry, it was a one-off – it only happened because of this daft feathery bracelet she was wearing.'

And I cringed back against the wall, thinking, OMG, the Pouncelator *did* work, but, argh, Rufus getting non-friend-y was just a one-off.

But then Lucien said, 'Jolly good. Damned irresponsible owner though, he should have warned us Bubbles had such a big buck on her.'

And I kind of choked on a strangulated giggle of relief and Lucien dashed into the hall and said, 'There there, don't cry, old bean!' (which was beyond ironic) then he held his hand to my forehead. 'Golly, you're burning up!

Let's get you home.'

I nodded and let Lucien fuss around and bundle me into his old Jaguar, because I did feel a bit dizzy and, more importantly, I felt highly unkissable. And as we sped through the lanes, he chatted away about Bubbles and how I must get back on her asap, so I don't lose my nerve. But I just sat feeling sad, because when Rufus leaned into the car to say goodbye he chirped, 'Chin up mate.'

There is now no doubt left in my mind, I will never get a proper boyfriend. Not even a totally rubbish one who I don't like.

Oh, hang on, what's that ringing – please don't let it be ankle bracelets. Mum's out with AJ watching the Lower Snoring Players destroy *Dirty Dancing* and she threatened to have Geraldine pop in to check up on me. No, you know, that sounds like . . . it is . . . it's my bike bell . . .

**Exu!!!
!!!!!!!!!!!!!!!!!!!!!!!**

Posted Friday 20th August, 22:29

OMG I thin kkm y ggf harnds arre tooexcittttted to tiyype orr fthingk

I think I mirrght bee Offfficially In Shockk.

Giiave mee a minuute . . .

Exuding Meaningful Body Language At Sunset
(Without Pouncelator, Without Make-Up)
Male Human Pet Control: Experiment 8c

Posted Friday 20th August, 23:01

God, that was weird. I just went all sort of fluffy-headed. I had to dance about in the garden a bit until my brain filled up with proper journalistic sentences again.

Rufus turned up. Had you guessed? He'd ridden my Chopper back from Knight Ridge. And this time I acted fast. As soon as I recognised my bell, I crept out of the back of the willow, so I could emerge casually from the woods at the top of the garden.

He was wobbling along the lane with his knees sticking out. As I watched, he looked up and glared, which was definitely unfriendly and very encouraging. So I glared back and sashayed in a lazily confident manner down the lawn (only quite fast, because it's so steep). At the bottom, I met my own reflection broken up into tiny squares in the cottage window. It cringed and pulled an appalled face, as it realised I was looking the epitome of friendly in an ancient *Snoopy* hoodie and stripy pyjama shorts. I considered nipping into The Nook to glam-up, but it was too late, Rufus was already pushing open the side gate.

'Your bike nearly killed me,' he barked. 'It's lethal, did you realise only two gears are working properly and your front brake's totally shot?'

I shrugged, clutched my shorts bum to stop my arms crossing and made my eyes exude attractiveness. 'Quits. Your horse nearly killed me.'

'She's a cob, actually – and technically, not mine.' He hissed that, but didn't look angry, for once, which made me think maybe he can't help hissing, so I decided not to get angry back. Besides, I had to concentrate on killing my 'mate' image. While my brain racked itself for the best bit of Savvy Rose's advice to accomplish this feat, my eyes watched Rufus closely as he pushed my bike towards me, trying to spot things that made him special.

It was quite shocking as I realised that loads of things I'd considered despicable before, I quite liked now. I'd got used to his scruffy hair and weird eyes. His square shoulders and chunky legs were nice too. And his chest and stomach and tanned forearms and quite big hands and slightly hooky nose and curly lips and sharp jaw and the blueish shadow around his jaw and his manly ears were all very acceptable. His jeans were exactly the right kind of blue too and his T-shirt had a picture of a cartoon ringworm on it and I even liked that, even though worms so aren't my thing.

And as I thought all this a voice started nagging in the back of my head . . . *Stop it, don't make a fool of yourself, back off, play hard to get, make him prove he likes you,* etcetera. But I just kept telling myself, *he is extremely happy to see me* over the top until Rufus stopped right in front of me.

'Should I prop this here?' He nodded at the wall outside the back door, which is where I usually leave my bike if it's not raining. And it wasn't raining, in fact the sun was still warm, even though it had started painting pink and orange stripes above the trees, so I opened my mouth to say, yes, but an idea popped straight into it so I said 'No' instead. Then I remembered Tash naturally lowers her voice when she talks to cute boys. So I made my voice a bit huskier and said, 'I keep it over here . . .'

Fighting a battle with my old instincts, which wanted to laugh flippantly, I led the way around the corner of the cottage to our tiny wooden shed. When I got to the door, I opened it and stood back, without making any sudden movements, to let Rufus push my bike inside. He slid his eyes sideways as he passed and I decided to believe that was an attracted look. Then I followed him in, which wasn't easy as the shed was already nearly full with animal food and bike and boy.

It was dark inside, even with the door open, and there were only a few centimetres of glittering dusty air between us. So I said, using my deeper voice again, which I'd decided would fit in with Savvy Rose's advice as it is exactly the tone I use when I'm trying to calm a horse down, 'I just need to prop this fork against the wheel to stop it falling over.' That made me cough a bit because it was quite a long sentence to say huskily. It was also a fib, but I needed an excuse for following him in and couldn't exactly say, 'I'm bored of chasing you round fields, so I've decided to trap you in the shed like we did when Jude Law escaped once.'

Then I took the big garden fork off its hook and made a lot of fuss about leaning it in exactly the right way against the back wheel, to stall for time. While I was faffing, Rufus asked, 'Where's your mum?'

'At the theatre, she won't be back till gone eleven.' As I said that, I realised it sounded quite suggestively meaningful and my cheeks started to burn and my legs got quite keen to get me out of the shed. But the air had gone really quiet suddenly. And I don't know whether it was Savvy Rose's advice finally sinking in, or my cheeks not wanting to show themselves in daylight, or the raw pet boy magnetism Rufus was exuding – but something made me freeze.

I took a deep breath, crossed all my fingers and turned towards Rufus. My eyes had adjusted to the dark, so I could see his face more clearly now. He was looking at me. It was hard to read his expression, but it definitely wasn't terrified or disgusted. So I dared to drop my gaze to his lips, then lift it back to his eyes. And he did that weird staring through me thing again, but this time it felt like he was quite interested in what was going on in my head. Then his fingers touched my chin and tilted my face up and I squeezed my eyes shut because I had a horrid feeling he was going to say, 'Chin up mate,' and I didn't want to see his face turn friendly when he did. But he didn't say that, he didn't say anything. His fingers slid along my jaw to my neck, then stroked down across my collarbones, then up under my hair, then I felt hot breath on my cheek and smelt mint and then . . .

Important Notification Of Major Experimental Research Result: 1

Posted Friday 20th August: 23:42

Rufus snogged me.

Sorry about the suspense. It just felt like it deserved its own post.

In fact, Rufus didn't just snog me – he snogged me properly.

He didn't turn into a puppy or a hoover or try out about a thousand different tongue techniques like boys at parties do when they're obviously just practising or trying to win a bet on who can last longest without breathing. He didn't pant or thrust or sprout extra sets of hands.

He snogged me slowly, like he meant it, right from deep inside him. And the more he snogged me the more I meant it deep inside me too. And I didn't even have to imagine he was R-Patz to get me into an exciting fizzy condition, like I had with pretty much every boy I'd snogged before.

But when he finally pulled away, he said, 'God, I was way out of order, wasn't I?' And for one horrific second I thought my lips must have been giving off some kind of annoyed vibe without me knowing, especially as he carried on, 'I take it all back.' But while I bit my lip and tried not to scream he laughed, 'You are definitely *not* a stupid little cow.'

I realised he was talking about the night we'd met, so I laughed too and said, 'And you are definitely not the rudest, stupidest, most despicable boy I've ever met.'

He winced, 'Ouch. Did you call me that? I don't remember.'

'No.' I grinned. 'But I thought it. A lot. You were hideous.'

'Sorry. I know it's no excuse, but I was out of my mind that night . . .'

It occurred to me then that as Rufus was responsible for looking after Flying Flint, Lucien might have sacked him if things had gone wrong. 'I guess you were worried about losing your –'

'Look, whatever,' he cut in, and I felt his body go rigid and pull away a bit, just like mine had in the cinema. 'It's not worth talking about, okay?'

I nodded but a chill prickled down my spine. I felt I'd missed something crucial, like when you nip to the loo during a film and when you get back the hero on the screen looks the same, but you know something's happened that's changed them, but you don't know what. I didn't know what to say either, so I just said, 'Phew, I'm thirsty, do you want a drink?'

'Yeah, good idea.' He smiled then, a bit sadly, but grabbed my hand and led me out of the shed. And once he'd downed a pint of Honeyhill's finest lemonade, he cheered up enough to snog me against the fridge, then on the window ledge, then on the sofa right through *Ultimate Vampirical Chill Out Mix IV*, which is precisely sixty-eight minutes and twelve seconds long.

When Rufus said he'd better get back as he had an early start in the yard, I walked him down to the front gate and we snogged again there. And I imagined we were by the school gates with Portia watching, stunned that I had such a hot boyfriend, so totally into me that he hadn't even noticed she existed.

But just as I pictured Portia blowing her nose on her own school tie in a fit of regretful devastation, I felt a vibration against my hip and a heavy guitar riff blared out of Rufus's jeans pocket.

He jolted away and stepped back, leaving my front suddenly cold. I crossed my arms, then uncrossed them, then crossed them again, deciding they were okay for practical, temperature-raising purposes.

Rufus heaved an extra weary kind of sigh. 'Hell, sorry, I'd forgotten . . . it's probably my da– er my . . . I'd better take it.' He flipped his phone open and glared at the little turquoise screen when it lit up, then turned away to answer it. 'Yes? What? Like I said . . . yeah yeah yeah . . .'

His voice sounded flat, and ice cold, as if he loathed the person on the other end of the line. 'What's the point? I don't want to . . .'

I shivered, hoping he'd never talk to me like that. Even

at his worst, on the night we met, he hadn't sounded that venomous.

'*Why?* Why do you think . . . the 29th, I remember . . . and you expect me to believe anyth– yeah right – look, call me tomorrow, I really can't talk now . . .'

He started pacing. I started wondering whether I should be applying some kind of pet boy rule. Was it better to stand here pretending to be patient while he talked? Or should I act like I had far better things to do, wave a cheerful 'Bye' then go indoors? It took me another couple of minutes of listening to Rufus spitting moody 'whatever's into his phone to decide to go inside, when he huffed, 'Yeah, so you said, I really don't have time – no, look, I'm with my girlfriend.'

Important Notification Of Major Experimental Research Result: 2

Posted Friday 20th August: 23:51

'*I'm with my girlfriend.*'

Savvy Rose, you'll be deeply disappointed in me. Honestly, when I heard Rufus say 'girlfriend' my first thought was, OMG, lying cheating spawn of the devil, he swore he didn't have a girlfriend! And I spun on the spot, scanning the lane, fully expecting to see some local 'It' babe strutting towards me shaking a fistful of designer bling.

But the lane was empty. And then Rufus snapped,

 217

'Course you don't . . . a couple of weeks . . . she's from London originally . . .'

Maybe he was talking about *me*.

'Circe . . . yeah . . . Shaw. What, do you think I'm a total imbecile?'

It was definitely me! He'd described me as his girlfriend, officially, which could only mean, major drum roll please . . .

I could describe him as my boyfriend. Ta da!

My heart leapt about, but also got a bit worried as his voice wasn't exactly full of passion and tenderness. Think half vicious hissing snake, half deeply moody lout, with a dash of sneering rebellion.

So I didn't punch the air triumphantly or anything, but I didn't duck back into the cottage either. It didn't seem the right thing to do somehow, now he was my Official Boyfriend. Instead, I slipped my own mobile out of my pocket and pretended to be engrossed in new text messages which were all in fact old, 'Ooh Ben just did this amazing thing/Ben just did that amazing thing' gushings from Tash.

But as soon as Rufus hung up, a few minutes later, I pocketed my phone, made sure my arms and legs were all uncrossed and looked at his lips encouragingly.

He didn't try to snog me again though, he just tipped his head back, glared up at the stars and swore illegally. Then he said, 'Sorry, look I'm wrecked. I'll call you tomorrow.' Then he turned away and stomped off down the lane.

Honestly, it's a really good job I don't like him.

How quickly can an Official Girlfriend expect to know everything about her new pet boyfriend?

Posted Saturday 21st August, 06:45

Okay, it's only my first day as an Official Girlfriend*. And, I admit I am a bit extra inquisitive. But I haven't got one single answer for Rufus, just all these questions . . .

Why is he working full time at seventeen years old? If he's poor, why are his clothes posh? (They're scruffy, but not in a cheapie way.) And why does he talk like a rich boy? And why did he kiss me like he meant it in his heart, but not want to talk about the stuff going on in his head? And what about the stuff? Is it about Flying Flint? Or is there something else – the something I felt I'd missed? And why did he take a phone call from someone he didn't want to talk to? Why not tell me who it was? Was it his stepdad again? Or his so-called mum? Why is she a so-called mum? Has she decided not to exist any more, like my so-called dad?

Of course, all of this is utterly unimportant to me as Rufus is just for practice and there are no emotions involved. But it is still beyond frustrating knowing *nothing*. Also, if my plan to snog in front of Portia on the first day of term is going to work, I need my pet boyfriend to be available on 1st September. So there is one crucial question that must be answered urgently . . .

What's so special about Sunday 29th August?

 219

I checked the internet and our calendar and the local noticeboard in Ye Olde Newsagente window, but there are no other shows or events, not even a car-boot sale. It's not a full moon or a new moon, or any kind of weirdy beardy festival either. So, what then? Is it the day Rufus leaves The Middle Of Absolute Nowhere forever? Is he going to throw his head back and laugh callously as he casts aside his Official Girlfriend, forcing her to rebuild her shattered life brick by brick? Or does he just think she's a holiday fling type of girlfriend, so won't even bother telling her?

Savvy Rose, what I'm asking is, doesn't his girlfriend deserve to know? Can she demand proper answers? Today?

* Strictly speaking, if you count our first date as the hamstericidal ratlets visit on Monday, I have now been going out with Rufus for five entire days and nights.

The only teenager in the world not on Facebook

Posted Saturday 21st August, 07:17

I just had a flash of journalistic inspiration thinking I might be able to find some answers on Facebook, so I did a search, but there is no Rufus Strakes.

It was very annoying. It should be illegal for hot teenage boys not to be on FB, not that Rufus is hot or anything.

Before I realised how deeply unattractive Jake was, I dug up loads about him on FB as he'd written *Fifty*

Interesting Things about himself. Portia has about a gazillion FB friends by the way. I'm not one of them, of course. But that didn't stop her sending me an ironic gift of a virtual heart-shaped box of chocolates on Valentine's Day. Oh she is *so* witty and hilarious.

Comment

Posted Saturday 21st August, 11:11, by Savvy Rose

WOW! Totally awesome, Circe – you got your guy! Big fat US-style round of applause with extra freaking whooping!

So now – relax a little, honey. Don't get so cranky about the things you don't know about Rufus. Have you ever gotten to know a pet right off? Nope. Me neither.

It takes a little time, a little patience.

I remember getting a new puppy as a kid, a Dalmation called Duke. When I threw a stick for him in the backyard the first morning he growled. But after a few days I worked out he was more of a frisbee kinda guy – from then on we were best buddies.

You need to spend more time with Rufus, you'll learn more about him as you go along. But if you're determined to find out what he's up to on the 29th, tell him about something you're doing in the next week, it might encourage him to open up about his plans. Top tip: when you try this, sit next to him, not opposite, just like you do when you hang out book-end-style with Ben. Guys often find too much eye contact uncomfortable if they're talking about things that mean a lot to them.

But, hey, don't sweat it if Rufus can't make the 1st. Do you *really* need him? I can tell you're getting more fabulously sophisticated every day. By the time you go back to school the pathetic Portia won't dare tease you, if that's what she does.

Comment

Posted Saturday 21st August, 11:18, by Savvy Rose

Hey, honey, me again. Just a thought. Portia doesn't actually *bully* you, does she? I know you don't want to waste any energy on her, but maybe I could help you figure things out?

Thanks, thanks, thanks but no thanks

Posted Saturday 21st August, 11:30

Thanks for the congratulations Savvy Rose.

And huge thanks for all your help with my hot topic.

And thanks for the eye contact tip. I just stared Johnny Depp in the eyes and asked if he preferred chasing birds or mice and his pupils went all big then he ran off, which I think is quite good scientific proof of your theory.

But, really, no thanks, re. going into gory Portia details, there is totally no point. What she does isn't bullying, i.e. she doesn't beat me up or call me names in the playground or anything. She's actually the epitome of Oh So Lovely And Charming to me whenever anyone's around. She only kicks-off when no one's watching – and then she just whispers stuff, mainly.

Anyway, I *so* don't want to think about her. The sun's shining, I've got an Official Boyfriend and I'm off to meet Tash for a girlie afternoon.

We're going to shop till we drop, even though Dullford only has two boutiques and one of those only sells thermal bras. Tash wants to buy a pair of 'miracle' reshaping jeans to cure her supposedly oblong bum. I want a new fabulously sophisticated outfit suitable for getting to know Rufus better and encouraging him to tell me things.

Learning an important pet boy lesson the hard way

Posted Saturday 21st August, 19:55

I bought an entirely new head-to-toe look for £9.78! Tash took me to a charity shop crammed with 'worn once' designer gear thrown out by Middle Of Absolute Nowhere gazillionaires. I got a chiffon layered minidress, cropped lacy leggings and satin ballet pumps with ribbons that criss-cross up my ankles. Best of all, I found a big black floppy flower brooch.

Tash found her miracle jeans, and while she was analysing the roundness of her buttocks in the triple-angled changing-room mirrors, and I was staring in the opposite mirror trying on my floppy flower in a variety of unexpected places, I said, 'I think Rufus might be going on holiday or something on the 29th – next Sunday.'

Tash grimaced. I wasn't sure it was to do with my announcement or the fact that her head was on back-to-front checking her rear view. 'Oh, that's a shame . . .'

'I mean, he hasn't actually told me he's going away yet, but he should, shouldn't he?' I couldn't say why it was so important, because Tash doesn't know about my ulterior snogging motive.

'Sure, why wouldn't he?'

'Don't know . . . So, do you think I could ask him then? Savvy Rose thinks you need to get to know pet boys better before asking anything important.'

'Hmm . . .' Tash unscrewed her head from her left shoulder then screwed it round to her right, 'round or still rectangular-ish?'

'Definitely round – I don't think I've ever seen a rounder bum.'

Tash poked her tongue out. 'Just ask him. Besides, I'd like to know. That's the last Sunday of the holidays, Ben and I are heading up to Hyde Park for the day, there's a "well radical" digital design exhibition on that he wants to see.

I was going to ask if you and Rufus wanted to come too.'

'Oh my god, I would so love that – a double date with an actual boyfriend!' Tash's face (now upside down between her knees) looked a bit surprised. 'I mean, I've been on tons of double dates before, but never to Hyde Park – wow, I love it there, you know, all the grass and the trees and the . . . London-ness . . .' As I trailed off my phone started to vibrate.

It was Rufus. 'Hey Circe, where are you?'

'Hi, um . . .' I'd never actually spoken to him on the phone before and his voice didn't sound hissy at all, more sort of rumbling and meaningful. 'I-I'm er I em am um you know er . . .' I took a deep breath and told myself just how astonishingly lucky he was to have me as his girlfriend, then said, 'Shopping with my friend Tash, you know.'

'No – I don't.'

'Yes, you do, the honey girl, the farm shop, the jar – remember?'

Tash, now upright, grinned.

'Ah,' he laughed, 'the free invisible honey offer, how could I forget? I often wish I'd accepted it when I'm toasting my invisible bread in the morning.'

I laughed then too. 'Where are you?'

'Dorset, looking at Flint's younger brother. Lucien wants me to try him on the gallops, to see if he's any better.'

'Any better? What's wrong with Flint?'

'He's a bolter, it took me a week to work out how to stop him.'

That explained a lot. I smiled. At least he hadn't deliberately tried to kill me.

'Anyway, we won't be back till late now. And tomorrow morning Lucien wants me to mend a fence, and in the afternoon I've got to clean all the tack so . . .'

My heart started to thump. This was it. He was going to finish with me by being busy all the time, like Drew, who'd suddenly developed lots of Very Important Hobbies, even though I'd worn my hair at least seven different ways to try and please him. I held my breath, pale Circe triplets frowned back at me from the changing-room mirror.

'So . . . er . . .'

I closed my eyes and braced my heart.

'. . . do you want to do something in the evening – maybe go for a pizza at Gina's in the village?'

I nearly choked as I exhaled and my mouth stretched into a grin at the same time, 'Yes, I'd love tha–' I stalled, remembering Savvy Rose's side-by-side advice. 'You know, as the nights are still so light – could we just hang out in the park instead? Meet on the swings?'

'Yeah, why not? Seven okay?'

As I said, 'Great. See you then,' Tash widened her eyes urgently. 'Hold on, Tash is saying something.' I paused as if I was listening to her plan for the first time, then said nonchalantly, 'Tash and her boyfriend are heading up to London for a day next week – she just asked if we fancy going too, you know, for a laugh.'

'Oh, er, maybe, depends when.'

I crossed my fingers. 'Next Sunday, I think it's the, um . . . 29th.'

'Nope. Can't then.'

His voice had gone flat and I knew straight away that Savvy Rose was right, I was asking for too much too soon. But then the horrid hungry feeling started hollowing out my insides and I just couldn't help it, my mouth rushed on, 'Oh, I suppose you're working?'

'Working? No. Right, I should get bac–'

'Or maybe you're going away? It is the bank holiday weekend after all, a totally normal logical time to fly off for a few days or maybe a week or two, or a month, longer even . . .' I winced and saw my three faces turn tomato in the mirror.

'No. I'm not going on holiday . . . I wish.'

'Good. I mean, bad, I'm sorry you're not going away if you wish you were instead of doing the thing that you are doi–'

'Look, *whatever* . . .'

I winced, then before my fabulous sophistication had a chance to stop it, my mouth mimicked, 'Yeah, *whatever*.'

Rufus huffed, 'I've really got to go, all right.'

Then he hung up, without a goodbye, again.

As my phone went dead, I realised I'd plucked a silky petal off the floppy flower pinned unexpectedly on the hem of my dress.

 227

Vital boy-keeping rules at-a-glance for instant brain top-ups

Posted Sunday 22nd August, 09:03

I've just worked out that it's mine and Rufus's one week anniversary.*

I think this is an excellent time to remind my brain about the pet boy keeping rules as it's easy to take things for granted once you're going steady. It's obviously essential too, as when Rufus called yesterday a mere 'whatever' annihilated every single lesson I've supposedly learned.

I've written this instant guide and printed it off, so I can check it whenever I need to without having to turn on my laptopasaurus.

> *1. Fake being 'where-it's-at' and/or natural confidence at all times.*
>
> *2. Give yourself lots of compliments even if they're not true.*
>
> *3. Find out what kind of party you are then exude it.*
>
> *4. Don't worry about saying perfect things, but keep your voice nice.*
>
> *5. Lean forwards etcetera to stop your boy turning into a friend.*
>
> *6. Notice things about your boy to make him feel special, even if he's not.*
>
> *7. Dress to please yourself, not him, or you'll confuse*

 228

your personality.

8. Don't accidentally cover up your confidence with make-up.

9. Don't expect to know everything about your boy all at once.

10. Use equipment like pouncelators, sheds and swings as necessary.

My brain feels quite well reminded now, so I'm going to think up something I can tell him I'm doing this week to get him in the mood to tell me what he's doing next Sunday. I know he said he wasn't going on holiday, but I still can't shake the feeling that he is going away somewhere, and won't be back. So I must also keep building up my fabulous sophistication as fast as possible because school starts again in, hang on . . .

Oh . . . My . . . God . . .

Ten days.

* Strictly speaking, if you count our first date as when I went over to Knight Ridge on Sunday morning, I have now been going out with Rufus for seven entire days and nights.

There is something I'd really like to do

Posted Sunday 22nd August, 12:02

Mum and Ralph hogged the patio all morning, reading the

news to each other and giggling, so I stayed in my room practising sophisticated glares until they roared off to The Soggy Duck. Then I wandered outside and accidentally ended up in the shed replaying Friday night's juicy moments in my head. And that gave me an idea.

There was something I used to do in London when things got really bad. I'd go and sit on the front garden wall, in exactly the same spot I was the last time I saw my so-called dad. Then I'd close my eyes and watch the story of what happened that day, like a film in my head. But I'd change the ending to something good. He'd slam out of the front door of the flat, but grin when he saw me and turn and go straight back inside. Or he'd get as far as the gate and say what he really said, but I'd say something so extremely clever or funny back that he'd hug me and sit down next to me. Or he would make it out of the gate, but I'd run down the street after him and he'd grab hold of my hand and take me with him. Whatever the ending was, it made me feel a bit happier when I opened my eyes again, as if the more I rewrote the ending, the more I could forget the real ending had actually happened.

Anyway, it suddenly hit me that I could try doing the same thing with Portia.

All I need to do is go to Venetia's pool, watch the story of her party in my head again and change the ending, so I do something fabulously sophisticated that shuts Portia up. Then when I see her, I'll automatically feel more fabulously sophisticated. And Venetia did say I could swim at her place anytime, didn't she? I just need to buzz the gate and ask her butler.

Of course, I don't want to waste a split second of what's left of my precious holiday thinking about Portia. But maybe part of being fabulously sophisticated is dealing with bad things?

In an interview with Jess Bradley I found online, they ask her how she chooses her *Hot Topicals* each week and she says, '*Easy. It's always the thing that makes me curse. Some sexist comment I overhear on the tube, or a skeletal model in the press. Whatever gets me maddest wins.*'

Even though Portia is totally unimportant and irrelevant, I can't deny she also makes me totally spitting mad. So I guess that's proof isn't it?

Should I tell him it's our anniversary?

Posted Sunday 22nd August, 15.46

Could that help, Savvy Rose? I mean, once Rufus realised that we'd been going out for a week he might feel more like he had a duty to tell me about the 29th.

Please ignore the last post, I've worked it out already

Posted Sunday 22nd August, 18:03

You're probably out breakfasting at Tiffany's or something. Please bin my last question, I've decided definitely not to tell Rufus it's our anniversary. I'm not sure that male humans really understand them.

I remembered Mum's last wedding anniversary with my so-called dad. She fussed around in the kitchen for hours, but he forgot all about it so much he didn't even come home from his studio. And when I went downstairs the next day the table was still set with candles and our old cat Tigger was staring at his bowl like he was dreaming because there was an entire roast chicken in it.

Getting A Boy To Tell You Things Without Him Noticing He's Telling You Them
Male Human Pet Control: Experiment 9

Posted Sunday 22nd August, 22:33

One positive point about The Middle Of Absolute Nowhere in the summer is that the park is always empty in the evenings. The village muppets used to hang around, but now they prefer to pile into the chief muppet's 'babemobile' (lowered Fiesta) and backfire round the deserted streets of Dullford blasting out JLS and randomly shouting, 'Tits.'

My best friends are very fond of their bush, of course, but I'd already called Tash to make sure they weren't planning a romantic night out in it.

So, sure enough, when I got to the park, ten minutes early, the coast was clear, apart from a few ducks flapping about in the fountain. I headed straight to the swings and sat down on the one in the middle, so Rufus would be forced to sit next to me. I then wriggled about a bit to arrange my arms and legs confidently and practised exuding cooler-than-a-disco vibes at the ducks, who all flew off.

By the time Rufus strolled in, I was perfectly positioned, leaning on the right chain of my swing so my body angled towards the entrance alluringly. My right hand was stretched above my head hanging on to the chain to show off my floppy flower (pinned to a glittery hair scrunchy halfway up my arm). My right leg was crossed over my left and curled round it at the calf to show off my ribbony ankles. My left hand rested casually in my lap and when Rufus smiled over, I waved it in a beckoning way, then I smiled back, sideways.

Rufus stomped straight past me. 'Get over here – I've a surprise for you.'

'Oh . . .' I didn't want to move until he'd fully appreciated my pose. I rotated my head slightly in his direction without disturbing the rest of me. 'Don't you want to swing a bit first?'

'What? No – come on, it'll get cold!'

I frowned as he walked towards the park shelter. It was

notorious for gross village muppet goings-on before they got their Fiesta. Charlotte Floyd swore she'd seen them measuring their spanners in there one night. I hoped Rufus's surprise wasn't his spanner, I definitely wasn't ready to see it, even though we were going steady.

'I played safe, grabbed a Margherita. Hope that's okay.' Rufus had stopped at the picnic table in front of the shelter and was sliding a flat box out of his rucksack.

I grinned as I untangled my legs (with difficulty as they'd gone numb) then wobbled over to him. 'Perfect – I love cheese.'

'That's useful to know, for future reference, the Gorgonzolana looked tasty too.'

Future? My heart did a happy jig. Maybe he wasn't going away?

'Great, it's still hot – here.' Rufus peeled off an oozing slice and handed it over. 'God, it smells good, I haven't had a scrap to eat all day.'

I wondered if Lucien was really as nice a boss as he seemed. 'Isn't that against the law or something?'

Rufus made a noise that was half laugh, half sigh, and scratched his head. 'I was flat out, I lost track of time, then I had to speak to . . . there was a call – *stuff*, you know – I just wasn't hungry . . .'

My tongue started actually twitching, it was so desperate to ask about the 'stuff' and whether it had anything to do with the 29th. But he was looking straight into my eyes. So I just nodded as if I understood, then shoved nearly the entire triangle of pizza in my mouth to shut it up.

He laughed properly, 'Wow, hard core!' Then he put his hand over mine on the table and said, really quietly, 'Did it get you that way, you know, make you feel actually physically sick sometimes?'

'Um . . .' I wasn't sure what he meant.

His eyes did their brain-penetrating thing again. 'What happened with your dad – when he left?'

The world tilted a bit, as if I was still on a swing, I dragged my eyes from his and fixed them on the shiny black olive in the middle of the pizza. 'Oh, er . . .'

He squeezed my hand. 'I'm an idiot, sorry, I didn't mean to . . .'

The olive was the last thing I should have looked at, of course. My so-called dad loved them. They were always served at the shows of his paintings, scattered in tiny bowls, rolling like big pins on cocktail sticks in long-stemmed glasses. The horrid hungry feeling began scooping me out. I opened my mouth, planning to say, 'Ha ha, no, I'm fine.' But then I remembered Savvy Rose's post about telling the truth. I swallowed, hard. 'Not sick, no, more, um . . . hollow . . .'

And as I said it I dared to look back at Rufus, right into his eyes, and all he did was blink, but that blink told me he got what I meant. We ate our way through the rest of the pizza in silence. Only it wasn't a bad silence, like the silence in Mum's 'tired time'. It was a good one, like we knew each other well enough not to have to fill the air with jokes or deep philosophical ideas, or anything really.

As we ate, the shadow from the shelter behind us stretched over the picnic table. So when we finished I had a really good excuse to suggest we move over to the swings, which were still lit by sunshine. It took us about fifteen minutes to get to them because we snogged quite a bit on the way. And once we were on them, we swung maturely i.e. just bobbing slightly. And then he grabbed the chain of my swing and tugged it so our rubber seats crashed, then he held both chains together and we snogged again. A lot.

The sky was navy blue by the time I said, as casually as I could with an entirely fizzy body and sore lips, 'Hmm, I've been thinking about my plans for this week. It's quite important as it's the last week of the holidays so I want to make the most of it. And you know where I'd really like to go?' (I'd rehearsed that, can you tell?)

And Rufus kissed me on my nose and said, 'No, where?'

And I made sure I didn't look into his eyes as I said, 'Swimming – at a friend's place. She had a party there at the end of term and it's stunning, but it was also horri– horribly crowded. But the house is empty all summer, so she said I could go back any time.'

'Sounds good.'

I deliberately swung a bit higher and stared straight ahead then, to give Rufus a chance to tell me about his plans for the week, but nothing happened. So I slowed down and asked, 'What about you, um, do you plan to do anything interesting – or *special* – this week?'

And Rufus laughed and caught the chain of my swing again so I zig-zagged in the air and he pulled me off the seat and into his arms and breathed right into my ear, 'I do, yes, something really special . . .' Then we snogged again* with my heart pounding like mad because it knew he was about to tell me about the 29th.

But when he finally pulled away he just curled his lips in a particularly snaky smile and whispered, 'I'm coming swimming with you.'

* I apologise for all the snogging, I am aware that we are almost as bad as Tash and Ben but I feel I need to be accurate as this is a professional journalistic report based on scientific facts.

Walkies (and hopefully talkies)

Posted Monday 23rd August, 05:37

I know. I'm awake before Clarence. I'm tempted to shout 'cock a doodle-do' out of my bedroom window to get him back for all the times he's woken me up, but I'd wake Mum up too. It's still dark, but I've got to get up to go over to AJ's, borrow Meg, then take her to meet Rufus at the pond for a dog walk at seven.

I'm borrowing Meg because I fibbed that I often take her for walks, so it doesn't seem like I'm making a massive effort to see Rufus again this morning, even though I am. It's the only time we can meet in the next two days as he has to go back down to Dorset with Lucien for a night to pick up Flint's brother.

I'm desperate to have another go at finding out about the 29th. And a dog walk is obviously a good way of being side by side and getting him to tell me things. We can also pass Venetia's place so I can buzz and check she really did tell her butler it was okay for me to pop in for a swim.

When I said to Rufus about going to the pool, I hadn't even thought about taking him along. But I can see now it's an excellent idea. Even if he can't make the 1st, at least I'll be able to remember we snogged in the exact spot Portia pulled off her pathetic stunt, replacing a hideous memory with a delicious one.

Going For Walks And Playing Games And Trying To Stop Playing Games
Male Human Pet Control: Experiment 10
Posted Monday 23rd August, 09:49

AJ lives in a wooden shepherd's hut in a wild, overgrown meadow on the other side of Bluebell Wood. He was a bit surprised when I turned up. He yanked open the door, flinched, and crossed his trailing-sleeved nightshirt arms (yes, you read right, a trailing-sleeved *nightshirt* – he's even a poet in his sleep).

'Circe! Hell. What's happened? Are you okay, do you need to talk about something – about your poem?'

God. Don't poets ever think about anything other than poems?

I shook my head. 'I just need to borrow Meg – it's an emergency!'

He laughed then, 'Gosh! What is it? Has a flock of rabid sheep broken into The Nook? Are they giving Johnny Depp a good bleating?'

Aren't adults hilarious? I rolled my eyes. 'No, I need to take her for a walk, of course.' I looked at my watch. 'Urgently.'

'Oh. Of course.' He grinned and passed me Meg's lead which set her bounding round my feet. 'Here you go then. Send my love to your mum.'

'Grmph, whatever,' I huffed, then forced a smile, after all AJ had lent me his dog at short notice, and he's all right really, apart from being a 'just friends' man.

Anyway, I clipped Meg's lead on so she wouldn't round up random things on the way to the pond and we made it there at exactly seven.

Rufus turned up with Digby a few minutes later and I was a bit shocked when I saw him as I couldn't stop smiling, even though his T-shirt was ripped and his face looked blue from not sleeping enough or shaving at all. He dropped a kiss on my cheek, which also shocked me as it sent an instant fizz right down to my toes. 'Morning, so, what route do you normally take then?'

I stared at him blankly.

He laughed. 'Wake up sleepyhead – which way do you like to go with Meg?'

'Oh – sorry – um, it's nice along the lanes, I'll show you.'

I set off in the direction of Venetia's house. It had taken me about ten minutes to run back from there into the village, spitting fury and chlorine. So I guessed it would take about twenty to walk, which gave us more than enough time to get Rufus back to Knight Ridge by eight, when Lucien wanted to hit the road to Dorset.

We let the dogs off the leads and after a bit of mutual bum-snuffling, they fell into step, proving that traditional domestic pets are much more straightforward than male human ones. I frowned at Meg's glossy black-and-white head bobbing happily alongside Lucien's lurcher's grizzly shoulder. 'Digby's not very big is he?'

Rufus laughed. 'I know, it must be seriously embarrassing for him when he has to introduce himself to other dogs.'

'Why did Lucien call him that then – was it sort of wishful thinking, like my mum's pet names?'

'Nope. That's down to me – when I first met him I really thought he was the biggest dog in the world.'

'Oh . . .' Something odd itched in the back of my brain

but I couldn't work out what it was, so I gave up and concentrated on thinking of a subtle way to bring up the 29th. I scanned the scenery for inspiration. The trees were spattering sunlight on the lane ahead and golden hills rolled away all around us. If you're the kind of person who likes having Absolutely Nowhere To Go and Absolutely Nothing To Do you would probably say it was beautiful. I had an idea. 'God, it would be good to get away wouldn't it – absolutely nothing ever happens here does it?'

This cunning double-question was specifically designed to make Rufus answer, 'Yes, it would – I'm so glad I am going away to blah-blah on Sunday.' And/or, 'No, it doesn't usually, but at least blah-blah will be happening on Sunday.' I kept my eyes front so Rufus would feel unwatched enough to tell me everything.

'Ha!'

I flinched and risked a sidelong glance. His lip was curling disdainfully.

'I can tell you're a city girl Circe – you are *so* wrong about that!'

I frowned, then grinned. 'Oh, so you don't want to get away – you're not going?'

'No, yes, whatever.'

Deep sigh.

'I mean, you're so wrong about nothing ever happening here.' As Rufus hissed that, he clamped his hands to my shoulders from behind and turned me to face the thick hedge running the length of the lane at head-height. 'Look closer. What do you see?'

'Um . . . a hedge?'

'Genius. And? Look again.'

I held my hand above my eyes to block out the sun. 'A ditch, wild flowers, lots of bees . . . um . . . two butterflies . . .'

'Higher!'

'Oh . . . trees, a wood pigeon . . .' I squinted, 'some crows, on a haystack – sorry, no that's thatch – a roof . . .'

'Ha! Yes. A roof!'

I couldn't work out what his mind was thinking from the weird tone of his voice and badly wanted to turn round to see what was going on in his eyes, but his hands had me pinned down. 'So?'

'So – loads of stuff happens here, but it's all hidden! People get away with stuff because they can hide behind their hedges. You see them around, in the village, and reckon you know pretty much who they are, but you don't, they're *liars* – you don't know anything!'

Rufus's fingers were digging deeper into my skin, but I didn't twist away because the no-eye-contact thing was working so well and I had a strong gut feeling that his seemingly random rant had something to do with the 29th. I waited, feeling his heart pounding against my back.

But then he let go of my shoulders and just breathed hard for a bit. And when he finally spoke again, his voice wasn't angry any more, it wasn't even hissy, just sad. 'No one's who you thought they were – nothing is what you thought it was . . .'

I badly wanted to say something helpful to cheer him up, but my mouth was full of far-too-personal questions, so I didn't dare open it in case they all fell out. Luckily, Meg and Digby started barking then, obviously impatient to move on to some new smells. Rufus jumped, sort of shook himself into a laugh, then looked at his watch and said, 'Woh, it's half-seven, where's the time gone?' as he grabbed my hand and tugged me up the lane.

And I yelled internally, *it's gone on your rant and you've managed to say loads without saying anything at all as per usual and now you're going to pretend it didn't even happen!*

Externally, I remained fabulously sophisticated, of course, and said, 'Mmm, time flies when you're having fun.' But then I realised I was saying something totally different to what I was thinking and that was like playing manipulative mind games, which is exactly what Portia does when she says charming things about me in front of people while she's obviously thinking horrid things. And that reminded me my experimental target was just to keep a pet boy for long enough to snog him in front of Portia. And that I was only keeping Rufus strictly for that purpose, so I shouldn't give a flying fig about his big fat boring secret. And that made me think, yawn, this is so not a big deal.

So then I exuded a bit of natural confidence by leaning into Rufus's shoulder and said in an especially nice tone of voice, 'I know it's over a week away, but could you meet me after school on my first day – next Wednesday – at the gates?'

And Rufus let go of my hand which made my eyes squeeze shut even though we were still walking along, quite fast, behind the dogs. And I thought, this is it, he's going to tell me he's emigrating to Australia/going to prison/turning into a girl.

But then he slid his arm round my shoulders and said . . .

'Yeah.'

Just like that.

Woooooooooooooooooooooooooooooooooooooooooooo!!!
Hooooooooooooooooooooooooooooooooooooooooooooo!!!
Posted Monday 23rd August, 10:30

Woooooooooooooooooooooooooooooooooooooooooooooo!!!

Rufus is going to meet me at the gates of Hell House and I am so going to wipe the smirk off Portia's face. For good.

I know this for a fact as when we got to Venetia's house I noticed there was a bug-eyed mirror on the bend in the lane opposite her gates to let cars see other cars coming. So before I buzzed Chivvers the butler, I leaned back against the gates and beckoned Rufus with my lips and got him to snog me.* Then I peeped at our reflection so I could work out the best arms and legs positions to seem most loved-up. And I looked best with one foot kicked up behind me and my hands on Rufus's waist and he looked good whatever he did to be honest, just the right height and broad-backed and definitely the epitome of beyond buff.

Portia is going to totally die of deep regret and major humiliation!

And . . .

Hoooooooooooooooooooooooooooooooooooooooooo!!!

I am going to get to wipe out the memory of Portia's pathetic performance at Venetia's pool.

After our snog, I buzzed the gate and Chivvers answered, 'Hitch-Scott residence.'

And I announced in a fake plummy voice, 'Good morning, sir, I do hope you are well, I am a friend of Venetia's and she said I might avail myself of the swimming pool facilities while she's away.'

And he said, 'Your name please?'

And I said, 'Circe Shaw.'

And he rustled around, then said, 'Ah yes, I have a note here. Do come in.'

And the gates started to whirr open so I babbled that I didn't have time right then, but I'd like to come back on Wednesday afternoon with a friend if that was convenient.

And he said, 'As you wish, Ms Shaw, I will prepare some iced tea.'

How cool is that?

* I swear, this is actually even easier than making a dog sit once you get the hang of it.

The trouble with having a BFF and a BBFF who are also BF and GF

Posted Monday 23rd August, 19:06

Mum and AJ are playing Scrabble indoors, so I've come out to my office to get away from all the squealing and find some peace to do my real homework (which has been a bit totally neglected due to my 'special project'). But now a barrage of texts has trampled my concentration into shattered ruins.

First Rufus texted

> Duller than Dullford here.
> Got to sit thru 10-course din.
> Yawn. Wish you were here.
> Correction. Wish I was there.

Which made me feel warm and happy all over like a proper girlfriend.

Then Ben texted

Hey Witchy!
R U home?
Want 2 hang out?

Which also made me feel warm and happy that my BBFF hadn't totally wiped me from his entire memory since he'd met my BFF. So I texted back

Come over.
Bring earplugs.

But then Tash texted

Lips sore.
Sent Ben home.
Fancy goss?

Which, I probably don't have to tell you, made me feel a bit annoyed with them both, then annoyed with myself for being annoyed as annoyed is definitely not a fabulously sophisticated feeling.

Then Tash followed up with

BTW how's pet boy?
Is he obedient yet?
Is he going away?

And my head filled up with confused thoughts and my heart filled up with mixed emotions then they had a major dramatic fight. And anyone who has tried to fight their head with their heart or vice versa should know it's no fun at all, especially when you've just spent an hour writing an essay on Protozoa.

And as if that wasn't all emotionally complicated enough

Posted Monday 23rd August, 19:25

Sorry. Just had to nip in to tell Mum to keep it down after she shrieked 'BARFINGLY IS NOT A WORD, DARLING!' so ear-piercingly that Jude Law buried himself under a lettuce leaf.

Anyway, where was I? Ah yes, internally fighting. So, after that stopped (my brain won, sort of) I called Tash and confessed I'd invited Ben over already and asked if she wanted to join us. She said no, she'd leave us to it, as long as I gave her an instant update on Rufus. So I told her he was very well thank you and mainly obedient and probably not going away, then I spilled all the juicy gossip about the last two experiments. She was very impressed and said it was a pain we couldn't all get together as she'd like to see my pet boy training skills in action.

Then she said, 'So, what *is* Rufus up to on Sunday?'

And, as I am more than a bit fed up with this totally irrelevant question, I huffed, 'No idea and it really doesn't matter to me because I don't actually like him and he is just a practice pet boyfriend as you well know.'

And Tash gasped, 'Wow, do you *really* not like him *one insy bit*, even after all that "lush" snogging?'

Luckily, as my brain had sort of won its argument I was able to say, 'Pah. You are forgetting that I am a professional. That was all strictly experimental research.'

But then she said, 'Ah, what a shame . . . hmm . . . So, now you know how to do the pet boy thing and you've written your journalistic blog reports, you'd better finish with Rufus asap, hadn't you?'

And I said, a bit defensively, 'Had I?'

'Course, Circe. Durr. I mean it was all fine when we knew he was despicable and hated you, but it sounds like he's pretty cool and likes you now, so it's not fair to lead him on, is it?'

And I couldn't disagree, because I knew she was right. But I also couldn't agree, because my heart was blocking my throat the way it used to with Jake, which also meant I couldn't actually speak.

So I just grunted, 'Umph'.

Then I pressed a few buttons to make it seem like my mobile had malfunctioned and hung up.

If Ben was a biscuit he'd be an irritating one

Posted Monday 23rd August, 22:07

Okay, apart from when he's playing our daft 'What kind of blah-di-blah are you?' game, Ben is definitely not a questions person. I think it might be part of his family's Looking On The Bright Side tradition. I suppose if you ask questions about serious and/or sad things you risk getting answers that make it more difficult to even find the bright side, let alone look at it. He did ask me once about my so-called dad after he left. But my answer actually helped him find the bright side, I think, so he stuck with that and he's never asked again, which suits me perfectly.

But then tonight, after literally years of not asking me anything serious at all, he said, 'So, why isn't your lad up for coming to the Hyde Park gig, then?'

I was so shocked I fell into a coffin and got my head snapped off (we were playing *Vampire Vault III* on Ben's DS).

'Yesss-ow!' Ben punched the air and scraped his knuckles on the wall. We were jammed into my room as the garden was too dewy to sit in, and Mum and AJ were still squealing things like 'Xylox' and 'Quoits' at each other downstairs.

'Argh!' I grumped. 'Unfair – you deliberately put me off because I was about to claim the Cape of Carnage and beat you to the next level.'

'No way! That's well out of order – you prattled on non-stop all through my go.'

'That was different. I was talking about *unimportant* stuff, deliberately – so I wouldn't put you off.'

'Okay, I did kind of tune out. But hold on a minute – you told me about Rufus, didn't you – about his "totally stunning" riding?'

'Um . . . yes.'

'So, he's *unimportant* then, isn't he?'

'Yes, he is, utterly unimportant, one hundred per cent.'

'So me talking about him can't have put you off either can it?'

'No – I mean, yes . . . no no yes no yes *YES*!'

Ben grinned. 'Be ashamed, Circe Shaw, be *very ashamed* – you are one *baaad* loser!'

'Umph-grr . . .'

'Ha! So, why isn't this Rufus up for hitting London then?'

'Oh . . .' I stretched and yawned, buying time, scratching around in my brain for a good reason, until I ran out of yawn breath and had to settle for, '*stuff*, whatever, you know.'

'Right, yeah.' Ben nodded slowly, as if he did know, but I could tell he didn't.

My brain had an idea then. I shuffled round so I was sitting beside him, fixed my eyes straight ahead and said, 'Ben, if you had *stuff* going on, would you tell your girlfriend about it?'

'I don't have stuff going on, Witchy.'

Sigh. Ben can be a bit too straightforward sometimes.

'I know you don't, this isn't a factual sort of question like in my interview, it's purely theoretical – pretend you *do* have stuff going on.'

'Like what?'

'Family stuff or something, secrets, skeletons in cupboards . . . stuff that annoys you, that you might not just tell any random person – would you tell Tash?'

'Yeah, course.'

'Hmm . . . But you've been going out with Tash for over five weeks now. What if you'd only been going out for, say, eight days – would you still tell her?'

'I reckon so, I trust her.'

'So you'd tell her *anything* – whatever kind of stuff it was?'

'Yeah, well, er . . . I wouldn't tell her stuff that might mess with her head, you know, hurt her.'

'Really? That's interesting, like what?'

'Like stuff she didn't need to know, I dunno . . . Like tricky stuff to do with another girl, an ex or something. Or confusing stuff, like when I was seeing that girl Carla last year, but couldn't work out if I only liked her outside – you know, her bum-length hair and her bum and that – but not her inside.'

'Oh.' My stomach flipped then, remembering how many times Rufus had stared at me like he didn't much rate my inside – or my outside, come to that.

While I calmed it down with a bit of deep breathing, Ben popped a ping-pong ball out of his combats, balanced it on the back of his hand, snatched his hand away and caught it before it hit the floor, then passed it to me.

I took up the challenge, grateful for the distraction, and we did best-of-threes then best-of-sixes then best-of-twelves, like toddlers in a trance. Then AJ roared 'Zombify!' downstairs and kind of snapped us out of it. Which, come to think of it, is quite a clever use of words, even for a poet.

Perhaps I'm gazing out of the wrong sort of window

Posted Monday 23rd August, 23:23

I'm sure Jess Bradley would only have to gaze out of her Soho window for a split second before coming up with a sassy solution to her entire romantic life. I've been staring out of my skylight for an hour, but my brain has just got blanker and blanker.

Some emo might help

Posted Monday 23rd August, 23:43

Given up on the window, but wondering about Rufus and

 253

29th and whether I'm doomed to spend all eternity in a blank void of mystery and heartache is now keeping me awake. And I desperately need to sleep because I have to catch up with my homework tomorrow or I'll get detention on the first day of school and miss my chance to wreak dramatic vengeance at the gates. Reminding myself that Rufus is pure research hasn't helped take my mind off things. Nor has reading my latest tragic vampire novel, so I'm going to plug in my earphones and blast out all my angst with extreme emo.

Or a bit of goth rock

Posted Tuesday 24th August, 00:13

Emo just not angry enough. I'm going to try some proper heavy goth.

Or even some trad classical

Posted Tuesday 24th August, 00:29

No good. Gothy growling's too scary with closed eyes. I'm now going to bore myself to sleep with one of my so-called dad's old cello concertos.

Or my *Twilight* soundtrack

Posted Tuesday 24th August, 00:48

The cello track was a seriously bad idea.

As soon as I closed my eyes, the music started kind of curling through my brain, disturbing memories, teasing things out . . .

I started to see shiny green leaves, a bright blue sky. I saw our old garden, an uneven winding path, grass so full of daisies it was almost pure white. Then I saw myself . . .

I'm cross-legged at my so-called dad's feet, grinning up at him. Music's wafting through the air and he looks like he's doing some mad dance – stretching high then ducking low and waving his arms about, completely out of time – but he's actually painting. There's a canvas as tall as him propped against a twisted tree trunk and he's splashing on oranges and reds and blues and yellows, the colours of the flowers crowding all around us. And, as he paints, he laughs a lot and tells me stories about them, about how the roses are all a bit stuck up, and how the geraniums gossip in Italian accents and how the lavender just can't stop giggling.

And I didn't just see all this, I heard it, I heard the birds in the trees, a plane overhead. I heard my so-called dad's deep voice booming out above the cello strings. I heard it as clearly as if he was here, with me.

And now I can't sleep even more.

R-Patz is my only hope.

Does anyone know where I can buy a new brain?

Posted Tuesday 24th August, 01:26

This one's really starting to annoy me. I've had about three minutes' sleep, maximum. The *Twilight* soundtrack sent me off into what should have been a lush dream. I was at a bench in the school biology lab and R-Patz was next to me explaining the history of flowers (which he knew really well, obviously, because he's been going to school non-stop for about forever). After a few delicious (and very educational) moments, Portia appeared, surprise surprise, and hissed, 'Keep away from her – don't you know *what she is*?' R-Patz just ignored her though and wrapped his arms tight around me. But then in the middle of the hug he got broader and morphed into Rufus and then he got taller and turned into my so-called dad and just as I lay my head against his chest he disappeared and I started falling and falling and spinning and all I could hear was Portia's laugh getting louder and louder and louder . . .

Right. I'm going downstairs to get a bun.

Hot and cross

Posted Tuesday 24th August, 01:56

Mum just planted yet another Rufus question in my mind and also confirmed that she is officially odd. God. Isn't it enough that I already have one problem parent?

I just found her downstairs on the sofa, eating a bun and staring at a candlelit Scrabble board. There were words all over it, but as soon as she saw me she clapped it closed as if I'd caught her ogling a seedy saddo mag.

'Hot isn't it?' She smiled brightly, as if she was a normal mum. 'I can't sleep, so I thought I may as well play a bit more Scrabble, you know, limber up – AJ's lethal.'

I nodded as if Scrabble practice entirely alone at one in the morning was not even slightly strange and said, 'I'm starving.'

'No wonder, crisps won't get you far, you and Ben should have sat down for supper with us – you could have joined in our game, darling.'

I hid my face in a cupboard to mouth, 'As if.'

'Well, at least Jude and Daniel are eating properly again, thank goodness, they seem far happier now. Do you miss the hamstericidal ratlets?'

'Um . . . a bit,' I fibbed, 'but I'm really glad Rufus has got them.'

'Ah, me too . . . he named them after famous orphans, didn't he? Poor Rufus.'

My ears transformed instantly from utterly disinterested to totally pricked up and I snapped, '*What?*'

But Mum just yawned and started walking upstairs. 'Right. Bed. I'm assisting on a big op on one of Henry's best stallions tomorrow, then I've got to drive over to the rescue centre to pick up Don Draper.'

I waited till her bedroom floorboards creaked overhead, then stamped on the spot and screamed silently at Johnny Depp, who just blinked back at me as if I was the deranged person in the house.

All the annoyance and bun sugar is keeping me awake

Posted Tuesday 24th August, 02:55

Okay, it hadn't occurred to me before, but the ratlets *are* orphans, so orphans' names *are* logical names. But why 'poor Rufus'? He's not an orphan, is he? He has a so-called mum and a stepdad, at least.

The worst thing is

Posted Tuesday 24th August, 03:12

All I want to do is pick up the phone and call Rufus to make sure he's not feeling tragic because he really is a 'poor Rufus' for some unknown mystery reason. This is very worrying, though I can't work out why.

OMG every illegal swear word you can imagine and a few more on top

Posted Tuesday 24th August, 03:28

I've worked out why.

Signing off for a bit

Posted Tuesday 24th August, 09:44

Hardly slept. Freaked. Need to pull socks up/self together etcetera. Over and out.

Comment

Posted Tuesday 24th August, 11.31, by Savvy Rose

Hey, Circe. Oh my gosh, I'm sorry to hear that and after you've been so awesome and you're on the home run and all.

What's up, honey?

Please let me know if I can help – I'm working all day but I'll check your blog over lunch – around five in the afternoon British time. And I should be home by six tonight – eleven your time.

Comment

Posted Tuesday 24th August, 17.11, by Savvy Rose

Gee, where are you, Circe?

I'm worried now. It's kinda frustrating being cyberbuddies, not being able to drop by to check you're okay. I hope you're talking to your mom, or Ben or Tash, at least. Could you just post up a little 'Hi'?

Hi

Posted Tuesday 24th August, 17.17

It's no major drama, really. But there's no point talking about it. I know angsty teens have a bad reputation, but don't worry, I'm not starving myself to size zero or painting my room suicidally black or anything. I promise.

Comment

Posted Tuesday 24th August, 17.22, by Savvy Rose

Oh, honey. I get that you Brits are big on the 'stiff upper lip', but bottling-up has never gotten anyone anywhere good, trust me. Okay, talking things through can be tricky, but maybe writing will be easier? Wanna give it a go?

Sorry Savvy Rose

Posted Tuesday 24th August, 17.31

You've been so amazing, helping me fake natural confidence etcetera to trick Rufus into thinking he likes me. But now I'm severely mortally ashamed because I've totally wasted your time. I just don't think I can see it through.

I understand that you probably won't want to be my number one (and only) reader any more. So goodbye from The Middle Of Absolute Nowhere and massive thanks for everything again. Blow a big kiss to the Statue of Liberty for me, I always think she must be lonely out there in the river when all the other statues and skyscrapers are cuddled up together in Manhattan.

Comment

Posted Tuesday 24th August, 17.37, by Savvy Rose

Hey, what kinda lightweight cyberbuddy do you think I am? Us New York City chicks don't scare so easy.

But, oh my gosh, you've gotten the Rufus deal *all wrong*. You have not tricked him into *thinking* he likes you, honey – he *does* like you!

Faking confidence has just helped you relax, forget your fears and draw out all the good stuff that's always been deep inside you. You've learned to use your mind and body – what you think, what you say, how you move – to show the best of yourself. Think about it. You haven't pretended to be someone you're not, you haven't dressed as someone you're not. Rufus has even seen you in your sweats without a scrap of make-up.

Rufus has fallen for the real you!

That is the honest truth, Circe, I swear. Does it help any?

Not sure

Posted Tuesday 24th August, 19.46

I guess you're back at work now, but I needed time to think properly. Okay even if I go along with that, even if he does like the 'real me', he is quite a complicated advanced pet, so he could easily change his mind at any time. And that wouldn't matter if I had stuck to my plan to keep him as a practice pet boyfriend who I don't like. But now it does matter because I've gone and totally messed up.

I worked out last night that I do like him. I like him a lot. Way too much. So I made myself remember bad things about him to try to get back to despising him. I've written a long list of serious defects (far longer than the one I had for Jake) and I keep reading it, over and over again, but it's not working at all. I feel like I'm trying to climb up a down escalator, however fast I run towards hating him I just end up back at really liking him, only more exhausted from trying not to.

Don Draper is a goldfish

Posted Tuesday 24th August, 19:58

Sigh. Mum just dashed in, dumped him on the kitchen table with a 'Be a darling and clean his bowl out, would you?' like I don't have my own life to live, then drove straight off to meet AJ at The Soggy Duck. I really don't know why some people bother to have children at all.

Comment

Posted Tuesday 24th August, 22.07, by Savvy Rose

Halle-freakin-lujah with a big fat yee-hah on top!

But this is fantastic news, Circe – about Rufus I mean, not Don Draper, though that is one slick name for a fish.

Don't you get it?

You've hooked yourself a pet boyfriend you actually *like*.

What's wrong with that? Nada.

Having the hots or a crush or lust or hearting someone or whatever you hip Brits call it nowadays – it's one of the best feelings in the whole freaking world.

Grab it, honey – enjoy!

So Rufus could change his mind? You could change yours too. No one knows for sure what's going to happen in the future. But if there's one good way to guarantee yourself a crummy life, it's by not letting yourself get close to guys you dig, not daring to let yourself feel real deep.

Trust me, honey, life is not just for living – it is for *loving*!

Maybe my life's just for cleaning out fish bowls

Posted Tuesday 24th August, 22.18

I'm sure all that's fine for normal people Savvy Rose. I know I should be ecstatic to have my first proper boyfriend with the added bonus of actually liking him, but I'm not. It's freaking me out.

Look, I'm seriously embarrassed about this, but I think I'm a bit sort of, well, *scared*. And I know Ralph probably does have some kind of statistical point and it's all down to my so-called dad making himself beyond scarce, but it's still pathetic. It's not fabulously sophisticated either. And it's got to be the epitome of totally not confident.

Comment

Posted Tuesday 24th August, 22.30, by Savvy Rose

Circe Shaw, you are confusing confidence with fearlessness. Show me a human being, guy or girl, who doesn't get scared sometimes and I'll eat the contents of my shoe closet – and that's a whole lotta high heels to chomp through. Fear is *normal*, we all get scared, but the more we do things we're scared of, the braver we get – look at how far you've come already.

But this is definitely not normal

Posted Tuesday 24th August, 22:39

Okay. You know that hollow feeling I get sometimes? It's back. And this time it won't go away.

It started as soon as I realised I properly like Rufus. It's horrid, like being hungry all the time but not just in my belly, in my heart and throat and head too.

I normally get rid of it by internally lying, kind of pretending what's making me hollow isn't true, until I end up sort of believing it. I got into the habit when I was sitting on the garden wall, rewriting the story of the day my so-called dad left. It started as a kind of hope. After I hoped it, I dreamt it a few times. Then I let myself imagine it properly, filling in details. Then me and Ben were cleaning our bikes in the garden one evening and he mumbled, 'What's happened to your dad, Witchy?' And the answer fell out of my mouth in one piece, 'Oh, nothing much, he had to go away to live on an island to paint pictures of all the rare flowers and things before they die of extinction.' And I didn't even blush or stutter or anything, even though that's not at all what happened.

Comment

Posted Tuesday 24th August, 22:46, by Savvy Rose

Honey, maybe you need to tell me what did happen?

Sort of nothing

Posted Tuesday 24th August, 22:53

Almost nothing happened, Savvy Rose. Other people asked that, at first. The phone was always ringing, and arty gallery people kept turning up and taking pictures away and nosing around the flat as if we were hiding my so-called dad in a cupboard or something. But we weren't, of course. I wish.

Comment

Posted Tuesday 24th August, 22:55, by Savvy Rose

Something must have happened with your pop, Circe, or why is he 'so-called'?

I don't want to pry, but I have a hunch this is why you're so scared of liking Rufus – that getting it off your mind could help.

Prepare yourself to be totally underwhelmed by boredom

Posted Tuesday 24th August, 23:02

God, I doubt it, but okay then. I hope you don't think it's going to be really exciting because there's been a big build-up. The real truth actually couldn't be more totally boring if it tried. This is what happened with my so-called dad.

He went for a walk around the block.

And never came back.

Ta da.

The journalistic key facts are tha– oh, woh, the hollowness is getting wors– hold on, give me a sec

**Prepare to be totally underwhelmed by boredom
again if you can bear it**

Posted Tuesday 24th August, 23:33

Right. The key facts . . .

Three years ago, on Saturday 30th June, at 14:05 hours precisely, I was sitting on our front garden wall stroking Tigger while I waited for Ben to finish his lunch.

A door slammed behind me, so I turned round, expecting to see Ben coming out of his flat on the floor above ours. But it was my so-called dad. He climbed the steps up from our basement and grinned, I think, when he saw me (although I might just have wished that to cover up a real memory of a glare or something). Then, when he got to the front gate, next to where I was sitting, I saw the scarlet and orange streaks in his hair and said, 'Have you finished the geraniums?' and he said, 'What?' like he'd never heard of geraniums before, even though he'd spent the last week painting them. And I said, 'Ger-aye-neee-ums!' in a funny voice, but he didn't laugh, he just said, 'Oh, no.' And I frowned then because he'd said he was definitely going to finish them before lunch, so I asked, 'Are you going to the art shop, have you run out of colours?' and he said, 'No, I just need some air, I'm going for a walk round the block.' And I do remember wondering why he needed air when he'd been painting in the garden all morning. But I didn't say anything. Then he rubbed Tigger under the chin, turned away, and strolled up the road with his hands stuffed in his pockets like he really was just going for a walk round the block. And I watched him go. I didn't beg or cry or hang on to his legs or anything because I didn't know I needed to.

Anyway, as I said, don't worry about me, Ralph's right, statistics show that I'm just a percentage. The exact same thing happens to hundreds of daughters all over the UK every day. My so-called dad rejected me. Big deal.

Comment

Posted Tuesday 24th August, 23:44, by Savvy Rose

Oh, Circe, I'm sure you've got that wrong too. It sucks that you watched your pop walk away like that, but he didn't reject *you*. He didn't split with *you*, he split with your *mom*. I'm sure he'd hate to think you were feeling so sore – missing out on dating guys because of him. Parents screw up, honey, they screw up in ways they didn't even know existed before they had kids. He and your mom had problems, I guess, stuff going on you couldn't understand – maybe they couldn't even understand. Wherever he is, please believe me, I'm certain your pop loves you.

Yeah right. Whatever.

Posted Tuesday 24th August, 23:46

269

Comment

Posted Tuesday 24th August, 23:57, by Savvy Rose

Oh my gosh, now you're mad at me too. I'm sorry, but I get why. I get that it's tough to believe that people can do the dumbest things but still love you deep down inside. I'm not going to try to convince you right now, but you'll get it one day. Till then, will you try something for me? Don't worry, it's nothing to do with your pop – it's another pet boy thing . . .

Try to trust Rufus.

Trust him like you trust your cat, Circe. You adore Johnny Depp, don't you? But without even thinking about it, you trust him every day when you open the door and set him free. He sounds like a smart cat. He could stray off to find himself an owner who'd cuddle him more, or feed him on caviar and cream, but he doesn't, does he?

Okay, I admit, some cats will stray whatever you do, they can't help it, it's in their nature. But imagine if you never let yourself have a cat, just in case it wandered off one day, think of everything you'd miss out on.

Furballs on my toes, snails on my pillow, decapitated things in the kitchen

Posted Wednesday 25th August, 07:50

Ah, the joys of owning Johnny Depp. I don't know how poor

Vanessa Paradis has put up with it for so long.

You're right, Savvy Rose, I totally do *not* get the mean outside, all loved-up inside idea.

But, okay, I do admit that maybe blogging about my so-called dad did help a bit with the fear thing. I slept really well last night, so I can think better this morning and I've decided I *am* going to try to trust Rufus. Or try to try, at least.

To be honest, I don't have any choice as he is my only hope for a snog on the first day back at school. Also, going swimming with him might show up some new major visible fault like doggy paddle or deeply unattractive kneecaps, which would help me Officially Get Over Rufus if I need to in the future.

School can be unexpectedly educational

Posted Wednesday 25th August, 12:08

Finished my English lit. homework in record time, thanks to inventing new extra large slanted handwriting. It's excellent as it fills pages really quickly and looks quite fabulously sophisticated from a distance. But it's also quite difficult to read, which is useful for hiding mistakes such as the lack of any actual facts.

The homework subject was interesting though, all about understanding stories more by looking at the

 271

authors' real lives. It turns out some of the best writers had Dark Pasts they had to rise above to use in their work deliberately or sometimes even accidentally.

This made me think a lot and I dug out the jar poem I wrote in AJ's workshop. Before we started writing, AJ told us poetry is about working out our real thoughts and feelings and trying to express them in a true way. The mauve 'lady' put up her hand then and said, 'Ah me, how I do flutter over thee,' in quite a growly voice. So I was mainly trying not to actually die of laughter until AJ explained how using an object as a metaphor can help us understand ourselves better, and I thought that was worth a try as understanding myself is exhausting even on a quiet day.

AJ gave us ten minutes to stare at our objects and scrawl down all the things that popped into our heads, before finding ideas and patterns to turn into a poem. Then we had to read the poem out loud at the end (which meant we had to literally write one and couldn't just doodle).

After the mauve lady read her poem out, which was mainly about bottoms and crying, AJ just coughed a lot. But after I read mine he asked if he could talk to me about it some time. And I winced, 'God, no, it's obviously mainly rubbish.' And he said, 'I rather suspect not.' Which is a typically mysterious AJ thing to say, so I just rolled my eyes.

But when I read the poem again today it did make me gasp a bit, because although it's still rubbish, it does seem true too, accidentally. So, there you go.

Anyway, this made me realise even the bad bits of life can be useful. And you're right, Savvy Rose, I don't see why my so-called dad should get away with messing up my entire love life, even if it is a non-existent one.

So, extra long drum roll please, I have made a major life-changing decision . . .

I am now going to use my fabulous sophistication to rise above my Dark Past and triumph against the odds.

It's not easy rising above a Dark Past when you've got a dodgy present

Posted Wednesday 25th August, 12:15

Rufus just texted me . . .

> Meet there at 2?
> Stuff's come up.
> Will need to
> split by 4.

This is annoying. I'd finished all my homework with twenty minutes to spare, which should have given me plenty of time to rise above my Dark Past, but now all I can do is obsess about Rufus's 'stuff'. Has he got a Dark Past too? Or so-called mum issues or stepdad problems or . . . or – what? I am so bored of not talking about what's really going on. And even if I wasn't bored of it, if I wanted to do it I could just stay at home and do it with Mum, who is the world's foremost expert.

Comment

Posted Wednesday 25th August, 12:18, by Savvy Rose

Whew. Glad you've forgiven me, honey. Just a quick post before I head out to work. Have you thought of asking your mom about Rufus's 'stuff'? She knows Lucien, doesn't she? Maybe he's told her something. Can't hurt to try, can it?

Very deep sigh

Posted Wednesday 25th August, 12:22

It can actually. Hurt to try talking to Mum, that is. No. I'm tired of tiptoeing around. If Rufus and I are going to have any kind of future, I need to know the truth. I'm going to ask him myself, after all his 'stuff' has affected our plans twice, which is at least once more than a proper girlfriend should put up with, I think. Also we have now been going out for ten days which is much longer than the average teen celeb marriage, so I probably do have some human rights. I'm going to check with Tash.

Hang-ups and hang-ups

Posted Wednesday 25th August, 12:37

Tash was a bit huffy at first, and so much has happened in my brain since I hung up on her that I forgot I had. I also forgot there was meant to be something wrong with my mobile, so I had to wave it around and talk from a distance in the middle of the call to remind her. She's happy I like Rufus though, so I don't have to finish with him. And she said I should ask him about the 'stuff'. She even thinks maybe he wants me to ask. But I think that's the difference between being a genuinely confident optimistic sort of girlfriend and still just a learner.

Ten . . . nine . . . eight . . .

Posted Wednesday 25th August, 13:21

The countdown has begun . . . At precisely 1.30 pm, in less than ten minutes, I, Circe Shaw, will embark on the ultimate pet boy experiment.

I'm in my office in the shade as it's baking. It must be the hottest day of the summer so far. The air's wobbly and smells of roses and the bumble bees are all crawling along on the ground as if they wish they could take off their furry stripes.

I'm already in my cossie so I can practise draping myself

around. I've decided to wear my dark green school one-piece because it's confidence-boosting knowing nothing important will fall out of it. I also need all the fabulous sophistication I can get if I'm going to rise above my Dark Past and pull off the trusting Rufus idea, so I've pinned my floppy flower unexpectedly on one hip and piled my hair up in a tousled knot I copied from a mag.

. . . seven . . . six . . . five . . .

Posted Wednesday 25th August, 13:25

In just a few minutes I will be on my way to a cool swimming pool to meet a hot boy who happens to be my Official Boyfriend. And who likes me. And, yes, I like him too. And that might sound miraculous and scary but it is in fact extremely ordinary and not even slightly worrying at all.

. . . four . . . three . . . two . . .

Posted Wednesday 25th August, 13:28

And nor is the fact that we are going to be totally alone. Together.

We will sip iced tea and Rufus will tell me what his 'stuff' is and it will be quite uninteresting really and we will throw our heads back and laugh.

 276

Then we will snog in the deep end. A lot.

And Portia's poison will be wiped from my entire memory forever. At least.

Oh. My. God.

Am I ready for this?

. . . one!

Posted Wednesday 25th August, 13:29

Yes. I so am.

Dark Past? Ha! What Dark Past?

Sparkly future, here I come . . .

Comment

Posted Thursday 26th August, 11.05, by Savvy Rose

So . . . How did it go? I'm in total freaking suspense . . .

Trusting Him To Tell The Truth And/Or Not Stray Male Human Pet Control: Experiment 11

Posted Thursday 26th August, 22:31

EXPERIMENT ABORTED
APOLOGIES FOR ANY INCONVENIENCE

 277

Comment

Posted Thursday 26th August, 23:06, by Savvy Rose

Oh my gosh. Honey, what happened?

Sorry, but I don't want to talk about it. Ever.

Posted Friday 27th August, 10:08

Comment

Posted Friday 27th August, 10:10, by Savvy Rose

Hey, I'm sure it can't be all that bad. Please, Circe, spill.

**No point. All a total waste of. It's Over. She's right.
I'm wrong. End of.**

Posted Friday 27th August, 10:21

Comment

Posted Friday 27th August, 10:27, by Savvy Rose

What do you mean? Who's right? Your mom?

No. Portia.

Posted Friday 27th August, 10:33

The Oh So Lovely And Charming Portia Thornington is right.

There. I said it.

I said it out loud too. Into my mirror. Looking myself straight in the eyes.

I am no longer in extreme total denial.

Comment

Posted Friday 27th August, 10:38, by Savvy Rose

What do you mean, Portia's right? Right about what? You said she was pathetic. What changed? Denial about what? Come on, honey, let me help, please. It sounds like you've hit rock bottom – telling me what happened can't make it worse, can it?

It couldn't be worse

Posted Friday 27th August, 10:51

I'm far lower than rock bottom. And it's pouring with rain here, which is like some kind of hilariously ironic metaphor as I can't squeeze out one single measly tear.

I'm sitting in the kitchen making sure Johnny Depp doesn't eat Don Draper. Mum's working, of course. Tash has gone to market with her dad and Ben's at a karate thing. Not that I could tell any of them what's happened. Tash phoned to get all the gossip yesterday but I pleaded heat exhaustion and said I'd tell her when I see her on Saturday, though I won't of course. I don't know what I'll say.

I did actually try to type up an accurate journalistic report on the experiment when I got back from Venetia's on Wednesday, but my head and heart kept yelling at each other and my hands kept veering off the key facts, so I dumped it in my drafts file. There's no way I want to go over it all again to rewrite it into some kind of sense, but if you can cope with deciphering total ranting hysteria I'll post it as it is.

Comment

Posted Friday 27th August, 10:59, by Savvy Rose

Please do, honey, I'm tearing my freaking hair out over here.

Trusting Him To Tell The Truth And/Or Not Stray

Male Human Pet Control: Experiment 11

Posted Friday 27th August, 11:08

[Saved Wednesday 25th August 16:43]

Aaaaaaaaaaaaaaaaaaaaaarrrrrrrrrrrggggggggggggh!!!!!!!!!!
Screaming and screaming internally. AND YELLING
PROPERLY OUT LOUD IN CAPITALS. What was I thinking?
What kind of mad insanity have I dragged myself into? I am
delusional to the furthest most bitter extremes of rampant
female human imagination. At least. Every illegal swear
word in every language on the planet.

I guess I've been totally carried away to the land of
virtual cloud cuckoo by this whole blogging thing, by the
holidays, the heat even. Maybe my teenage hormones are
raging too much. Maybe I should get them removed? Can
you get them removed? If you can't, I might have to stay in
FOR THE REST OF MY ENTIRE LIFE.

I'm hiding up in my room because Mum must not get
even slightly near me while I feel like this. It says on the
calendar that she's eating out with Ralph tonight, but she'll
be back from work to shower and change soon, so I left a
note on the fridge. *Everything fed. Put DD on top shelf as
JD tried to murder. Napping now, do not disturb under
any circumstances, even emergency.* I added a PS too . . .
Definitely not ill, just tired from homework. This will stop
her trying to come into my room to take my temperature or

do one of her consultations. If she asked, 'How are you?' right now, the appalling truth might fall straight out of my mouth and then where would we be? Back at square one again, that's where, with her in bed 'tired' and pills lined up in the bathroom and bills piled up in the hall and strangers with clipboards shaking their heads and muttering about 'unknown whereabouts' and 'fostering solutions' and sitting me down and telling me to be grown-up and brave and saying, 'Don't upset your mum, she's upset enough about your dad' etcetera, and me nodding a lot then hiding all the photos of him because I thought it would make Mum less upset because when she did get up for a bath or something I could see her eyes went blurry when she looked at them specially the one of their weddi–

OMGOMGOMG!!! WHAT AM I ON? Blah blah blah. Where was I? Trying to type up my experiment as it is my trainee journalistic duty even though I just want to totally obliterate it from my brain forever and ever amen. At least.

Okay. Deep breaths. Channel Jess Bradley, stay professional, stick to the key facts, type fast, get it over with . . .

So, I started out this afternoon feeling pretty fabulously sophisticated and confident and quite where-it's-at too. Rufus was already outside Venetia's when I got there and we didn't waste any time but snogged straight away. I meant to peek in the mirror to double-check my best loved-up look, but the kiss was so amazing my brain didn't want to open my eyes. Rufus said 'Wow' afterwards and we both laughed and looked at the ground a bit. Then Chivvers buzzed us in and led us to the pool and showed us the music system and the fridge with a pitcher of iced tea inside. Then he announced, 'I'll be in the office, Miss, should you need anything further.' And he actually bowed.

While Rufus put on some smoochy sounds, I laid our towels on a pair of sunbeds, slipped off my dress and draped my arms and legs out confidently. Then he came over and tugged off his jeans and T-shirt and he didn't reveal deeply unattractive kneecaps or anything else even slightly unattractive. He looked beyond fit and I couldn't help fully appreciating all the best bits of him from behind my sunnies and he grinned, so I think he realised and it made him feel special. Then we laid back and sipped our drinks and I babbled a bit about Venetia being sweet before remembering that he was probably his own favourite subject. So I asked him what he's into, apart from horses, and it turns out he plays bass and likes darkly haunting rock music and spooky films and classic ghost stories. And I really like all that too, so I didn't even need to pretend to have things in common.

We decided to swim then and Rufus didn't try to throw me in or divebomb to deliberately soak me or anything. He took my hand and we walked down the steps together with the cool water sliding round our ankles, then our knees, then our thighs. When the cold hit my waist I shivered and dived under and came up in front of him and he pounced on me and we splashed about, laughing like mad. Then we had a race and I won. But when Rufus caught up with me he pinned me in the corner of the pool at the deep end between the metal steps and the diving board, which was exactly where Portia trapped me at the party after she'd grabbed my ankle and held me underwater so long my lungs felt like they were on fire and I thrashed and fought until I came up spluttering and gasping for air only a few metres away from where Ben and Tash were snogging but they didn't turn round and I didn't have any strength left to lash out and I didn't have any breath left to yell it was all I could do to keep kicking to keep my face above the chopping water, keep clawing at the slippery blue tiles to get a grip on the rough cement stripes between them, keep sucking in air to fill up my lungs. I coughed up a mouthful of chlorine and Portia giggled as if we were mucking about, 'Hey, babe, I've got some really juicy gossip! Have you heard about the creepy saddo in our year who's never *ever* got off with a boy at the school gates but still leeches around so she can get off on watching *everyone else* snogging. Gross.' Then she dug her sharpened talons into my arm, leaned in, and hissed in my ear, 'No one gives a damn about you, Circe Shaw, remember that. Not a soul. You could drop dead right in front of your so-called best mates and they wouldn't even notice.' Then she winked, 'God, you're so lucky I saved you!' And I still couldn't speak, but I pulled a face to show I knew exactly what she'd done and that she wouldn't get away with it, even though I hadn't worked out how she wouldn't. Then she said, quietly, but so charmingly that anyone who did overhear would assume she was being her usual lovely self, 'Ah, poor Circe the curse, all alone, doomed never to love or be loved – no wonder you want to *drown yourself*.'

BITCHBITCHBITCH YELLING PROPERLY OUT LOUD IN CAPITALS AGAIN That's it. That's Portia's idea of a laugh. Pathetic isn't it? It's the kind of rubbish I've had to put up with all year. Chirping 'Morning Curse!' every day in registration, so cheerily that everyone assumes she's saying 'Circe'. Tutting, 'Do you think I should warn him?' if a cute boy talks to me. Sighing, 'No point you learning all this babe,' behind me in sex ed. Soon her whispers were following me everywhere, hissing at me down corridors, in the playground, through toilet doors. In the end I started to hear them even when they weren't there.

I would never have let Portia get away with it in London. But at Hell House being the newbie outcast with the second-hand uniform was tough enough, without picking a fight with the most popular girl in school. So I just avoided her, ignored her, hoped she'd get bored and give up sooner or later. But she didn't.

And the worst thing is, it's all my fault. Portia was in charge of looking after me for my first week at Hell House. She did it outstandingly, of course, showing me round, introducing me to teachers, complimenting me on my 'lush' curls and 'rad' accent. Then, on the Friday afternoon, she slipped her arm through mine and waved her chauffeur away with, 'I'm walking my gorge new friend Circe home.'

When we got back to The Nook she said, 'Oh . . . my . . . god . . . does your whole family fit in there?'

I nodded, 'Just about – but it's only me and my mum.'

And she gasped, 'Oh *babe*, where's your dad?'

And, it was like she'd mesmerised me with all her arm linking and hair flattering and, without even thinking, I told her everything, just like that. How I'd watched my so-called dad disappear, how Mum fell apart, how I beat myself up for not being pretty enough or clever enough or funny enough to make him stay with us. How, deep down, even though I was so much older and wiser now, I still felt that way.

Portia nodded and bit her lip and her eyes filled up. And I felt happy for the first time since we'd moved, because I thought I'd made a good friend. A friend who actually knew the truth about me.

I couldn't have been more wrong. When I sat down beside her in registration the following Monday, she smiled sweetly then leaned in and whispered, 'Do you know what your name means?'

And I said, 'Yes, Circe was a famous sorceress in Greek mythology.'

'Really? What was she famous for?'

I answered straight away, because my so-called dad had actually told me once. 'She saved Odysseus from the deadly singing sirens – from being shipwrecked.'

Portia tutted, 'Oh babe, that's what my dad would call

"glossing over the truth".'

I frowned. 'What do you mean?'

Portia rolled her eyes. 'Circe was a notorious evil witch – she cursed all the men she met and turned them into pigs.'

And I was so stunned by what she was saying after all I'd confided in her that I just gaped.

Then Portia's face contorted into a vicious little smirk. 'Maybe that's why your dad really disappeared Circe – you cursed him.'

Okay, don't get me wrong, I'm not a total doughnut, I know the witch story isn't true, that believing it is as daft as believing R-Patz could pop me on his back and run straight up a tree, but it still made my heart clench. And it's made the horrid hollow feeling grow stronger again, just as it was starting to wear off a bit. And I hate that someone as pathetic as Portia has managed to do that to me.

OMG AGAIN!!! WHAT'S GOING ON WITH MY HEAD? I am the epitome of blah blah blah. Maybe it's actual sun-stroke? Okay. Fabulous sophistication. Facts. Focus. Where was I? Right. Yes, back in that same corner of the pool . . .

So Rufus was pinning me exactly where Portia had trapped me, which was exactly where I wanted to be, remember? I expected it to help me do my trick of replacing a horrid old memory with a shiny happy new one. So I did the staring at lips thing, which I hardly had to bother with, to be honest, Rufus seemed to not mind snogging at all.

When we kissed again it tasted a bit of suncream and

chlorine but I didn't care because it was still nice, and it got nicer and nicer. And in the end it was so nice my mind stopped thinking about confidence etcetera and my hands stopped gripping the sides of the pool and curled around his neck.

I was way out of my depth, so he was keeping me afloat, keeping my face above the water. But I let myself go, totally, literally. I let myself trust Rufus. Not just with my heart, with my body too. And it didn't just feel like floating, it felt higher, wilder, totally free – like flying . . .

Then . . . *Circeee, oh Circeee* . . .

That's how it started. With my name, with a sweet, simpering voice in my head. Portia's voice, whispering . . .

Oh Circeee . . . You don't really trust him do you? He doesn't really like you. You're not good enough for him . . . not pretty enough . . . not clever enough . . . not funny enough . . . He'll leave you, just like every other boy – just like your dad . . .

I snapped my eyes open even though I knew Portia wasn't there, that all I was hearing was my own stupid fear making things up. But seeing the empty pool didn't help, her whispers kept coming, louder and louder . . .

Oh Circeee . . . What's all his secret 'stuff'? Maybe it's nothing to do with his family? Maybe you're just a practice girlfriend for him? Maybe he really fancies someone else? Maybe he loves someone else. Maybe she's coming back from her holiday on the 29th. You're too scared to ask, aren't you? Maybe it's ME . . .

Bile burnt up my throat. I gagged and pulled away from Rufus so fast I slipped straight under the water. When I came up, I was coughing and spluttering, just as I had with Portia.

But Rufus didn't help me, he just glared, then hissed in his most hideous mocking voice, 'Charming.'

'Ch-ch-char . . . h-how d-d-dare . . .' I was gasping too much to get my words out, but it was as if Rufus had thrown a lit match on to a pile of dried-up passion in my soul or something. As soon as I'd sucked in enough air, I spat back at him, 'Charming! *Charming?* Ha! I suppose you think it's charming not to tell your girlfriend *anything* about *anything*?' I kicked furiously, retreating to the side of the pool. 'What exactly is *stuff* Rufus? What is your big oh-so-important secret? Why exactly do you have to leave early today? AND WHAT'S SO SPECIAL ABOUT SUNDAY?'

Rufus just did that thing with his eyes flashing and boring through my head. But this time he looked like he really wished he didn't know what was going on inside it.

'Aaargh! Stop doing that weird eye thing! It's so *pathetic* – and disgustingly melodramatic!' I squealed, punching the water with my fists, 'Why can't you just tell me? Oh. My. God. That *is* it! You totally fancy someone else don't you?'

Rufus ran his hands through his wet hair, which made him look infuriatingly gorgeous, and raised one eyebrow.

'And don't do the eyebrow thing either! This is not ironic or funny or even a metaphor! Ugh – you're actually *in love* with someone else aren't you? You're in love with some A-lister heiress or Lady Mucking 'It' girl and I'm just a distraction because I'm *not good enough*. What is it? Am I too boring or curly or maybe just too plain poor? Ha! That's it, maybe you fancy swanning about acting Lord Huffing Mucking in a place like this? Well tough, that is so not going to happen is it? Take a look at yourself, you're just an ugly, stupid, despicable groom – AND YOU SMELL!'

Once I'd shrieked all this into the air between us, I just stared at it, horrified, while Rufus backed off towards the metal steps behind him. If I was a normal girl who could cry, I probably would have burst into tears and apologised then because his face had gone dead white and his eyes had gone all deep and cloudy, as if there was an actual storm going on in his head. But I'm not normal, so I just thought, *Oh no you don't – you are* so *not going to leave me* – I *am going to leave* you! Then I dragged myself up and over the side of the pool, grabbed my stuff from my sunbed and fled.

The last time I fled, I did it in a very dignified way, calmly pulling my school uniform over my sopping bikini, waving casually to Tash and Ben still cuddling in the water, pointing at my watch and mouthing 'Thanks' across the pool to Venetia, then striding out as if everything in my world was just peachy. This time, I didn't hesitate at all, I ran barefoot down the gravel drive, dressed while I waited for the gates to whirr open, then ran and ran. And ran.

I didn't stop running until I hit the edge of the village. And it was only then that I noticed a stripe of blood on my thigh and realised I'd ripped off my floppy flower on the side of the pool. Imagining it sinking down under the water made me feel so tragic, I thought I might actually cry. But I didn't, of course. I just laughed a bit hysterically, because it occurred to me that on the bottom of a swimming pool was quite an unexpected place to pin a floppy flower.

I'm not boasting about the crying thing by the way. I'm not being internally strong or anything. I wish I could cry. I mean, I wouldn't want to be blubbing all over the place for no reason, like Geraldine. But not crying at all is rubbish. I haven't cried since I asked Mum where my so-called dad had really gone and she shouted non-stop for an hour, then went to bed until the first clipboard lady turned up.

MORE YELLING I am the epitome of an unprofessional deviant. I've done it again – wantonly wandered totally off the journalistic subject. Jess Bradley would be ashamed. But I'm too sad and shaky to do any better now. Maybe I'll feel calm enough to rewrite it tomorrow. Or maybe I'll just delete my entire blog and prepare to fail all my exams and train the intelligentish bit of my brain to accept its grisly secretarial destiny. ARGH! Enough. Shut up Circe shut uppppppppppppppppppppppppp

All is lost, at least

Posted Friday 27th August, 12:12

So, as you can probably tell, Savvy Rose, *Experiment 11* was not a big success. In fact, I achieved the exact opposite of what I set out to do. I also failed as any kind of journalist by spewing out a random prattling rant. I probably didn't even rip my floppy flower off my swimsuit, I bet it threw itself off in despair.

Anyway, now I don't know what to do. All I know is I've scared off my first proper boyfriend. And even though I spent all yesterday hoping and wishing and trying to connect my brain to Rufus's psychically to lure him to The Nook (which I do with Johnny Depp when he won't come in at night) he hasn't texted or called or anything. And it's horrible, I miss him like mad already.

Even better, in another stroke of my own brilliant wisdom, I managed to prove Portia right. My name *is* a curse. Even if I know it's not true in an actual magical sense, if I hadn't been named Circe, she wouldn't have been able to whisper all that rubbish. If she hadn't done all that whispering, it wouldn't have been in my head poisoning my thoughts against Rufus, and I wouldn't have morphed into a squealing banshee in the middle of the best snog in the history of my entire almost non-existent love life.

But please don't bother, Savvy Rose, in case you're thinking up some pet boy rule like, 'Gee whizz boys are like dogs, very loyal even when you call them names.' I know that's not true in this case. Rufus loathes me and even if he doesn't, he is more a cat-type than a dog-type anyway and cats are definitely less forgiving.*

* This is a proven fact. Foxy, the vicar's Jack Russell, growled at Johnny Depp the first time they visited our cottage and Johnny's never let her (or the vicar) come back in again.**
** Mum pretends to be sorry about this, but I think she's quite glad really.

Comment

Posted Friday 27th August, 12:46, by Savvy Rose

Oh my gosh, Circe, I'm so choked up – and so freaking crazy I could probably write a hundred pages. But hey, I get that you're a teenager and you guys like to cut to the chase. So I'll keep it short for now, but please if you want more, just holler. I hate that you're hurting so bad, so I'll make sure I check in online every morning, at least, from now on – around dawn my time, ten yours.

First, and this is crucial, I want you to read this line over and over, till you've got it fixed in your head real good . . .

You are NOT a curse. Your name is NOT a curse, in ANY sense.

Circe is a beautiful name, honey. There are always heaps of different interpretations of classic myths, I'm certain your folks read the one where Circe enchants all the men around her with her great wisdom and general gorgeousness and wins the heart of the hero.

Anything that went wrong wasn't because of your name, it was because Portia poisoned your thoughts about it. And, take it from me, an airhead like her would have found something mean to say, whatever your name was.

Okay, so now, what you should do. Ouch. It involves that big old Trust word again, so deep breath . . .

1. Tell your mom about Portia.

That girl is not just pathetic, she is a fully-fledged bully and your mom needs to know what's going on. Honey, folks can get real tired sometimes. What your mom went through with your pop must have been tough, I guess she needed to rest up for a while. But it sounds like she's doing okay now – trust her to look after you.

2. Tell Tash about Portia.

Tash sounds like she always thinks the best of people, which is admirable. But she's your buddy, Circe, trust that too. If you tell her the truth and she doesn't believe you, sorry, but you're better off without her.

3. Tell Rufus everything.

Okay. I know. Scary. But I really think it's worth a try. And, hey, you've nothing to lose, have you? Tell him about your so-called dad, about why you find it hard not knowing about 'stuff', about what happened at the pool with Portia. Trust him and you might be surprised by how much he understands. He's obviously got some problems too. Have you wondered where his parents are, why he's not living with them, why he's living with his grandpop?

So, *Experiment 11* sucked – it was a disaster with a big fat D. But everyone messes up sometimes, Circe. You didn't plan to freak out on Rufus, you'd just been bottling everything up too long. And all is definitely *not* lost. You've learned how to keep a boy as a pet – and kept one for ten whole days! This is just a blip, a mistake you needed to get out your system, maybe. In fact, you could use it to turn your life right around – hell, *I* trust *you*, I know you can!

Circe, it's time to trust *yourself*. Now – go girl!

I need to think

Posted Friday 27th August, 13:02

I might be a while.

A yes, a maybe, an okay, a shrug and a very unfabulous journalistic error

Posted Saturday 28th August, 11:20

Savvy Rose, first, thanks so much. I can't believe how lucky I am to have such an amazing cyberbuddy. You've made me think properly instead of being devoured by my own natural teenage instinct to wail power ballads into my hairbrush and pout out of windows and eat buns in between. Here's what I think . . .

Re. not being a Curse, I will read that out loud each day and try to believe it.

Re. point one, I know telling Mum about Portia seems like a good idea from a distance of about 3459.34 thousand miles away. But any closer and it looks impossible. From where I'm sitting (at the kitchen table) it looks more than impossible. We communicate mainly by fridge. I suppose I might try writing a post-it and sticking it next to *Need more coco pops*. Maybe something vague like, *Friend being teased at school – please leave wise advice by shopping list before 1st Sept.*

Re. point two. Okay. You're right. I'm going to see Tash this afternoon and I promise I will tell her.

Re. point three. Well, Rufus still hasn't texted or called or even turned up to throw the hamstericidal ratlets back in my face, which was a terrifying thought involving having my nose bitten off, but was also my last desperate hope. I just don't know. I feel like I don't know anything at all about Rufus really, even though we were going steady for nearly ten days. About the only thing I do know though is that he's a groom – Lucien is his boss, Savvy Rose, not his grandad. My mistake no doubt, and yet another crushing blow to my journalistic self-esteem. I must have typed a key fact up in a confusing way to make you think that.

Weird

Posted Saturday 28th August, 11:30

I can't actually remember typing anything about Rufus living with his grandad, even by accident, so I'm going to do a word search on 'grandad'.

Weirder

Posted Saturday 28th August, 11:32

No 'grandad's anywhere. Maybe I used 'grandpa' or 'grandfather' or 'gramps' or even your American-style, 'grandpop'. I'll try them . . .

No. Nothing. None of them came up. I'm going to search for 'Lucien' now and make sure I didn't write anything accidentally misleading like 'Lucien looks related to Rufus but is too old to be his dad' or something.

And weirder

Posted Saturday 28th August, 11:35

No. nothing like that either. As you can probably imagine, Savvy Rose, because I'm a trainee professional journalist dedicated to accurate reporting, this is driving me a bit bonkers. Where did you get the grandpop idea? Can you find the right post for me? I just counted and I've written over 70,000 entire words, so it's difficult to check them all. Can you remember where you read the misleading thing? Or maybe you didn't? Maybe you're just confused because you're so busy living it up in the big apple that never sleeps? Maybe one of your own men lives with his grandpop and you mixed your pet up with mine? Or maybe you just took a wild guess?

But what if?

Posted Saturday 28th August, 12:12

What if it's true? I just assumed Rufus was Lucien's groom – he never told me he was. Though, of course, he never actually told me anything much.

Rufus doesn't look anything like Lucien either. But Lucien's face is about fifty years older and mainly wrinkles and I've only met him once in daylight.

It does sort of make sense though. When I imagine it

 298

being true, the whole story of me and Rufus shifts somehow. Little niggling bits of puzzle in my brain fall into place, like why Rufus would be invited to a posh dinner with Lucien's friends and why he thought Digby was the biggest dog in the world – who'd think that? Only someone really small – a child, *a grandchild*.

I need to do some detective work. Luckily, I know just the person to help.

Going round and round and being dead straight all at the same time

Posted Saturday 28th August, 17:37

Just back from the park, feeling beyond confused but also quite calm.

I told Tash everything. I hadn't planned to, not all at once. I decided I'd only tell her today what happened with Rufus at the pool, and why, as in what Portia did at the party. Then I thought I'd tell her the truth about my so-called dad next week, so she didn't feel too bombarded by dull facts about my Dark Past.

When I got to the park, Tash was already sitting cross-legged in a triangular section of the roundabout, slowly rotating, smiling up at the sun, eyes closed. I caught the handrail and pulled myself into the section next to her. 'Hi, Tash.'

She yawned. 'Hey you. I was just thinking we should mark our last holiday Saturday with Über Grande Vanillatte Frapettocinos. Fancy hitting Gina's?'

'No, um, not right now – don't move, don't even open your eyes.' I leant back against the central plinth of the roundabout so our heads were side by side, but facing away at right angles. 'I want to tell you somethi–'

'Ooh. Pet boy goss – at last. So, how is the "despicable" Rufus, did he look fit in his swimmers? Has he got a six-pa–'

'No, I mean, yes, but no – it's not really that kind of something, it's actually quite boring, but sort of important...'

'God, Circe, you sound all deep and serious – are you okay?'

The scared bit of my brain jumped about then yelling, *say yes, say everything's just mega-peachy*. But I told it to shut up, swallowed hard, then started speaking, watching the scenery slide from the parched playing field to the table where I'd shared pizza with Rufus, to the swings where we'd snogged, to the fountain edged with ducks, then back to the field. And it was slow and difficult at first, but as I spoke I remembered what Savvy Rose said about trusting Tash, and myself, and it got easier and easier. And every sentence that fell out of my mouth was like a surprise to me, it's so long since I've let myself even think about all this.

I started right back at the beginning, from when my so-called dad began to work later and later at his studio, started to go to more and more arty parties. How it made Mum tap her phone on the table in time with the tick-tick-tick of the kitchen clock.

'One night she threw his ruined dinner at him, still in the saucepan. He ducked so it missed, but it smashed a window and Neighbourhood Watch thought it was a burglar and called the police.'

I described how he walked away that Saturday. How Mum laughed in the evening and said he'd be home soon enough, because he'd left his precious painting in the garden. But he still wasn't back the next day and the sun had crinkled his canvas and baked his palette into a multi-coloured scab. So I asked Mum where he was, and she said it had completely slipped her mind that he'd planned a little holiday as he'd been working so hard. And I wondered why he hadn't told me, but it did fit with him saying he needed air, so I let myself believe it. But a week passed, then two, then three, and I thought it was weird he hadn't phoned or even sent a postcard. Then a lorry from his gallery turned up and took his paintings away and left the flat all echoey. So I asked Mum again and she changed her story and said he was looking after an elderly aunt who lived abroad now and might be away much longer. But I could see by her blurry eyes that she was fibbing, so I cried then, and shouted a lot, and Mum shouted back.

'Then she closed the curtains and went to bed, Tash, even though it was the middle of the afternoon. And she didn't get up properly again for nearly three months.'

Tash grabbed my hand then. So I told her how once Mum did finally get up it was as if my so-called dad had never existed. How I'd been warned not to upset her, so I didn't mention him, and nor did she. She didn't even say anything when she cleared out all his things, so I wouldn't even have known.

'Then I was walking back from school along the high street one day and my knees actually collapsed when I thought I saw my so-called dad in the corner of my eye. But it was just his old suede jacket on a mannequin in a charity shop window.'

I stopped talking then, because my heart did its throat-blocking thing as I remembered how I had to lean against the window and force my legs to go rigid before I could go in. Tash didn't say anything, but squeezed my hand tighter.

'There were bits of him all over the shop. I found some of his stripy shirts and a green jumper and a paisley scarf and a couple of art books and his satchel too. This satchel. I had to haggle with the sales assistant and pretend I thought it was rubbish and mouldy, so I could afford it with the rest of my week's lunch money, but I managed to buy it back.'

Tash cried when I told her that, which reminded me of a certain pathetic person's fake tears, so I told her about Portia then and she said, 'Oh My God, Circe, what a total cow, I'm so sorry.' And then I told her about Rufus and we both swore illegally, quite a lot.

And being side by side did make it all easier to say, so that theory works between girls too. But we both felt a bit dizzy by then, so we climbed off the roundabout and Tash hugged me and asked if there was anything she could do. And I said, 'Actually, there is one thing. I think Savvy Rose has guessed a key fact about Rufus and I want to check it out. Can you call Knight Ridge for me, and if an old plummy voice answers, say, "May I speak to your grandson, Rufus?" and if a young moody voice answers, say, "May I speak to your grandfather, Lucien?"'

So Tash phoned, and I could tell Lucien answered, because she said in her best politely legal voice, 'Good afternoon, might I speak to your grandson, Rufus?' then she said, 'Oh I see, no. Thank you.' And hung up.

I sighed, 'I suppose he said, "Don't you mean my *groom* Rufus?"'

She shook her head. 'No. He said, "Sorry, my grandson's away with his, er, father until tomorrow night, can I take a message?"'

And I physically choked a bit then and she had to slap me on the back until I could splutter, 'O-oh-h M-my God. *What was he THINKING?* That's *it*? *That's his big secret?* He was going somewhere with his *dad*! Why didn't he just tell me? And why didn't he tell me Lucien was his grandad? Argh! But why didn't I guess? I have been the epitome of absolute doughnut. Even Savvy Rose guessed!'

Tash wrinkled her nose then. '*She did?* But that's a

massive coincidence isn't it? Why would a total stranger guess something like that out of the blue?'

Which, of course, is a typical suspicious lawyer thing to say, so I just tutted.

Taking time off from me

Posted Saturday 28th August, 18:53

I've been thinking more about what Tash said and my brain's been jumping to all sorts of mad conclusions. I'm ignoring it though as I reckon too many unsaid things have been emptied out of it too quickly, so it's made it refill with daft ideas.

In fact, I've decided to close it down – or at least stop thinking about boys and bullies and so-called dads and Dark Pasts for a few hours. Mum's going out to eat at Le Gingham Bistro with AJ, so I'm going to cuddle up with Johnny Depp and a bun and watch TV, then go to bed early. I need extra energy for tomorrow as I've decided to spend all day boosting my fabulous sophistication.*

* Obviously, all my hopes of a snog at the school gates have been torn from my wretched heart and tossed to the wind in melancholic smithereens.

Chalky Chick on one hand, *Noir Nuit* on the other

Posted Sunday 29th August, 09:48

Which does look quite fabulously sophisticated and is the perfect representation on the outside of how I feel on the inside, so is also the ideal nail polish choice for pet boy control. Although this is more than irrelevant information for me now, of course.

On one hand, I do actually feel lighter since I told Tash everything. She called from the train to London earlier and said she's sure Portia will be okay next term. I think she's being a bit optimistic, but it was still good to be able to talk about it.

On the other hand, I'm in a black gloom about what happened with Rufus. How I ruined everything. For nothing. I keep imagining him with his dad, maybe doing a slightly embarrassing hobby he didn't feel ready to own up to, like stamp spotting or something.

But, most of all, on the middle hand, I'm mainly a bit amazed, thinking about you, Savvy Rose. Not just how brilliant you've been to me. But how you were so keen for me to get to know Rufus. How you guessed Lucien is his grandfather.

And now I've got a big fat scary question blocking up my head. And I know it's ridiculous. But I also know I'll never get it out again unless I ask it. So, apologies in advance, feel free to virtually pelt me with bagels for even thinking this. But also please please please reply immediately, or sooner, so my brain can stop being amazed, it's beginning to hurt. I deliberately held off asking till now as you said you'd check my blog each morning at ten-ish UK time.

Okay, very deep breath . . .

Although you're thousands of miles away, the world is quite small and everyone's only six people apart from everyone else according to Facebook, so it is actually possible . . .

You don't by any wild chance accidentally *know* Rufus do you?

Or maybe you know Lucien?

Posted Sunday 29th August, 10:05

He seems the kind of man who'd know lots of interesting international types of people. Maybe you made him a tweedy jacket once or something?

Savvy Rose? Where are you? You said I should ask, you said you'd be checking. Don't disappear on me now of all times – *please!*

Posted Sunday 29th August, 10:17

The Middle Of Absolute Nowhere to The Most Exciting Place Anywhere

Posted Sunday 29th August, 10:35

Mayday, mayday. Come in Manhattan!

Savvy Rose?

Posted Sunday 29th August, 10:46

Or maybe it's not Rufus, or Lucien . . .

Posted Sunday 29th August, 10:51

. . . maybe it's Mum. She knows all sorts of people and I think she did some vet training on a ranch in America before I was born. You're not some kind of a work colleague or friend of Mum's are you?

Oh. My. God.

Posted Sunday 29th August, 10:57

No. Please. No.

Posted Sunday 29th August, 10:58

You're not are you?

Posted Sunday 29th August, 11:00

You're not *Her* are you.

You're not *Mum*?

Posted Sunday 29th August, 11:02

Mum?

Posted Sunday 29th August, 11:03

Comment

Posted Sunday 29th August, 11:12, by Savvy Rose

Darling, I'm so sorry. I'm on the patio. Come down. Please.

Ha ha ha LOL

Posted Sunday 29th August, 11:14

Hilarious. Fantastic joke Savvy Rose. Oh you zany New Yorkers have such a far-out sense of humour.

Comment

Posted Sunday 29th August, 11:17, by Savvy Rose

Circe, you're under the willow tree wearing a black vest and denim shorts.

Oh very clever. Lucky guess. Try harder.

Posted Sunday 29th August, 11:19

Is August 29th April Fools Day in US time or something?

Comment

Posted Sunday 29th August, 11:21, by Savvy Rose

Daniel Craig is sitting on a carrot, Jude Law is sitting on Daniel Craig's head.

XXXX!!!!!!!!!!

Posted Sunday 29th August, 11:29

Ha ha ha hahahahahahaaaaaaaaaaaaaa, I just plucked some leaves to peek and that *is* true. And Mum *is* on the patio with her laptop on the table in front of her. But it can't be, can it? *She* can't be . . . *Can she?* I'm laughing out loud properly now, I'm not sure I can stop. But something in me refuses to believe this is actually happening. No, not just something – *everything* – every single organ in my body and every single cell in my brain. And all my natural human instincts and logical senses are refusing to believe it too. So they must be right.

Oh.

My.

GOD.

Mum's standing up . . . now she's walking towards me. Calm calm it could still be a massive nightmarish coincidence, it still might not be true.

'Darling. I'm so sorry.'

Mum just said that, she's standing right in front of me now, in my official *secret private* office, *under my willow*. I'm not looking at her, my eyes are totally refusing. I don't think I'll ever be able to look at her again.

If she is Savvy Rose, think of everything she knows about me, what she knows about Rufus about snogging about Portia about my so-called dad about what I think about *her* oh xxxx xxxx xxxxity xxxx xxxx hahahahahaaaaaaaaaaaaaaaaaaa I'm just going to carry on typing because I think if I stop I might actually explode *how could she?* HOW DARE SHE? *WHAT WAS SHE THINKING?*

image 310

'Circe, stop typing like that, please, you'll hurt your fingers. Let me explain . . .'

Explain, she says! *Explain?* How can she *ever explain*? She has broken every parent and child bond of trust and motherhood pledge and teenage human rights law in the entire universe. At least. She did not just *read* my diary – she *wrote* it. And she's lied and cheated and . . . OMGOMGOMG she knows about spanners – SHE KNOWS I PICTURED RALPH'S SPANNER!

!!! !!! arrrrrrrrrrrrrrrrrrrrrrrrrrrrrrrrrgh I'm so angry I can't tiipype any moe just going to carryh onn to kssp yer backss. Kjf;oia3ejfvl,mz;liejfa'pk'poje'fjlzdlk joidoijooojllk;v nz km'aiejr'#pkf:Lm'/lkjfa'ioja'p orj'lfm/ adlmfa'fla'ofk#f#fmvm !!!!pou d[09ddkjlk d000 d;faur;e/ amf;a v[eo 'ejofaiura; kjf/lkanf'aiu'afm'a;lkz zzz oh

Good, the leaves are rustling . . . she's going away. Okay. Calm calm CALM. Think *think* . . .

Comment

Posted Sunday 29th August, 11:35, by Savvy Rose

I never meant this to happen, Circe. I promise you. But I was worried. That night we went out to treat Flying Flint, you were so jumpy – so *angry*. And I didn't know what to do, how to get through to you – darling, you never talk to me . . .

I NEVER TALK TO *YOU*?

Posted Sunday 29th August, 11:37

Argh! That's about the BIGGEST JOKE I've ever heard in my ENTIRE LIFE!

Since when did *you* ever talk to *me*? Since my so-called dad left, it's bee– well, you *know* don't you? You've already *read* it all. It's like there's a big fat ghost between us with his name on it – but oh no, don't dare to even *think* about mentioning it, don't dare ask a question.

So what did you do? Did you think it was a lovely caring maternal idea to sneak into my room and steal my laptopasaurus when I was asleep or something? Hack your way deep into the innermost seething core of my personal private life?

Comment

Posted Sunday 29th August, 11:47, by Savvy Rose

Oh, Circe, of course I didn't. I know it's hard to believe, but it was an accident.

When we got back from Lucien's that night you'd fallen asleep typing. I came out of the bathroom and heard your laptop motor whirring. I was worried, as I said, so I peeped in. The screen was lighting your face blue but you were sound asleep, snoring. I moved the laptop and, I admit, I was curious about what – or who – had been keeping you up. There are some strange people in the virtual world, Circe, all parents worry about the internet – it's one of our human rights! So, I looked at the screen. It had frozen on your post about our evening. I only read the last few lines before I switched it off, but it was like being punched hard, right in the heart.

I remembered the blog address in the morning. Not deliberately, but it's catchy – *totally hot topics* – not easy to forget. I resisted going anywhere near the internet all day. And I tried to get you to tell me about it yourself when I got back from work – you called it an 'unwelcome spontaneous consultation' as I recall, and you clammed up, as usual.

By the time I got home from dinner with AJ that evening, I was about fit to burst. I couldn't help myself, I typed the url into my browser, just out of curiosity, fully expecting to be blocked by a security code or password request. But, as you know, there wasn't one, so it opened straight up.

I intended to have a quick look, check nothing awful was going on for you. But you're so funny, darling, I got drawn in, I flew through the posts. And I know it's no excuse, but as you'd put the blog out there for anyone in the world to see, in theory, I told myself I had a legitimate excuse, that it was like dipping into a magazine, not at all like reading a secret diary. Of course, I was also concerned about what you'd written about Portia at the pool party, or rather, what you'd left *un*written. But, the truth of it is, I kept reading because, well . . . it was like finding my long-lost daughter again. Honestly, Circe, it was like a little miracle to me, you've been so distant.

I'm not quite as dense as you think, you know. I saw you flinch when I asked about school. I noticed you never mentioned a boyfriend. I realised you must be missing your dad, of course I did. But you'd never tell me anything. Your blog was an irresistible opportunity, at long last I had a chance to speak to you, to do what you never let me do – to look after you . . . .

HOW DARE YOU!

Posted Sunday 29th August, 11:50

I DO *NOT* SNORE! Ever. I'm far too fabulously sophisticated.

And also, *how dare you?* You are the strange people on the internet! I should report you to the police or the BBC or someone. I mean, I know you're a bit naturally weird, but couldn't you just make a tiny effort to act like a normal mum for once? Why did you have to create some fantasy alter ego? Couldn't you at least email me in your own name? Or, pardon me for being the epitome of conventional, but couldn't you just have knocked on my bedroom door?

Comment

Posted Sunday 29th August, 11:55, by Savvy Rose

Would you have listened, Circe? Would you have let me in? No. Of course you wouldn't. But I didn't even consider my options, it was a spur of the moment thing. The *Saville Row* label on the waistcoat AJ had left draped over the sofa inspired the name and job. And I thought you'd listen to a New Yorker because of Jess Bradley. *Voilà*. Savvy Rose was born. But I only intended to write one post – to boost your confidence a little. You sounded so fed up about not having a boyfriend or even a real-life blog reader.

And the pet boy thing – you made all that up too?

Posted Sunday 29th August, 12:03

Comment

Posted Sunday 29th August, 12:05, by Savvy Rose

No. I didn't lie to you about any of that. I promise. I thought if I could just plant the idea in your head that boys would fall at your feet if only you showed them the same confidence you show animals, you'd work the rest out on your own. I should have known better, of course – you just kept coming up with more questions. I resisted answering for days – you might remember? But in the end, it seemed worse to leave you confused than to write to you again. And I believe thoroughly in everything I told you, Circe. The only fibs were the bits about wild times in The Hamptons and so on – and even they were true, they just happened twenty years ago, when I was studying in The States. And, you have to give me some credit – the pet advice worked, didn't it?

But you are the epitome of rubbish with men

Posted Sunday 29th August, 12:05

At least. Savvy Rose sounded like men pant after her wherever she goes – she's totally sassy and sorted. I'd never take advice from *you*. You're hopeless at keeping pet men! Your so-called soulmate husband strayed off for good and now all you do is flirt pointlessly with a penniless poet and a brainless ad-man.

Comment

Posted Sunday 29th August, 12:15, by Savvy Rose

Ouch. Though, for the record, darling, your father never stopped loving me – he just couldn't live with me any more. And, Ralph and AJ and I are fine, on the whole. I'm enjoying a little fun after an awful lot of sadness. But they both know I'm not ready for anything more serious – having the two of them around proves it if they ever need reminding. Besides, I *am* still married to your so-called dad.

Oh, and incidentally AJ is rather well off, but thinks money inhibits his creativity. And Ralph, you know, he's really quite a sensitive soul underneath all the hair gel. He might be a little too fond of his statistics, but he is genuinely concerned about you. Rufus was being particularly obnoxious when Ralph met him at the show, I'd told him about the ratlets and he spat lots of nasty stuff about his mum being a tart and turning him into an orphan overnight. Ralph wasn't impressed.

My entire world is officially upside down
Posted Sunday 29th August, 12:35

So you are a man magnet? AJ is loaded? Ralph is sensitive? But Rufus? Rufus is *not* an orphan – what's all that about?

Comment
Posted Sunday 29th August, 12:59, by Savvy Rose

Oh, Circe. Poor Rufus. His mum has run off. It's partly why I encouraged you to get together in the first place, why I dropped hints about his problems. Rather naively, I suppose, I thought you might talk to each other, even if you couldn't talk to us wrinklies.

Lucien told me everything that first night. He was trying to keep a stiff upper lip, but I could tell he was beside himself with worry even though I'd assured him that Flint would be fine. As soon as I asked what was wrong, it all came pouring out . . .

Rufus had turned up at Lucien's – who is his mum's father – that afternoon, raving and ranting, filthy and exhausted after cycling from his parents' place, nearly thirty miles away. He'd woken to find his mum gone, his dad packing a case. When Rufus asked him if they were going on holiday early, he said, 'No. There's no easy way to say this, so I'm just going to tell you straight. Your mother had an affair eighteen years ago. Now she's done it again – this time she's swanned off to France with some toyboy actor. And again she's left me with her debts and her son and I've had enough, I'm dragging her back here to face the music if it's the last thing I do.' And when Rufus said, 'What do you mean, *her* son?' he said, 'Exactly that, Rufus, her son. It's high time you knew the truth. I agreed to raise you, I care about you like you're mine, but you're not mine.'

That's why Rufus was marching Flint round – it was entirely unnecessary, today's injections relieve colic almost instantly. Lucien was keeping Rufus on the move to distract him, help burn off his rage. We had to keep up the pretence for a while, of course, once he'd stomped off and left you to it. Sorry about that, darling.

Anyway, that's probably also why you mistook Rufus for a groom. Lucien told me he planned to keep him as busy as possible, so he wouldn't have the time or energy to knock doors down all over the county trying to hunt down his real father.

Poor Rufus

Posted Sunday 29th August, 13:02

But, hold on, he's with his dad today, isn't he?

Comment

Posted Sunday 29th August, 13:10, by Savvy Rose

He's with his stepdad, the man he's called 'Dad' all his life. According to Lucien he's been scouring the Mediterranean looking for Rufus's mum and her toyboy. He promised Rufus he'd meet him today whether he found her or not, and help him begin to track down his real dad. Lucien knows nothing about it. His mum refuses to name him. His stepdad only knows that he lives somewhere around here.

OMG

Posted Sunday 29th August, 13:15

No wonder being with Rufus was a bit like being on a particularly moody kind of rollercoaster. When I first realised my so-called dad didn't actually love me I felt exactly like that.

Comment

Posted Sunday 29th August, 13:22, by Savvy Rose

Circe, don't. Your dad *does* love you, he always will. He always has – he was enchanted the moment he set eyes on you, it's why we called you Circe. But, well, he's a very complicated man, darling – the most difficult kind of pet.

I knew what I was taking on from the day I met him, long before you were born.

We were both travelling in the Greek Islands. He was paying his way by painting, of course. I was slaving at a donkey sanctuary, supposedly relaxing after my finals. I was unromantically forking manure on to a muck heap when he strolled up, all mad hair and big grin, and insisted on painting me as I worked. He wouldn't take 'no' for an answer and I thought he was a right prat, to be honest. But, by the time he'd finished, not even an hour later, I was lost. He'd switched something on in me, and I just couldn't switch it off, even when I realised what kind of man he was. The kind of man your grandma called, 'Undomesticated'. But I took a risk on him, because I loved him. And I know it's a terrible cliché, but I don't regret it, not for a minute.

Okay, I can't pretend your dad didn't break my heart. I certainly can't deny that I'm not still furious with him sometimes. Or that I will ever forgive him for removing himself so completely.

But one thing I do know, Circe, without a shadow of a doubt. Your dad didn't leave because he didn't love you. If anything, it was quite the opposite.

Oh

Posted Sunday 29th August, 13:23

I see. So I might be a bit totally wrong then?

Comment

Posted Sunday 29th August, 13:24, by Savvy Rose

Wrong about what?

I've never even thought it properly, I'm not sure I can type it

Posted Sunday 29th August, 13:25

Comment

Posted Sunday 29th August, 13:26, by Savvy Rose

Darling, please try.

Okay, but I might throw up on Johnny Depp

Posted Sunday 29th August, 13:27

He's curled up by my deckchair and my stomach feels like it's crouching down and trying to sneak out of my body.

Right. Deep breaths. I am a journalist in pursuit of the key facts . . .

Don't you think it's my fault at all then? Not even a bit? That Dad left, I mean. I thought . . . you know, because you didn't tell me why, because you made stuff up . . .

Comment

Posted Sunday 29th August, 13:29, by Savvy Rose

Oh, Circe.

 322

Totally weeping under a willow

Posted Sunday 29th August, 15:50

But I'm smiling too. Honestly.

Mum was under here with me. She's making tea now – and getting another loo roll, just in case. I've already snivelled all the way through one. It's like I've turned into some kind of rampant human fountain. I keep thinking my eyes must have dried up, but then another bucketful pours out. I suppose three years' worth of tears is quite a lot. Johnny Depp ended up drenched, he's fluffing himself back up in the sun now.

It's weird talking to Mum again, but we've stuck to the side-by-side rule, so that's helped. And when I clammed up for a bit she drawled, 'Oh my gosh, freaking get on with it, honey!' in a Savvy Rose accent. And it was a bit shocking, and reminded me that she is the epitome of a bad mother and I can never forgive her. But it also reminded me how much I liked talking to Savvy Rose and that Mum actually *is* Savvy Rose and so maybe I could get used to liking talking to her too, now I know she won't flip out and go straight to bed if I accidentally upset her.

We talked about Dad first and even laughed about the blushing ladies who always trailed him round galleries. Then we giggled a bit about AJ's mauve lady fan who Mum says is actually Lord Something-Or-Other and owns half of Dullford. We talked about Portia then and I promised to tell

323

Mum if she tries anything this term. I crossed my fingers in my shorts pocket though, because I really think I must be fabulously sophisticated enough to fight my own playground battles now I've been through yet another Major Family Trauma.

Finally, we talked about Rufus. I think it's a totally hopeless case. I feel even more awful about the things I said at the pool knowing what I know now, and if I was Rufus I'd never forgive me. But Mum thinks it's worth a try. She says a good pet boy is worth fighting for and she thinks Rufus is really 'solid' even though his family stuff has made him so moody. She still stands by Savvy Rose's advice to tell him everything. But I'm pretty tired of talking now, to be honest. I might just text, 'Sorry' so he doesn't think I'm the worst kind of heartless monster.

Oh, and I'm going to upgrade my security setting on the blog to beyond top secret, so Mum can't get in any more. She's promised faithfully that she wouldn't dare even *think* about trying to read it again. But come on – would *you* trust her?

The general usefulness of stars
Posted Sunday 29th August, 23:04

I'm lying in bed looking up at the stars, wondering things, which is definitely what stars are best for.

I wondered about them scientifically first, as in how many gazillions there are and how many are actually space satellites or astronauts' lost helmets etcetera.

Then I wondered if my dad can see the same pattern of stars where he is, wherever that is, and if he's looking up at them wondering if I can see them.

Then I wondered if Rufus is lying in his attic looking up at the same stars too, wondering things about his real dad.

Then I remembered the starry poem in the film we saw. And that gave me an idea for something I could do about The Rufus Situation, which I think might be quite fabulously sophisticated and confident and romantic at the same time.

I don't really trust my brain to be a good judge now though, as it's been through quite a lot today. But if the something still feels like a good idea in the morning, I'll do it. As Savvy Rose says, sorry, as *Mum* says – it is worth the risk.

The morning after the day before
Posted Monday 30th August, 09:02

Well . . . my idea feels a bit scarier today, but it does still feel like a good one. Besides, I don't fancy going to the park with Tash and Ben, for obvious reasons, so it will give me something more interesting to do than staring at Johnny Depp staring at Don Draper. I can also write it up as my last ever pet boy experiment, then move on to a new hot topic. Maybe an easier one? Maybe Tash was right in the first place and I should stick to *How to love your hair even if it's giant*, or something.

Allowing Him To Get Close Even If You Think He Might Bite
Male Human Pet Control: Experiment 12

Posted Monday 30th August, 10:24

Please note that this is not like previous experiments as the male human pet specimen will not actually be physically or mentally present during its undertaking.

This is a letter. Remember letters? I know, I know, I'm meant to be an official cyberteen product of the virtual revolution and a letter is all very trad and *Wuthering Heights*. But I'd like to point out that Jess Bradley interviewed a posse of edgy East London artists the other night and they were all dandied up in cravats and top hats – apparently old-fashioned is about *the* most modern thing to be right now. Anyway, this is not just any old letter, it's a letter in fountain pen and including a heartfelt poem, even though it is a

rubbish one about an empty jar. I've already written it on a
sheet of Mum's thick cream writing paper, using my best big
slanted handwriting. I haven't dotted the 'i's with hearts (*so*
Year 10) but I have sketched a tragic gothy cupid in one
corner. Here's what it says:

Dear Rufus,

*I'm so sorry about what happened in the pool. I suddenly
got upset about things that were mainly nothing to do
with you, and some other things I didn't even realise I
was upset about. But that's still no excuse, I was really
enjoying our swim etcetera and I deeply regret that I
was a total doughnut and spoilt the afternoon.*

*I'm also really sorry about your 'stuff' (stepdad/dad/
mum/toyboy situation). I didn't know about it at the
time, but now I do it makes what I said even worse,
especially as I know a bit about what you're going
through. You probably think I'm just saying that to get
you to forgive me, but maybe the poem below will help
you believe me. Unfortunately, it is totally rubbish and
AJ mentally blackmailed me into writing it, but it does
accidentally describe how I feel about my dad situation.**

Message in a jar

I took a jar
that used to be full
of honey
as warm and sweet
as love

I took a jar
that used to be full
and I looked inside
and it turned
into a mirror

I took a jar
and filled it up
with notes for you
and all they said was
'Why?'

I understand if you never want to see me again. I definitely understand if you don't want to talk about any of this. I didn't talk about my stuff for years, but I've talked about it so much the last few days my mouth is now officially bored. So if you would just prefer to snog that would be excellent. Or not. Whatever.

My best regards to your grandfather and the hamstericidal ratlets.

Yours sincerely,
Circe (Shaw)

* I lied about my dad, sorry. He might not be on an island, I don't know where he is.

I'm going to cycle over to Knight Ridge now and drop it into the letterbox by the gates as I don't entirely trust The Middle Of Absolute Nowhere postman because he wears brown sandals with blue socks, which tells me all I need to know about his eyesight.

Wish it luck.

Night before school, feeling weirdly okay

Posted Tuesday 31st August, 20:04

So here I am, thirty-one long, mainly hot, summer days later. I can't believe I was worried I'd have nothing to do. So much has happened I feel like I've hardly had a holiday at all. It's a good job we don't have to stand up in registration and tell everyone what we did, like we used to in primary school. This is what I'd say:

> 1. Worked on fabulous sophistication via
>   journalistic blog.

2. Gained a bit of confidence thanks to advice from sassy 'total stranger'.

3. Bought essential unexpected floppy flower for bargain price of 75p.

4. Got a pet boy and kept him for ten days.

5. Lost everything in the deep end of a swimming pool.

It's not exactly happily ever after is it?

My mum is also a liar and imposter and I'm not sure if I will ever really be able to forgive her, even if it has got us talking a bit more. She claims she planted the 'grandpop' clue deliberately, so I'd find her out and she'd have a chance to tell me the truth. But I'm not so sure. She also keeps reminding me she only went through with the whole thing for my own good. But that's just standard so-called grown-up speak for, 'Remember, mere offspring, I am always right and that is that.'

And my dad? Well, I'd love to report that he suddenly appeared in a beam of sunshine, just as Mum and me started talking. But this is a real story, not a fairytale, so my dad is still on The Longest Walk Around The Block In History. He's somewhere out there doing who knows what with who knows who and we have no idea if he'll ever bother telling us where he is, or coming back.

I did pluck up the courage to ask the ultimate do-not-even-think-about-going-there question. The question that grumps around in the back of my head every time I see a news story about someone everyone thought was missing who turns out to be dead instead. Mum hugged me so hard my ribs creaked, then she said Dad's not dead as she'd 'just know' and we'd also have been told by law, and her eyes didn't go blurry, so I believe her.

But she refuses to try to hunt Dad down, even though he should be paying her to feed me nutrition etcetera. She insisted it wouldn't help anyone in the long run, because he won't have any money anyway, and it would stop her living in a forwards direction. She said I can look for him myself when I'm older, if he hasn't already turned up (apparently, because of taxes and voting, he can still find us even though we moved house). I'm not sure how I feel about tracking him down myself, but luckily I'm not older at the moment, so I don't have to worry about it yet.

Mum also said it might be good to celebrate Dad's birthday in future, to think about him together properly, maybe go to a gallery or something. And this morning she came down from her room with what looked like a wodge of old newspapers and it turns out she'd secretly kept one of his paintings, the one he did of her when they first met. It's only a small one, but we've put it up over the sofa and it makes everything look brighter, just like he did.

After we hung the painting, I confessed about the photos of Dad I'd hidden inside an old jigsaw box. When I got them out, they made us both cry at first, but now they're propped all round the cottage. And seeing his mad hair and big grin all over the place makes me feel a bit more whole, a bit less like I have a gaping windswept void in me where one half of my biological physical genetics should be.

Anyway, considering everything, I feel pretty good. I haven't heard from Rufus and it still hurts. But I keep telling myself that he was only a practice pet boyfriend who I didn't like. And if I say it enough, one day my brain might actually believe it.

It's quite possible Portia will staple me to the blackboard tomorrow

Posted Wednesday 1st September, 18:35

But I don't care.

I used my fabulous sophistication against her today and, major drum roll with extra cymbals and a trumpet or two . . . it worked! Okay, Portia is now totally spitting and probably persuading her darling daddy to complain to the prime minister and have me arrested and thrown in a special delinquents' school where I will rot for the rest of my doomed days surrounded by deviant psychopaths. But, hey, whatever.

When I walked into registration, she was already holding court in the middle of the classroom, batting her lashes and having her shiny *Head Girl* badge admired. As soon as she saw me she chirped, 'Morning Curse!'

I took a huge deep breath as I sat down at my desk. Then I stretched my lips into my most confident sort of smile and asked, 'What did you say, Portia?'

She tossed her bleached hair and flashed her bleached teeth and repeated, 'Morning Curse!'

There was absolutely no doubt what she'd said this time and all the chattering and giggling in the class hushed to silence. And I thought, stuff this for a game of chocolate soldiers, which was something Dad used to say when I was about six and I'd completely forgotten until that moment. But even though it was childish instead of fabulously sophisticated, it did seem quite sensible. So I tutted and said, 'Oh My God, it really is *difficult* for you to pronounce Circe isn't it? It's sir-see. Everyone else can say it. Why don't you try again?'

Portia's face went dark and her shocking pink nails stabbed into her desk. Even though my whole body flinched internally then, I forced my eyes to stay fixed to hers. But then my ears heard crepe soles squeaking along the corridor and Mrs Stave bustled in saying, 'Morning morning morning!' then, 'Heavens, what a glorious tan, Portia.' And Portia tore her eyes from mine to smile charmingly and the moment passed.

Luckily, Tash and I had the first lesson together, so I told her what happened and she stuck to me like glue for the rest of the day. Portia did glare a few times, when no one was looking. But she didn't even try to whisper anything, not one single malicious syllable. And I know the battle's nowhere near over yet, I know it's just a start, but it's still a pretty good one isn't it?

And something else happened today too. Actually, it's probably totally irrelevant and officially unimportant now, almost boring and pointless and really quite unnecessary. I don't know, should I bother telling you at all?

Hmmm . . .

What? You really want to know?

Posted Wednesday 1st September, 18:38

Are you the absolute epitome of sure?

Posted Wednesday 1st September, 18:39

Beyond sure?

Posted Wednesday 1st September, 18:40

Oh, okay then . . .

Posted Wednesday 1st September, 18:41

When the bell went at the end of the day, Tash and I walked

out to the gates together, laughing over a daft joke her brother had texted.

Portia and Jake were already there, snogging, of course. So were Venetia and Milly. And Tim and Mita and Joanna and lean Lee and Charlotte and the chief village muppet.

Ben was there too, waiting for Tash, because his college doesn't start until tomorrow. And she was so happy to see him, she forgot she was sort of guarding me and shot across the lane and swooned straight into his arms.

I knew I should either walk over to them confidently, or sashay off down the lane fabulously sophisticatedly. But all I really wanted to do was jump up and down on the spot screaming, which didn't give my brain much hope for me to be honest.

So, there I was, frozen on the spot, surrounded by loved-up couples, ending the first day of the new term just as I'd ended the last day of the old one. Alone.

Then I felt something touch my hip – a tiny static prickle. I winced and stiffened to rigid, assuming Portia had charmed someone into prodding a compass into me. But then a voice really close to my ear said . . .

'Stay still, I think this belongs to you.'

And the voice was deep and drawly and a bit radically plummy and had a slight mocking hiss in it.

It was definitely the most gorgeous voice I've ever heard.

It belonged to The Rudest Stupidest Most Despicable Boy I've Ever Met.

My smile stretched so wide it hurt. I looked down. Rufus's big square hands were fumbling to pin my floppy flower back on my hip.

'It's a bit wilted, and it lost a couple of petals when I ran it through the tumble-dryer, but I couldn't bring myself to bin it.'

I looked up. Rufus was wearing his scruffiest jeans and his faded T-shirt with the worm logo and his hair had straw and a streak of mud in it. He looked so hot that at least a gazillion butterflies hatched in my stomach and started fluttering all over my body, but not in a scared way – in an excited way.

He reached out and tucked a curl behind my ear. 'I got your letter, Circe – and the jar poem. It helped, thanks.'

I just carried on grinning because my brain was entirely blank with happiness. Then I heard a familiar, 'Ooh!' and I saw Tash nudge Ben and they both smiled over, and next to them Venetia nudged Milly who nudged Tim who nudged Mita who nudged Joanna who nudged lean Lee who nudged Charlotte who nudged the chief village muppet who nudged Jake who peeled his lips off Portia who squealed.

Portia pouted at Jake, then her eyes narrowed as she followed everyone else's stares over to me. I grinned back. I was still incapable of doing anything else. As she slid her eyes from me to Rufus, her mouth actually fell wide open. Then she licked her lips and I swear she arched her back.

I looked up at Rufus and my heart dropped to my boots when I saw he was watching her too. And before my brain had a chance to stop my mouth, it said, 'Pretty, isn't she?'

He frowned down at me. 'Who, the blonde?'

I nodded, my heart back up and blocking my throat.

'God no. She looks like she's made of plastic.'

I started to laugh then. Not in a charismatic vampirical way, not even in a triumphant way, just in relief, I think. I laughed until tears blurred my eyes and a stitch stabbed into my sides. And Rufus laughed with me at first, but then he pulled me against him and shut me up. Not with a sneer, or a hiss, or even an illegal swear word.

With the most deeply meaningful snog I've ever had.

At least.

When we finally came up for air, he took a step back, cupped my face in his hands and tilted it up. Then his eyes flashed and lasered deep into mine, and he looked like he really was interested in what was going on inside my head.

And I didn't glare back or cringe internally or feel even a bit hollow. And I didn't put on any where-it's-at exudations or deliberately drape my arms and legs out confidently. But as I watched his pupils dilate, turning his eyes from almost transparent silver to jet black, I said, without even thinking about whether it would make him feel special or not, 'Rufus, you know, your eyes are totally amazing – they really are just like a cat's.'

And Rufus raised one eyebrow. Then he curled his lips into the kind of grin that makes you realise that a boy really does have all the best kinds of romantic bad intentions.

And then he said, 'Meee-ow.'

 THE END

(Or is it?)

Journalistically Legal Blog Postscript

Although The Middle Of Absolute Nowhere is where I actually live, facts like addresses and surnames have been changed for secretive reasons. Pets (non-human) are called by their real names, but any resemblance to actual attractive older sex symbols is strictly co-incidental.

Okay, this next bit seems beyond pointless as if you've been even a bit awake at school you'll already know it, but never put your personal details online. And if you meet a stranger in the virtual world never, ever agree to meet them in the real world, even if they swear they're a gazillionaire R-Patz look-alike. As if.

There's more info on staying safe and fabulously sophisticated online at **thinkuknow.co.uk**

If an invisible so-called parent is annoying you, try **childline.org.uk**

And if a poisonous Portia is hissing about in your life, check out **cybermentors.org.uk**

Circe x

Why I'm no longer wrapped casually around a posh boy

Posted Monday 24th October, 18:24 by Diane Messidoro

Once upon a time I was a teenager called Diane Cox who dreamed of becoming an author. But I hadn't a clue what to do about it. I didn't know any writers. I didn't have any qualifications. My teachers rolled their eyes.

So, instead, I went to work in a posh shop where I spent most of my time cuddling posh boys, whenever I could catch them. And there I might have stayed, wrapped casually around Lord Someone-Or-Other, were it not for some very special, very helpful people . . .

Nicky Reed giggled through my tales of strutting riding instructors. Cheryl Foster showed me daring. My mum pleaded, 'Learn to type!'

PR supremos, Libby Mudditt and Sue Malec mistook me for an efficient secretary, took me to events involving racing drivers then encouraged me to write about them (or most of them). Liz Hulme gave me a chance to pen features. Steve Somerset offered me a job writing about books.

Jax Donnellan and Clare Sychrava read my work, laughed in the right places and hugged me when things weren't so funny. Berry D'Arcy lent me her brilliant left-brain when plots thickened. Debbie Fagan believed in signs.

Buns helped too. Debbie Bostelmann lit me up with carrot cake, while her dad, Bob, put me right on colic cures. Sarah Rayner and Hattie Gordon empathised over bangers and mash. Hugo Lines talked art over curry. Then there was Rachel Stelling (pizza); Hilary Freeman (gnocci); Eleanor Ashfield and Giles Wigoder (fat chips aboard the Good Ship Empty), Kim Gilchrist and Maeve Rutten (oliebollen).

The dashing boys of Frith Street especially Rory Aitken,

Ben Pugh, Eran Creevy, Matt Golding, Chris Quigley and Sam Smith coped with me wafting about in 'the romantic corner'.

Mon adorable famille Messidoro: Camille and Yvonne; Magalie; Therese; Jean; Michel, Denis and Patricia didn't mind me hiding behind trees with my laptop.

At Birkbeck, poet Paul Bavister taught me about metaphors (and that isn't a metaphor). Novelist Mary Flanagan understood. A babble of strangers became a band of friends: mistress of viscerally poignant pudding, Miranda Bowen; Emma Dunton; Nigel Crowe; Mary Jane Gomm; Victoria Grigg; Thaddeus Hickman; Mary Murphy Ford; Ann Palmer, Birte Peterson and the fabulous Liz 'the science' Simpson.

A few people might not realise they helped, but they did. On Arvon courses Jenny Colgan and Mike Gayle fired me up: five years later Jane Harris, Richard Beard and Glen Duncan cheered me up. Nick Stringer, Becky Swift and Julia Bell spurred me on.

The RNA's Nicola Cornick recommended me to my wonderful agent and editorial whizz, Broo Doherty. Louise Willder, Alice Berry and Kristen 'Artypeeps' Harrison put me in a room with a truly inspiring publisher, Leah Thaxton. A year later, an amazing editor, Philippa Donovan, knocked me off my boots with the perfect response to my script. Cally, Mike, Jo and the Egmont team made me feel I'd come home. Andrea conjured up a cover to swoon over. My dream came true.

So now I'm wrapped gleefully around a French boy, my own gorgeous pet: rarely obedient, but always up for a cuddle. For everything, Didier, *merci* will never be enough. I'll think of something else, perhaps a chewy snack?

And thanks everyone, really, I am beyond gratefully chuffed. At least.

DIANE MESSIDORO

Diane Messidoro spent her teens shimmying in glittery disco boots, swooning over smouldering moody boys and falling off horses. Now she's officially grown up, she spends her time far more wisely; shimmying in glittery disco boots, swooning over smouldering moody men and not getting on horses. Diane has been studying the strange behaviour of the male human species since chasing her first crush across a playground. She hopes 'How to Keep a Boy as a Pet' will inspire girls to take charge of their romantic destinies – or at least save their natural sparkling pizzazz from being trampled into tragic smithereens! She lives in a leafy corner of London with two disobedient pet cats and an occasionally obedient pet husband.

Diane doodles about boys, boys and beautiful brains at

howtokeepaboyasapet.co.uk

 electricmonkeybooks.co.uk

and

dianemessidoro.co.uk

'The End' is officially just the beginning!

If you loved How to Keep a Boy as a Pet visit…

howtokeepaboyasapet.co.uk

and

ELECTRICMONKEYBOOKS.CO.UK

· Discover your Official Crush's pet type!

· Debate the hottest new topics.

· Be a guest star blogger.

· Be first to read the next book,
  What Not to Do in The Dark

WIN
the coverboy's
T-shirt!